Cerébrum

By

Nicoline Evans

Author: Nicoline Evans – www.nicolineevans.com

Editor: Emily Kline – www.ekediting.com

To my beta readers and everyone else who has offered support (in all ways, shapes, and sizes) during this entire process—THANK YOU!

Dedicated to those determined to survive

Guides and Maps

GUIDES:

MAPS:

Chapter 1

Cerébrum

Silence.

Darkness.

All-consuming solitude.

Scritch, scritch, scritch.

"Who's there?" Grette shouted, jerking away from the sudden arrival of sound.

"Shh," the stranger replied. "He likes silence."

"Who likes silence?" Grette asked in a whisper.

"The warden."

"I thought I had lost my ability to hear," Grette confessed.

Scritch, scritch, scritch.

A small flame burst into life.

"I can see," Grette exclaimed, her periwinkle eyes glimmering with tears.

"Shh!"

Grette scanned where the light touched and gasped. Hundreds of broken souls sat huddled all around, their hopeless gazes staring upward at the flickering flame.

She turned her focus to the light-bringer—a strange-looking man made of smoke and embers.

"What's wrong with them?"

"They are lost minds, just like you."

A small droplet of fire extended from his fingertip.

"Where am I?" she whispered.

"Cerébrum."

His scarlet eyes shifted eagerly.

"Who are you?"

"I am a friend."

Grette lifted her stone hands to the flame. She could see through them.

"Am I dead?"

"That's a complicated question." He flicked his wrist and made the flame dance. "Some might say you might as well be dead. No one leaves this place."

She looked again at the faces around them. None were familiar.

"Where did they all come from?"

"Where did *you* come from?"

"Namaté."

He huffed. "Of course. Another mortal child of Matrigaia."

Grette hesitated. "Gaia?"

"Same deity, shortened name."

"Yes, she is my goddess; my divine mother."

"She's mine, too. And every other mind here." He sighed, puffs of chalky ash plumed from his figure. "All casualties in a much bigger war."

"I thought I was done with war," she confessed as a familiar heaviness returned.

"You are. No more fighting or picking sides. You are out of the game. You've lost."

"I don't understand. Whose war?"

"Life and death." He sensed her confusion. "Matrigaia and Kólasi."

"Oh." Grette thought of her last moments in Orewall: the black-stemmed stonespur flowers covered in gossamer threads. "Kólasi sent those flowers."

Her fellow inmate shrugged. "Perhaps."

"My name is Grette," she offered.

"You can call me Orso."

"And this place?"

"Cerébrum is one of Kólasi's prison planets. This one ensnares minds."

"And there is no way to leave?"

"Not that I know of." He paused. "No exit that we are capable of achieving, at least."

The weight of each breath deepened as Grette struggled to combat her worried thoughts.

"How long have you been here?" she asked.

"Impossible to tell—time doesn't exist here."

"Try," Grette requested.

"Long enough to know that no one leaves."

"Ever?"

Orso shook his head. "I sensed your vigor. You seemed worthy of the flame."

"I appreciate it."

"I've tried sharing the light with others, but they all surrendered to the darkness soon after. It doesn't take long for this place to break a mind."

"But you haven't surrendered."

Orso lifted his finger to his face, illuminating a rebellious sparkle in his scarlet eyes.

"I never surrender."

"I won't either."

"I hope not," he encouraged.

He clenched his fist and smothered the flame.

Total darkness resumed.

Lost in the obscurity again, but this time, with a sliver of hope.

If they could challenge Kólasi's darkness with fire, surely there were other rules waiting to be broken.

Grette snapped her fingers repeatedly.

Though she was a figment of her former self, a hollow semi-translucent shadow, she felt compelled to try. Within her mind's casing in this prison, her purple tanzanite and marble fingers made contact.

Stone against stone, the familiar friction fanned a spark.

Grette smirked.

Light would prevail.

Chapter 2

Vapore, Namaté

Atop the highest branch of the ancient cypress tree, Ciela waited for a fleeting moment of pure silence and solitude.

She had to speak to the Mother.

She needed to inform her of Kólasi's invasion.

Moments of stillness were harder to come by now. The swampy shores of Vapore teemed with gossamer-covered buttonbushes and spiderworts, and it was no longer safe to touch the ground. Kólasi's rooted webs of darkness had sprouted everywhere and the Gasione warriors could not sleep on the beach. Instead, they rested on the lower branches of the cypress tree, absorbing starlight as quietly as possible.

Their breathing mimicked the soft swirling breeze. Their heartbeats matched the gentle ebb and flow of the waves.

They were too close.

Too loud.

Ciela opened her piercing marigold eyes. She needed distance from her resting warriors.

Glorious eagle wings spread wide, she lifted into the sky and spun into an aella—it was the only safe way to travel beyond the poisonous dome shrouding Vapore. Between the golden death flies, the zombified creatures of Namaté, and Kólasi's unpredictable visits, surviving was easier when they could not be seen.

Ciela rose into the sky and scanned the daytime energy.

No ethereal hum, no golden rays of death, no pulsating pull toward Fibril.

Kólasi was elsewhere.

He came and went frequently, leaving his mind-stripped zombies to recruit the surviving creatures of Namaté to his abyss—or wherever they went.

Besides herself and her warriors, small factions from most lands still managed to evade Kólasi's invasion: King Calix of Crystet had been taken by the mindless during their initial shield build, so his sister Gwynessa ruled in his wake. Alongside her stood a handful of her closest confidants. King Feodras of Orewall and many of his comrades. But the majority of their populations were lost to the dark roots of chaos.

Elecort's population barely endured their most recent battle, but all who had survived were kept safe from Kólasi under Queen Elixyvette's care. She extended her protection to the Metellyans as well—a selfish or selfless act, it was too soon to tell.

All the Woodlins were accounted for and hiding in Occavas. Using the scepter of alchemy, they created a dome of light over Radix de Wicker that Kólasi's diseased webs and roots could not penetrate. While they had successfully evaded the darkness beneath their shield, they had also become unreachable to the rest of the survivors. Every time Ciela tried to talk to them through their dome, the Woodlins could not hear her and instead, always answered her by pointing upward, leaving her increasingly frustrated.

The infected threads of Radix de Fibril had spanned the ocean and weaved a thick net around the dome. The webbed tendrils pulsated with desperate golden rage, eagerly awaiting an opportunity to strike—Kólasi wanted the Woodlins most of all. A single crack in their light shield and the slinky strands would creep through and seize their wooden brains.

There were no surviving Mudlings or Bonz. Though their foggy-eyed, empty bodies remained in Namaté, their minds were elsewhere.

An unknown fate—something Ciela did not wish to tempt.

She remained in aella form as she flew toward Elecort. She had yet to discover *how* Elixyvette kept two populations safe, and was determined to discover her secret.

Though the saturated city of electricity had been rebuilt to its former glory, there were not enough surviving Voltains to fill the space. While each survivor claimed a home in the districts, most spent their time inside the refurbished castle with their Queen, while the Metellyans lived full-time in the districts. The Metellyans maintained the intricate wire system, while also sharing their own metallic conductivity to keep the land abuzz. A fair trade, perhaps—labor for safety—but Ciela suspected there might be other less visible layers to this arrangement. The Voltains had farmed Metellyan prisoners for centuries, harvesting their bodies for coils and cogs, and using their metal bodies to create extra electricity to power the entire land. If this arrangement wasn't already disadvantageous for the Metellyans, it would likely turn so soon.

Ciela dipped toward the castle and entered through an open set of sky lights over the throne room. She hovered high above, keeping her distance to avoid being detected.

Elixyvette sat tall atop her throne of electrified coils, and Prince Elior slept silently in a bassinet beside her. The Voltains were spread across the great hall tinkering with small projects and socializing. There was no fear, no urgency, no desperation. They simply existed, as if the world were not on fire beyond their borders.

While the rest of Namaté's survivors—besides the Woodlins—lived in daily terror, the Voltains enjoyed peace and tranquility, seemingly unbothered by Kólasi's reign of horror.

"How?" Ciela called out, unable to control her frustration.

Elixyvette glanced upward, unbothered, toward Ciela's voice.

"Nice of you to spy on us again."

Ciela shifted out of aella form. "How are you doing it?"

"Doing what?"

"Keeping your people and the Metellyans safe from Kólasi?"

Elixyvette raised her brow. "You and I never worked together before, why start now?"

"A deal with the devil never ends well."

"I made no deals."

"Then how?"

"I have Gaia's protection." Elixyvette smirked.

"Lies!" Ciela spat.

Angering the Gasione queen brightened Elixyvette's magenta glow. She addressed her devoted subjects, "Please leave."

"Should I take Elior?" Helaine asked.

"No, he will stay with me."

She bowed and departed with the other Voltains.

Elixyvette continued, "While I've made no deals with Kólasi, I suppose I *could* make a deal with you."

Elixyvette was playing mind games, and Ciela's impatience worsened. "I just want to know how you've staved off the devil."

"Charm and beauty, I suppose."

Ciela growled. "Your selfishness will find you again in the afterlife."

"Gaia's nirvana awaits me."

"We both know that isn't true."

Elixyvette smirked. "Surely, Her nirvana awaits *you*, so I'm not sure why you're so worried about our mortal woes. Soon, you will revel in an eternity of bliss."

"It's not my time."

"Nor mine."

Ciela paused, then revisited Elixyvette's former offer. "What kind of deal do you want to make?"

Elixyvette's steel-pink eyes blazed with mischief.

"I will tell you my secret in exchange for a task."

"What is the task?" Ciela asked.

"However you healed your wings, do the same for my son." She lowered his blanket to reveal crude scars across his neck.

"What happened?" Ciela asked.

"Rúnar tore his neck wires and stole his voice." Elixyvette ran a gentle finger along Elior's scars, then balled her hand into a fist. "Then the drakkina returned his voice, but the price was his glow. He has no natural electricity running through him. She said he would grow stronger in time, but he's made no improvements." Her eyes glistened with angry tears.

"While I want to help, I cannot. Gaia returned my wings at Her own discretion. No prayers, no magic—simply Her will."

"Then leave!" Elixyvette barked. "You are of no use to me!"

"I understand that you are grieving the health of your son, but we really need to work together."

"I want nothing from this wretched, unfair world. I hope it burns."

"Did you hear nothing that I said? Gaia healed me. Why? Because I proved myself worthy. Perhaps if you served Her with the same devotion you give to yourself, She might grant your greatest desire."

"She will grant me no kindness," Elixyvette seethed. "We both know that."

"Perhaps. But it's your only option."

"I'd rather watch the world burn."

"You are delusional with grief."

"I am angry."

"So am I," Ciela retorted. "But at least I'm using it for good. I haven't given up. If you did the same, maybe you'd receive more blessings."

"I'm the one safe from Kólasi's wrath. I'm the one sitting pretty." Elixyvette's infuriating self-righteousness had returned. "Worry about yourself."

"I will," Ciela replied. "And when I figure out a way to save myself and the others from this nightmare, I'll be sure to remember your selfishness."

Ciela rocketed into the air and left through the skylight.

No new answers, just more frustration.

Elixyvette considered Ciela's advice and warnings.

Perhaps there were other ways to get what she wanted.

For now, Elixyvette cherished her ancient relic—Jasvinder's eyes kept safe those who mattered to her most.

Chapter 3

Crystet

The terrain teemed with brain-dead Glaziene, ravenous for Kólasi's approval. Every living person they snatched for Him filled their mindless bodies with dark joy.

Only the sky was safe.

Without the ability to fly, the few Glaziene survivors were bound to the castle grounds, which Gwynessa had reinforced with magic from the lost relic of Gaia. It was the only thing strong enough to keep both Kólasi's infectious roots and His zombified minions away.

"Any luck?" Ario asked, quietly entering Gwynessa's blood-stained childhood bedroom—her personal crypt of nightmares. She sat cross-legged on the floor.

"No," she answered, holding back her tears. "I miss him."

"I miss him, too."

"I prayed to the Vorso," she admitted, gaze glued to the blood-filled floor cracks. "The evening after we lost him. I thought that if Gaia wouldn't listen, maybe the others would."

"I thought you didn't believe in them."

"I don't," she mumbled. "I was desperate."

Ario nodded. "I understand."

"The Vorso are a fairy tale. Calix's continued absence is proof."

"Prayers take time."

"Or maybe the gods don't care."

Ario lowered his gaze—he didn't know what else to say.

Gwynessa continued, "We don't need the gods. We need the drakkina."

"Yes, maybe, but take a break, please. You've been in here for days."

"Only they can combat Kólasi, and only I can reach them. I have to keep trying."

"Promise me you will come to dinner at least?"

Gwynessa sighed. "I promise."

Ario bent down and kissed her forehead, then left.

Alone again, surrounded by the horrors of her past, Gwynessa exhaled deeply. Spidering cracks filled with Kipp's blood stained the glass room—veins filled forever with her grief. The mantle on the wall still displayed Lorcan's and Trista's severed heads, mouths agape and stuffed with their hardened hearts. Their mummified expressions of horror haunted her heart. Next to the heads, Ignatius's glowing blue eyeball stared at her, as if it were still alive; as if it still held resentment toward her.

It was too much.

This tomb of nightmares no longer served her.

It no longer provided adequate motivation.

Terror, grief, and rage—that's all it gave. These suffocating feelings gurgled in her chest, boiling with vivacity. Their pull so strong, another familiar feeling clawed its way to the surface: heartlessness. A tried-and-true method to combat her own darkness; a lost friend begging to save her once again.

No.

Never again.

That demon was put to rest—eternal slumber for her devious heart. And though she'd never choose to numb the pain again, perhaps revisiting this crypt of memories did not serve her well either. This room was a curse—each visit a debilitating waltz with all she had lost. Every moment spent here was time stolen from all the love that had survived.

Gwynessa rose to her feet.

She came to this room of horrors to escape the nightmare persisting beyond the castle borders, but fear could not conquer fear. Only light and love could save them now.

Perhaps the festering heartache radiating from this den of melancholy had thwarted her attempts to reach the drakkina. Maybe the darkness was too loud, maybe it drowned her out.

It was time to try again from a source of light.

It was time to leave this room of ancient misery in the past.

Gwynessa side-glanced at the mantle of horrors.

"I do not forgive you," she said, "but I forgive myself for who I became because of you."

Her eyes tracked the bloody streaks of bereaved love covering the floor and walls.

Near the door, she traced her finger over a deep stain.

Her most loyal friend.

"I'm sorry I could not save you. I blamed myself for your death all these years, but I was just a child. There was nothing I could have done differently." She sobbed. "I'm sorry your fate was linked to mine."

She kissed the spidering bloodstain.

"I will love you forever," she whispered, her eyes glistening with remorse.

Unable to stomach this awful feeling a moment longer, she stepped through the door and closed it behind her. Gasping for air between sobs, she locked the door, keeping her horrible mementos sealed safely inside.

Heart racing, breath fleeting, she leaned against the cool glass wall and reminded herself that feeling pain was healthier than feeling nothing at all.

She cried until the feeling subsided naturally.

As her panic settled and her tears dried, she lifted herself off the wall and focused all her energy on her mission: reaching the drakkina.

Her heart needed to stay in place, intact, if she wished to reach Gaia's heart on her own.

She needed light.

She needed love.

She tried to think of a place within the castle that housed happy memories, but failed. The entire grounds were home to her wretched childhood.

There had to be someplace she could go.

Happiness surely existed *somewhere.*

The Wildlands, she thought.

She glided down the hall and into the throne room.

The king's chair sat vacant—the spot where Calix should be sitting, ruling this land from the comfort of his throne.

Instead, Gwynessa was forced to fill this space. She sat in the chair, prepared to honor him by saving him and their home.

Opulent shards of glass and crystal adorned to the backrest fanned over her head.

"So glad you decided to take a break," Ario said from where he stood beside Tyrus.

"Did you reach them?" Mina asked.

"No, but I am going to try something new."

Tyrus turned his forlorn gaze out the window to the former ice queen. Mina paused her crochet work to listen also.

"What's the plan?" he asked.

"I'll make my call from the Wildlands."

"No," Ario objected. "That's beyond the protective border of the castle grounds."

"I made that protective border," she reminded him. "I can use the lost relic of Gaia to keep me safe on this journey."

"I'm going with you," Ario said.

"No," Gwynessa countered. "I need to go alone."

"It isn't safe."

"No, it's not," she agreed. "But it will be easier to keep one person safe rather than two."

Ario grumbled to himself. "I don't like this."

"My greatest connection to the animals is within the Wildlands. It makes sense to try again from there."

Tyrus cut in, "I'll stand watch on the tower until you're back. If there are any issues, send up a flare."

"Thank you." She grabbed Ario's hand and kissed his knuckles, then promised, "I will be back soon."

He pulled her in close and buried his face into her hair.

"You better," he whispered before letting her go.

Gwynessa touched the lost relic of Gaia hanging around her neck, took a deep breath, and left the throne room before she lost her courage.

She made her solitary glide through the castle—the few survivors taking shelter there rarely ventured beyond the common rooms.

Outside, on the castle grounds, Gwynessa walked to the middle of the large yard, then glanced back. Atop the tallest tower, Tyrus and Ario stood watch, as promised.

She turned back around and continued her walk to the border. Thousands of foggy-eyed Glaziene villagers crowded the thin, sizzling purple shield. Energy muted, minds empty, motivation paused—they knew where the survivors hid and waited patiently for an opportunity to strike.

A few hundred feet from the protective shield, Gwynessa clutched the star relic hanging around her neck.

The closer she got, the more the outliers stirred. Their vacant stationary swaying turned into sudden fidgeting jerks as they sensed her presence.

Gwynessa activated the relic's magic and channeled her intentions. The glittering purple magic slithered out of the star and clung to her body, creating a form-fitted shield of protection.

When she reached the border, she paused before crossing through.

The foggy white eyes of her people snapped to her, zeroed in on her flirtation with disaster. She searched for Calix's sweet smile, his head of silver-blond curls, his bright silver-green eyes.

She saw Keane Bicchieri, owner of the ill-fated lodge. Claudio, the kind stable boy with two different colored eyes. Merliando, the most famous painter in Crystet.

No sign of Calix.

He wasn't among them.

"Can any of you hear me?" she asked.

They groaned and grumbled in reply.

A familiar face pushed to the front of the crowd.

Uncle Exton.

His foggy eyes held a faint golden glow.

"He wants you most of all."

It wasn't her uncle. The voice belonged to someone else.

"Who?" she asked.

"Kólasi."

"Why?"

"His favorite mortals to play with are Matrigaia's favorites."

"If you let me pass safely, maybe we can strike a deal."

"No deal making with mortals. Only mind snatching."

A golden fly flew out of Exton's ear. The moment it departed, her uncle's expression sagged.

It was now or never.

She had to trust in Gaia's magic and brave the terror, or resign herself and her loved ones to a half-life of hiding within Her magic.

Courage sparked, she walked through the shield, taking the first step of many toward freedom.

Chapter 4

Radix de Orewall

Feodras and the surviving Bouldes remained in Occavas. Their amethyst castle still lay in a pile of rubble above, leaving Radix de Orewall as their last safe place left to hide. And while it was safer here from the possessed Namatéans, they still needed a never-ending guard to deter Kólasi's infected roots of darkness. The magic of Occavas was not strong enough on its own to combat Kólasi's ethereal power, so the Bouldes took turns manning the borders of Radix de Orewall, using magic-fueled stones from Occavas that radiated protective energy and kept the sickly tendrils stemming from Radix de Fibril at bay.

It was tireless work, but critical—one lapse in their guard and their fight would be lost.

Stennis manned the schedule, making sure every inch of shoreline was attended between shifts. Cybelle and Carrick joined Feodras on daily trips to collect more stones. Feodras had a theory—a hope—that if they gathered enough stones to outline the border of Radix de Orewall, the combined energy might be enough to give the guards a break and turn their echoland into a true sanctuary.

"Ready for our daily adventure?" Cybelle asked. Though she healed from the torture she had endured, her ancient age held on to the scars and physical trauma longer than the others. A limp accompanied each step as she hobbled toward their Murk King.

"Soon, we'll have enough stones to cover the eastern shoreline," Carrick added, offering Cybelle an arm to lean on while walking beside her.

"It's taking too long," Feodras grumbled. "Everyone is growing tired. I don't know how much longer we can ward off the infected tendrils from Radix de Fibril."

"We are tired, but we are determined," Cybelle offered. "No one has lost hope, thanks to your leadership. Stay strong, and the others will follow."

"You're right. I just wish I had some direction, some solid hope to hold on to." Feodras's tiny shoulders slouched. "We are mortals trying to evade a god."

"You're right, it's not very promising," Cybelle agreed, "but whether we emerge on the other side of this mess brain dead or victorious, at least we can say we tried."

"And that we never *stopped* trying," Carrick added.

Feodras nodded. "Thank you. Sometimes I feel like the weight of this bears on me alone, but it doesn't. We are in this together."

"Always," Cybelle confirmed.

"Let's go."

Feodras led his friends to the shadowy quarry of Radix de Orewall. Tons of magic-enhanced rocks lay here, but with the majority of the surviving Bouldes rotating between sleep and guard duty, they had very few hands to help collect rocks.

Occasionally, Bedros, Haldor, Axton, and some of the other guards would skip their sleeping shift to help, but today, they all chose sleep.

Feodras didn't blame them—their new existence in nonstop survival mode was exhausting.

With only himself, Cybelle, and Carrick on collection duty, today's haul would be small.

As they lugged as many rocks as they could to their wheelbarrows and prepared to make the first of many trips to the eastern shoreline, a gushing whir of wind swirled overhead.

"We're busy!" Cybelle grumbled.

Feodras lowered his wheelbarrow. "Ciela, is that you?"

The whirring ceased as Ciela revealed herself. She did not land, though. She stayed safely hovered in the sky. "Elixyvette won't share her secrets."

"I figured as much," Feodras said.

"We have to find out how she's doing it."

"She must have powerful magic of some kind." Cybelle leaned against a boulder to rest. "There are ancient relics hidden all over Namaté. Maybe she found one of them."

"I know of the relics," Ciela scoffed. "Do you think those are strong enough to ward off a god?"

"They were made when Gaia created the scepter—a little piece from each land that still holds its original power. They all have Her touch." Cybelle shrugged.

"I hadn't considered this."

"It's a good thing we're thinking out loud, then," Cybelle stated bluntly.

Feodras added, "Gwynessa is using the lost relic of Gaia and that is protecting the surviving Glaziene brilliantly. Makes sense that magic touched by Her holiness can deter Kólasi."

"Then why isn't the magic of Occavas protecting you?" Ciela asked. "It's also touched by Gaia."

"It is protecting us, but the potency of the magic here is lessened due to how it spreads across the echoland. Within the relics, the magic is concentrated."

"Hmph." Ciela crossed her arms over her chest.

"We are currently gathering as many stones as we can to amplify the magic," Feodras further explained.

"Combining their power," Ciela mused, deep in contemplation.

"Correct. And we need to get back to work if we ever wish to finish outlining Radix de Orewall's border with these stones."

"What is Orewall's ancient relic again?" Ciela asked, consumed by her own private thoughts.

"Queen Amezite's stone brain," Cybelle answered. "No one has ever found it."

"That's not true, actually," Feodras revealed.

Everyone's attention snapped to him.

"The Murks found it centuries ago."

"You found it and never used it to help yourselves?" Cybelle asked brusquely.

"I never saw it personally—I wasn't alive during its recovery—but I've heard stories about it."

"And?" Ciela demanded.

"Legend has it that the first Murks found it. There were six of them: Cloch, Hajar, Marmor, Rupes, Pietra, and Skala. I was told the story as a kid, but from what I remember, they thought it was cursed—it was a remnant of Gaia's wrath—so they hid it where they thought no one would ever find it."

"Do you know where that might be?"

Feodras shook his head. "And no one *has* found it since."

Ciela huffed. "There's too many anyway."

"What do you mean?"

"I was thinking if we found all the lost relics and combined them, maybe we could create a source of power that rivals the scepter of alchemy. And with both sources of magic, maybe we'd stand a better chance against Kólasi."

Feodras, Cybelle, and Carrick shared curious glances, then leaned in, listening closely.

Ciela continued, "But if it'll be this hard to find the lost relic of Orewall, I can't imagine how hard it would be to find all the others. Only the lost relic of Gaia is accounted for."

"And whichever relic Elixyvette is using," Feodras added.

"Right."

"And Rúnar's heart is somewhere deep within Seakkan."

Ciela grumbled. "Never mind. It was just a thought."

"It's a good thought, actually," Cybelle encouraged. "Might be the best thought anyone has had yet."

"But it'll be near to impossible to execute."

"Surviving Kólasi is near to impossible, but we haven't given up yet."

Ciela hesitated. "You're right. I'm sorry. I'm struggling to stay positive."

"We all are," Cybelle empathized.

"Once we create a self-sufficient shield around this echoland, we will start hunting for our relic," Feodras promised.

"And I will begin searching for the others," Ciela offered.

Ciela lifted higher into the sky and spun in rapid circles until she turned into an aella. As her breeze vanished, the Bouldes turned to each other.

Feodras waited a moment longer before speaking, then after checking the area make sure they were alone, he confided, "I think I know where it is."

Chapter 5

Crystet

Safely encased by the lost relic of Gaia, Gwynessa made the long trek to the Wildlands.

Kólasi's minions clung to her as she walked. Every time they touched her shielded skin, the sizzling purple magic burned their fingers. And though it caused them to flinch and retreat, without their minds in place, they had no sense of self-preservation. They kept returning to Gwynessa, kept touching her and inflicting more pain upon themselves.

They filtered in and out around her, moving in a rotating wave of vacant determination. There was never a free moment from their smothering swarm.

Halfway through Grimmur Village, the suffocating presence of the mindless masses became too much to bear. She didn't have much practice using the relic to levitate, but if there was any time to try, it was now.

Concentrated on her intention, the magic slowly lifted her into the sky. She rose until her feet dangled safely out of reach of the tallest foggy-eyed Glaziene. It took a great deal of concentration to keep both the shield and her levitation activated, but she was safer and could travel faster this way.

She added one final task to her concentration: forward movement. Though she reached the edge of the Wildlands much quicker this way, the mob of minions still lingered below, stalking her flight pattern.

To her great delight, upon entering the Wildlands, she learned that her beloved animals were spared from Kólasi's takeover. When they caught her scent hovering above, they emerged from their hiding places within the Wildlands and joined the masses following her.

She reached Jökull Cliff.

Graveyard to her broken past.

Home to her rebuilt future.

::I need to lower,:: she said to her animals.

Kentara led the wolves, who herded the mindless Glaziene away from the cliff. They resisted, half-heartedly, but they were no match against the animals who had formed a long line that kept them at bay. From afar, the brain-dead Glaziene kept their hollow, vacant eyes locked on Gywnessa, waiting for their chance to reach her.

Gwynessa lowered, unafraid of their empty glares. The purple shield still tightly hugged her body and protected her from the infected roots littering the forest floor, and no one would get past her animal protectors.

She sat on the ground, fingers dug into the grainy glass soil, and called out to the drakkina.

::We need help.::

No reply.

With every ounce of her being, Gwynessa channeled her connection to nature. Her love surged through her body, bursting through her head, fingers, and toes.

::Can you hear me?::

A roar only she could hear boomed within her mind.

::Speak to me,:: Gwynessa pled. *::We need you to come back.::*

::Gwynessa?::

::Yes!::

::How are you reaching us?:: The voice belonged to Amari.

::I don't know, but I need your help.::

::We cannot come.::

::Why not?::

::Only Gaia can open the portal that releases us from Cruxeus.::

::Ask her to!::

A different drakkina chimed in.

::I told you there was darkness brewing.:: Gwynessa recognized Gwyneira's voice. *::I tried to warn you. You shouldn't have sent us away.::*

::I was wrong, I know.::

::We haven't peered through Namaté's door in a while. You were in control when we left. What has changed since?::

::The darkness you were feeling was Kólasi. He planted infectious roots here and is turning everyone into some kind of zombie.::

Silence.

Gwynessa's fingers dug deeper into the soil. *::Are you still there?::*

::Are they mindless or soulless?:: Amari asked.

::There's a difference?:: Gwynessa asked, appalled.

::Yes. And whichever they are determines which of Kólasi's prisons they were sent to.::

::How can I tell the difference?::

::Soulless is trickier to spot—their cognitive functions will operate normally, but they'll be different. They won't be their normal self. Impossible to detect on a stranger, but you'd notice the change in people you are close with.::

::And mindless?::

:: Mindless are easier to spot. They can't talk or think by themselves.::

::They're mindless,:: Gwynessa answered confidently. *::They grumble and cheer, but they only speak when the little gold flies enter their heads.::*

::Filii diaboli.:: Disdain welled in Amari's voice.

::What's that?::

::The Devil's sons.::

::Those flies are sons of the devil?::

::They travel in many forms while doing Kolasi's bidding. As flies, seas creatures, windstorms, terrain worms. The possibilities are endless, but they always wear Kólasi's signature gold color. Sounds like the filii came to you as muscas—flies. It's one of their most fearsome forms.::

::Muscas,:: Gwynessa repeated. *::Do you have any tips on how to beat them?::*

::Fire from the sun. Ice from the moon.::

::I don't have access to either of those things. Anything else?::

::Only elemental extremes work on the filii. Whatever weapon you use, harness its most intense form.::

::And it will kill them?::

::No.:: Amari laughed. *::They are gods. You cannot kill them. But it will kill the forms they took and send their godly essences back to the abyss.::*

::I see. So I need to find an elemental extreme that I can harness.::

::Correct.::

::And what happens to all the mindless people once the flies are gone?::

::They stay mindless. Without the muscas around to instigate their actions, they'll become more docile.::

::How do we get their minds back?:: Gwynessa asked.

::You don't. No minds, bodies, or souls ever leave Kólasi's prisons. Not without divine intervention.::

::Where is Gaia?:: Gwynessa asked.

::Reaching Her only happens when She desires.::

::She will want to help us.::

::You overestimate her love and patience.::

::What do you mean?::

::Your planet has been a great nuisance to Her for eons. She might see their imprisonment as proper punishment.::

Gwynessa choked on a sorrowful gasp.

Calix.

All of her people, and those from neighboring lands.

Gone forever.

She quickly swallowed her emotion.

Amari continued, *::Just make sure you do not join them.::*

Gwynessa inhaled deeply. The danger of their current reality suddenly intensified. She glanced over her shoulder and the ravenous gazes of the mindless Glaziene greeted her.

They wanted her mind; they wanted her to join them.

::Is there any way for you to come here and help?:: Gwynessa tried one more time.

::Only Gaia can unleash us from Cruxeus,:: Amari answered. *::Plus, we cannot defeat Kólasi on our own. We often help Gaia fight Her immortal brothers and sisters, but we hold no disillusions of our own strength. Only gods battle gods.::*

::I understand.::

::Call out to us as needed. For advice or support.::

::Thank you. I might need your knowledge and wisdom in the forthcoming days.::

::One last thing before I go,:: Amari began, *::How is Elior?::*

::Who?::

::The electric prince.::

::I've heard nothing about him.::

::Put him on your radar,:: Amari advised. *::He may be the answer to all of your prayers.::*

The telepathic connection sizzled as it broke.

Gwynessa lifted her fingers out of the soil, and as she returned all her senses to the reality surrounding her, the sound of wind clapping filled the space.

Noelani rose above the cliff's edge—her hastily made aquatic wings kept her elevated.

Eyes wide with fear, expression etched by unknown horrors, she sniveled.

"Help me."

Chapter 6

Gwynessa scrutinized Noelani harshly—her foggy eyes were their normal shade of fierce orange. No additional golden glow.

"How are you speaking to me?" Gwynessa demanded. "You are one of the mindless."

Noelani tremored. "I am dead." She paused. "Well, I should be dead, but He's keeping me alive."

"I don't understand."

"Ciela killed me." Noelani lifted her chin and pointed to three raw scars on her neck. She wore the deep, diagonal slashes like a lethal necklace. "I asked her to. Death was a gift. But Kólasi stole that from me."

"He brought you back to life?"

"I don't know what I am anymore. I teeter between here and there." Her eyes darted nervously. "I will be taken away again soon."

"Taken where?"

"To the darkness."

"I don't understand what you want from me," Gwynessa stated plainly.

"Help me stay here. Please," she begged. "I don't want to go back. I don't want to serve as His vessel anymore."

"I have no power against Kólasi."

Noelani lowered and knelt before the ice queen. "Please!"

Gwynessa threw her arm toward the legion of mindless Glaziene itching to get past her animal guard and serve her to their nefarious god.

"I can't even save my own people," she barked. "How do you expect me to help you? I am outmatched. I have no power."

"You have the lost relic of Gaia."

"If it cannot save me from the devil, it cannot save you, either."

Noelani sobbed.

"I'm sorry," Gwynessa offered.

As Noelani sobbed at her feet, Gwynessa granted her a moment of grace. She stood by her, allowing her to unleash her anguish in the company of another. Noelani's solitary suffering had been profound—lending a momentary ear was a small gift Gwynessa was willing to give.

"I recognize your distress," she offered. "I do not understand it wholly, but I empathize."

"If you saw the dark place, if you felt its consuming emptiness ... you'd try to help. You wouldn't let me go back."

"Where is it that you go?"

Noelani shuddered. "I don't know."

As the words left her lips, the life left her eyes. Her orange gaze dulled, and the pearly fog covering her vision intensified.

She was gone.

Returned to her state of mindlessness, Noelani rose to her feet, and her empty gaze fixated on Gwynessa. She extended her arms, reaching for the very alive woman standing before her.

Gwynessa lifted into the sky.

Noelani released an animalistic cry as her target evaded her grasp. Unable to speak, her instinctual noises revealed her frustration.

The revelation hit Gwynessa like a lightning bolt—Noelani's body was still here, but her mind was taken elsewhere. She wasn't physically taken away, only mentally.

Gwynessa scanned the crowd of mindless Glaziene, then returned her attention to Noelani. She was teetering back and forth between Kólasi's prison planet for mortal minds.

How? Gwynessa thought. *The drakkina said no one could leave once they were there.* She paused. *Unless they had help from the divine.*

The implication was grave and bewildering.

Based off what Noelani had said, the god playing with her fate was Kólasi, but why?

Realizing now that Noelani could play a huge role in saving the mindless and learning more about Kólasi's intentions, Gwynessa wished she had pried more information out of her before her mind was stripped away again.

Noelani's wet wings hung against her back as she jumped and growled, still reaching for Gwynessa. Without the golden muscas inside their skulls directing their thoughts and actions, basic motor functions among the mindless were less accessible. A blessing, really—if the mindless were easily able to use all their natural gifts, such as flying, swimming, web weaving, and sailing with motivated direction, it would be much harder to evade their recruitment. As it was, they were relatively lazy and apathetic. They had a mission, but little urgency. Only when the golden flies entered their skulls, or Kólasi visited, did their enthusiasm perk.

::Keep her here,:: Gwynessa asked of her wolves. *::But if Kólasi comes for her, do not risk your lives to uphold my request. Let Him have her.::* She turned to the owls perched in the evergreens. *::If He takes her, follow. At a safe distance, of course. See what you can learn.::*

The owls hooted with understanding while the wolves seized Noelani by her extremities and dragged her into the forest.

Still hovering high above the swarm of mindless below, Gwynessa focused her energy toward Vapore.

She had not yet traveled using the lost relic of Gaia, and now was not the time to try. There were too many threats and dangers lurking beyond Crystet's borders. Too many opportunities to be ambushed and stripped of her mind. Her family needed her back at the castle. She needed to stay here with the lost relic of Gaia to protect them.

Still, she *also* needed to reach her allies.

::Helgi.:: Gwynessa summoned her lead owl. Calling her name brought back memories of her beloved, departed, Hadid.

Helgi spread her black spotted wings and soared to Gwynessa.

::How can I help?:: the young snow owl asked.

Without lowering, Gwynessa used the magic of the lost relic to scoop up a large handful of dusty glass soil. She dumped it into a small pouch hanging from her waistband, pulled the drawstrings tight, and handed it to Helgi.

::Fly directly above Vapore. When you are at the center point of the dome, dump the contents of this pouch. It should be enough to let Ciela know that I'd like a meeting with her.::

Helgi hooted and flew off.

Gwynessa stewed in this new revelation.

Noelani—the ultimate instigator for so many of Namaté's recent problems.

Could she really be the key to saving them all?

Chapter 7

Cerébrum

Blinded by darkness.

Noelani whimpered, "Not again."

Afraid to move, afraid to make a sound, she hugged herself tightly and waited. And though it often felt like an eternity before Kólasi returned to rip her out of this hell, He always did.

Eventually.

Her perpetually wet, aquatic wings hung limp on her back. Since losing her original wings, these slimy extensions—a forced gift from King Morogh and King Rúnar—were her second set of wings. She had loved the metal dragonfly wings she had given herself using the scepter of alchemy, but Elixyvette stripped her of those. These scaled, aquatic wings were the nefarious duo's attempt to fix her so that she could serve them.

She'd rather be wingless—a grand sentiment coming from someone defined by flight.

Methodical droplets dripped off her slick wings. They made no sound as they fell, but Noelani felt each bead as it slithered down and fell. She counted, hoping it might solidify the concept of time in this vacuum of a prison.

It didn't.

On the one hundredth drip, she still had no idea if she had been there for seconds or weeks.

Eagerly anticipating Kólasi's ethereal pull, she tried not to panic or succumb to the darkness.

He would be back.

He always came back for her.

The darkness amplified the silence.

Isolated with her sight stripped, her other senses heightened—the stench of hopelessness, the sound of nothingness, the feeling of empty vastness.

What if He didn't come back this time?

Noelani shuddered.

She wasn't sure how to pray to the god of death and chaos, but she tried.

"Father, Brother," she whispered, unsure what He was to her. "Your holy darkness. I beseech You. Come back for me, please. I am Your humble servant, Your loyal vessel. I will be anything You need me to be, just don't leave me here." She sniveled. "Please."

Nothing changed. Silence, stillness, and darkness remained.

"In the name of Death, His devils, and all of their sins, I vow."

She wasn't sure how Kólasi liked to receive prayers and accolades, but it felt right.

Still, nothing changed.

Tortuous solitude in everlasting obscurity.

"You're praying to the wrong god," a voice offered from the darkness. The scent of charred embers accompanied the intrusion.

Startled, but clearminded, Noelani replied, "I already tried praying to Gaia."

"Have you tried her progenies?"

"Which ones? She has many."

"Any. They aren't as busy as Her. Perhaps they will answer."

"I only know the drakkina to be real."

"There are others."

"Who are you?" Noelani asked, spinning in a blind circle, searching for a face she'd never see.

"I am a friend."

"Do you have a name?"

"You can trust me."

"I can't even see you. How can I possibly trust you?"

"Try."

Noelani hesitated, then asked, "Do the drakkina have a specific prayer?"

"The drakkina can't help you. They are bound to their prison in Cruxeus."

"Then who? I don't know much about Gaia's other progenies."

"Your glass friends do."

The scent of smoke dissipated.

"The Glaziene?" Noelani asked.

There was no reply.

The shadow voice was gone.

Noelani considered this. Praying to a different god couldn't hurt.

A shiver ripped down Noelani's spine, followed by an infant's cry. Loud, shrieking, awful—was there a baby trapped in this prison, too?

She turned in circles searching for the source, but the crying stopped as soon as it had begun, and silence resumed.

Disoriented, she had no idea which way she was facing when she saw the light.

A flicker, then a flame.

It was far off in the distance, but as bright as a sun in this prison of eternal night.

Hope ignited, she ran toward it, but before she reached it, a familiar voice echoed through her head.

<<You are mine.>>

Kólasi snatched her by the brain and snapped her backward. In a blink, the darkness of this prison merged with the darkness behind closed eyes, and she was stripped away again.

Soon, light would greet her.

Soon, she would be home.

Chapter 8

Wildlands, Crystet

Noelani reentered her body

She flickered in and out as Kólasi took control.

Her weakened body was a vessel for the god of death and chaos, and while He used her to tour Namaté, she clung to consciousness. She could not speak or control her motor functions, and while she was able to observe and hear everything happening around her, the force of His possession often kept her in a daze.

Kólasi was in control.

Snarling wolves surrounded Noelani's body, which His divine being slithered within. The savage creatures formed a barrier between His vessel and the world beyond. He stood, raised her wet wings, and growled back at the beasts. Orange eyes glimmering with fierce gold, the wolves whimpered and stepped back. They did not lower their guard, but their resolve faltered.

"Let me pass." Though it was Noelani's voice, it echoed ethereally. Ominous, stern, commanding—the wolves obeyed their intuition and let Him pass.

The owls screeched in protest, circling overhead but doing nothing to thwart Him.

Smart choice, mortal monsters, He thought, laughing at their frailty. The animals were insignificant to Him—they existed on all of Gaia's planets. What He aimed to destroy were the humanoids unique to Namaté. Erasing those mortals from existence would cause Gaia the most strife, as they were harder to recreate.

Kólasi flapped Noelani's wet wings, splattering thick slime over the wolves. He lifted into the sky and then dove over the side of Jökull cliff.

Every visit followed the same pattern: lighthouse maintenance, a wellness check on the mindless, thorough examination of the remaining mortal survivors, and a blast of celestial energy into His sons.

Inside Noelani's vessel, He soared toward Fibril. There, His edifice of death stood tall and menacing.

Covered in dark webs teeming with contamination and emanating an ethereal golden glow, His lighthouse radiated with formidable opulence.

As He flew closer, its towering grandiosity filled His hollow heart with delight.

He had lighthouses scattered all over the universe, each one as special as the next. Some of His lighthouses served His prison planets. Others served His planets of chaos and death. Some created chaos within the mortal lands where they were stationed. His most grandiose lighthouses served His abyss and Matrigaia's nirvana. Each edifice had a function—and side effects—unique to its specific design.

This one captured mortal minds and transported them to Cerébrum, where their minds would remain imprisoned forever. Kólasi had three prison planets—Cerébrum for mortal minds, Corpeus for mortal bodies, and Spiritus for mortal spirits. He chose to make the mortals of Namaté mindless, as Cerébrum was currently His most malnourished prison planet. Each captured mind not only fed the dark ecosystem, but also bolstered Kólasi's dominance. He could not create mortal life—

He could only take it away—and each mortal He captured represented His power and control.

Kólasi circled the web-covered edifice made of charcoal and gold. Through Noelani's hands, He resealed every tiny fissure with gilded putty. He maintained this lighthouse regularly, so there weren't many cracks to fill, and when every inch was pristine again, He left to check on the mindless.

His mind-stripped mortal minions swarmed across the land and beneath the sea.

Over Orewall, the mindless Bouldes wandered aimlessly, trekking across the desert and dunes, waiting for a living mind to snatch. Dormant in this state, as their purpose was paused—there were no living minds around.

It was the same scenario in Soylé and Crystet. The mindless wandered aimlessly unable to find, or blocked from reaching, any survivors.

In Vapore, only the wing-pinned Commondores were mindless. All the other Gasiones flew free.

From the sky, Wicker had no visible survivors. The once lush forest was now a barren dust field covered in dead leaves and broken stumps. But Kólasi knew they hid within Occavas under protection from the scepter of alchemy. They were His most coveted recruitments, as Gaia loved them the most, but for now, they remained unreachable.

Coppel appeared vacant also, which frustrated Kólasi more—the metalheads should have been easy recruits. He turned His flight to Elecort.

As they were the last time He visited, the Metellyans were protected under Elixyvette's strong shield.

Kólasi seethed.

He knew that all the remaining survivors, except the Gasiones, were using different forms of magic to thwart Him—the Glaziene had the lost relic of Gaia, the Woodlins had the scepter of alchemy, and the Bouldes used the magic of Occavas, while the Gasiones just used their natural ability to fly. What were the Voltains using?

Kólasi steered Noelani's body closer to the top of the shield. The tickling buzz and droning hum of electricity from the land pulsated through the dome. Though it was strong enough to mask the vehement pull of concealed magic from mortals, Kólasi felt the magic radiating beneath.

Without needing to get any closer, He closed Noelani's eyes and channeled the magic. His vision left the vessel and located the source. Atop Elixyvette's head, hidden in her crown of electric coils and masked by her long dark hair, sat a pair of glowing eyes. Their irises burned a potent shade of fuchsia.

Another enchanted ancient artifact—they radiated the same energy as the lost relic of Gaia.

How many relics were there?

How many were still lost?

How many were found?

Kólasi stewed. He had heard of Gaia's reckoning on this planet eons ago, but never cared to know the details. They had never mattered until now.

The power pulsating from the fuchsia eyes taunted Him.

<<*Noelani!*>> His voice boomed, rattling Noelani's consciousness from the cozy depths of her mind.

I am here, she thought in reply.

<<*What do you know about the eyes hidden in Elixyvette's crown?*>>

Jasvinder's eyes, Noelani recalled. *There aren't many who know that she has them.*

<<*Then how do you know?*>>

She and I were allies for a brief moment. I spied on her prior to aligning. She betrayed me not long after. I never got the chance to tell anyone. Or to seek revenge.

He ignored the boring details. <<*How many similar relics exist?*>>

I'd have to think about that.

Kólasi skipped through Noelani's thoughts, searching for the information He desired. Due to her half-alive status, her memories weren't as clear as those of the living.

<<*Think!*>> He demanded.

Noelani stammered, *Th-there's the lost relic of Gaia. Jasvinder's eyes. Erm—* She paused, genuinely struggling to remember.

<<*I've felt power like this before,*>> He mused.

There are more, she confirmed.

<<*When I first arrived, right before I emerged. I felt the magic of a relic, then I felt the drakkina, but both were gone before I arrived.*>>

Rúnar's heart, Noelani remembered.

<<*And where would I find this heart?*>>

I don't know, she answered honestly.

<<*Go back to sleep,*>> He taunted, shoving her consciousness with an invisible hand. She stumbled and fell back into the pits of her mind.

He could not sense dormant relics, but He could summon those who might know their whereabouts.

"Rúnar!" He bellowed.

Foggy red light beaconed from beneath the sea.

Chapter 9

Seakkan

Kólasi dove Noelani's body into the ocean.

The minds of the ancient deceased were long out of reach and stored in Sensi's vault. The elder god of mortal minds, would never allow Him access to Her chambers—She, Viscus, and Vigor hated Him for His prison planets that stole their mortal spoils—so He'd have to rely on the muscle memory of the recently deceased.

Viscus, the elder god of mortal flesh, did not collect bodies. He could, but He often allowed the cosmos to deliver the pieces as they organically decomposed.

Aimed at the red glow beaming from the west, Kólasi swam at a godly speed to the source.

Rúnar swayed in place beneath the sea, his red gaze gleaming through the foggy veil of mindlessness.

<<*My son,*>> Kólasi greeted. <<*I need your help.*>>

Rúnar grunted in understanding.

<<*Where is your heart?*>> Kólasi bellowed telepathically. <<*I know that Sensi took your mind when you died—I'm sorry that I did not act faster to intercept Her retrieval—but I am hoping your body might remember.*>>

Rúnar stirred in his stupor. The water made his slow movements even slower. He turned and pointed to the east.

<<*Take me there,*>> Kólasi commanded.

Kólasi extended an arm and lifted Rúnar off his feet. Sand kicked up, creating a plume beneath the mindless glass king. As it settled, Rúnar floated forward, moving faster with Kólasi's help.

He led the god of death and chaos to a massive gorge near the coast of Fibril.

Rúnar paused and briefly glanced over his shoulder at Kólasi.

<<I need to see it.>>

Rúnar turned back toward the gorge and lowered into the dark ravine.

Kólasi did not follow.

The red glow from Rúnar's eyes slowly vanished the deeper he lowered.

Minutes passed.

When the faint glow returned and brightened, Rúnar rose from the dark void with his heart in his hands. It was blackened and had thin fissures that pulsated red. In his grip, the dormant magic was revived and Kólasi felt it's potent pull.

<<It will remain lost,>> Kólasi ordered. *<<You will lower back into the gorge with your heart and you will guard it. No one touches your heart except you and me. This is your only job. Do you understand?>>*

Rúnar nodded.

<<You will have help. I will assign a team of ocaemons to safeguard the gorge as well.>>

Rúnar gurgled something incoherent, but Kólasi understood.

<<Your soul? It is safely tucked away in the flames of my abyss.>>

Rúnar mumbled uncomfortably.

Kólasi laughed. *<<Gaia's nirvana was never in the cards for you.>>*

Rúnar shook his head.

<<Reincarnation? Incarna decided you didn't deserve that option. Not after aligning and working with me during your long stay in our

shared purgatory. My abyss is where you belong.>> Kolasi paused, assessing Rúnar's demeanor. <<*It was the right decision.*>>

Rúnar bowed, confirming his loyalty.

<<*You continue to serve me well. Now, go.*>>

Heart in hand, Rúnar lowered back into the gorge.

Kólasi extended His arms and summoned the nearest oceamons. A mix of cecaelia, sirens, and tritones were yanked from their solitary spaces of waiting and dragged to the gorge.

<<*You have a new job,*>> Kólasi informed them. <<*You will protect the edges of this gorge. No one goes down there except me. Do you understand?*>>

They all nodded.

Plan in place, Kólasi rocketed upward and flew through the surface of the sea. Back in the sky, He shook Noelani's body, freeing Himself of excess water, then took in the collective energy of Namaté once more.

Conscious, animated life existed in all directions.

Recruitment was at a stubborn standstill. All remaining survivors had found steadfast methods of evading capture.

His sons—the filii diaboli in muscas form—needed to do more.

While some still had enough life force to do their jobs of inhabiting mindless skulls, most had taken shelter in hidden nooks and crevices while waiting for an energy boost upon their father's return.

The time was now.

Kólasi inhaled deeply, drawing in every musca in Namaté.

The muscas buzzed violently as they were sucked into Kólasi's breath stream.

He swallowed them whole.

Deep in the pit of His celestial gut, the muscas fed on His divine golden innards. Fleshy power, tendrilled strength, vivacious mucus—they feasted on His dark matter.

When He felt like they had enough, He exhaled. The hurricane force of His breath shifted the ocean tides and ejected the muscas out through His mouth.

"You are renewed," Kólasi declared. **"Wreak havoc!"**

The golden muscas hovered around their father momentarily to express their gratitude before flying away.

"Lucifer, wait," He commanded.

One of the tiny golden muscas halted and redirected its flight back to Kólasi, who extended His hand.

The musca touched Kólasi's fingertip and then transformed into full form—goat hooves for feet, the horns of a bull, black wings tipped with white, blood-red eyes, a chiseled male body, and a handsome human face.

"Yes, Father?"

"What is the problem here? This planet and all of its humanoid mortals should be mine by now. Why are there still survivors?"

"We can't bypass their magic."

"You must."

"We need more power."

"Do I not give you enough?"

"You do, but it fades too fast." Lucifer paused. "We've been here too long. I can't speak for my brothers, but I need to get back to my netherworld. I left Belzebuth in charge, and I already fear the mess I'll be going home to."

Kólasi seethed silently.

Lucifer quickly corrected himself, "It's not that we don't want to help You. We live to serve You. Of course. It's just that we have other hells to raise as well."

Kólasi snapped his fingers and Lucifer morphed back into a golden fly.

The devil buzzed furiously, angry with his father for silencing him.

"Go on, little bug. Do as you're told."

Lucifer flew away, unwilling to defy Kólasi.

Once out of sight, Kólasi sent an extra burst of His power into His sons. It wasn't as strong of a dose as when they were inside of Him, but it was enough to let them know that He recognized their strife. He'd give them more next time.

For now, His work here was done.

He exited Noelani's body, which plummeted like a ragdoll into the sea, and then rocketed into the ether.

He had other edifices to monitor, other planets to terrorize.

Chapter 10

Vapore

Ciela shielded her head as daggered shards of glass rained over the cypress tree.

A quick and clear call from the other side of Namaté.

"Real subtle," Adaliah grumbled as she brushed the glass out of her hair.

The other warriors taking shelter among the tree branches muttered with similar aggravation as they shook glass from their feathers.

"The mother of monsters needs to speak to me," Ciela said, stating the obvious.

"No kidding," Dasan replied.

"Wish she had another way to summon you," Lovise added.

"I'll suggest something other than glass when I speak to her," Ciela said.

She spread her giant eagle wings wide, prepared to lift into the sky, when a gurgling disturbance turned every warrior's attention to the swamp.

From the depths of the murky acidic water rose Noelani.

She flickered in and out of mindlessness. Her orange eyes fought to be seen through the pearly fog, while her body tremored, jerking violently. She stumbled forward despite her body's betrayal.

"Help," she begged during a moment of awareness.

"How is she speaking?" Adaliah whispered.

Lonan, Lovise, Dasan, Haizea, and Mazin chattered quietly among themselves.

"It's me!" Noelani pled. "Please help me."

"We cannot lower to the ground," Ciela informed her.

Exhausted, but determined, Noelani spread her soaked wings and lifted herself high enough to speak face to face with the Gasiones. She blinked vigorously to keep the fog from settling over her eyes.

"Noelani," Ciela began, "are you really with us right now?"

"I am," she cried, her head hung in shame.

"Look at me," Ciela demanded. Noelani lifted her chin, but kept her gaze on Ciela's beak. "In the eyes," her queen demanded.

Noelani met Ciela's blazing orange stare.

"How are you here?" Ciela asked.

"Kólasi uses my body as a vessel to check on Namaté. When He exits, I get about an hour back in my body. I am running out of time now, though. It was a long swim to get here."

"Can you see everything He is doing while He is here?"

"I can."

"Tell us."

Noelani hesitated. "It's hazy. He pushes my consciousness down. It's hard to see everything, and hard to remember."

"You must try!" Ciela demanded.

Noelani wobbled where she hovered. She rubbed her eyes to clear the fog.

"I need to stay here," she insisted. "I need to stay in my body."

"Until you can figure out how to do that you must start paying attention."

"He spends a lot of time at the lighthouse," Noelani revealed as she scanned her fuzzy memories. "I saw Rúnar this time."

"Rúnar? Where?"

"We were in Seakkan."

"What did Kólasi want from Rúnar?"

"His heart." Her wet wings faltered as she remembered. "But He let Rúnar keep it." She flapped her wings harder to stay at eye level with the Gasiones.

"Why did He want his heart?"

"It all started after He saw Elixyvette with the eyes."

"Eyes?"

"Jasvinder's eyes."

The Gasiones listening shared a collective gasp.

"He knows about the relics," Ciela realized.

Noelani shook her head, clearing the haze from her vision.

"Yes," she said. "He asked me if there were any other ancient artifacts with power like the eyes, and I could only think of the lost relic of Gaia and Rúnar's heart. Now I recall the rest, but I couldn't at the time."

"Do not tell him!" Ciela demanded.

"He's in my mind. He can pry the information out of me if He so chooses."

"Do everything in your power to keep this information from him."

"Why?"

Ciela shook her head. "It's better if I don't tell you." Her expression shifted to one of deep kindness. "You are in a delicate position of power. You can either help Him, or help us."

"I want to help *you*."

"Then you must pay close attention while He possesses your body—we need to learn His intentions, motivations, and weaknesses. And you *must* guard your memories at all cost."

"I understand." Tears returned to Noelani's whitening eyes. "I don't want to go back."

"Where do you go when you're gone?"

"I don't know. It's pitch black. I can't see anything. It's maddening."

"If it's where *you* go, I imagine all the other stolen minds are there also."

"I hadn't thought of that." Noelani wore a pained expression. "My mind doesn't work right anymore. It hasn't since I first lost my wings."

"This is your chance for redemption. Remember that."

Noelani nodded as the fog overtook her orange eyes. The lines on her worried face softened as her mind left her body. Her wings lost their strength, and she lowered to the ground.

She was gone, mind stripped and returned to the dark place.

"I need to talk sense into Elixyvette," Ciela stated.

"You need to see what Gwynessa wants from you also," Adaliah reminded her.

Ciela cupped her face in her hand. There was so much to do.

"Come with me," she requested of Adaliah and Lonan. "The rest of you, carry on with the relic hunt. Most importantly, find *our* lost relic. The black feathers of Elzaphan *must* be somewhere in Vapore, or Radix de Vapore."

"We will find them," Lovise promised.

Ciela nodded and then rocketed into the sky as an aella. The warrior duo followed, leaving the rest to the wild relic hunt.

Ciela detoured to Elecort. Once they had safely crossed Elixyvette's magic border, they spun out of aella form and descended over the castle.

"Elixyvette!" she shouted. Her giant white wings pounded the electric air. A tingling buzz shook her feathers.

The trio dove into the throne room through the open sky lights.

"You must join our alliance," Ciela demanded of the unbothered Voltain queen.

"No," Elixyvette replied without glancing up at her uninvited guests.

Ciela lowered. Adaliah followed, staying close to the Gasione queen, while Lonan guarded from above, observing the whole room and all of its occupants.

"The fate of Namaté depends on your compliance," Ciela urged.

"I'm fine with the Voltains and Metellyans being the sole survivors of this temporary invasion. I don't care what happens to the rest of you."

"Kólasi will not stop until all of our minds are seized."

"I can hold Him off until Gaia returns."

"Did you not consider *anything* I said during our last meeting?"

"I did." Elixyvette lifted her chin to meet Ciela's furious gaze with one of her own. "And I decided that you are not a holy messenger. Your connection to the gods is not greater than mine, or any other mortal of Namaté." Her steel-pink eyes blazed with a fury that went much deeper than her dislike for Ciela. "As for your wings, *gifted* by Gaia … you having wings must serve the greater good. She doesn't give gifts without reason, and She doesn't pick favorites."

"You're missing the point—"

"No, *you* are. I will not bow to you or anyone else. I am the master of my destiny."

"And what of your son's?"

"Do not speak of my son," Elixyvette seethed, her rage worsening.

Ciela scanned the room and found baby Elior sleeping quietly in the arms of a handmaiden. His sickly gray flesh gleamed under the maiden's emerald glow, and unless Ciela's memory was glitching, he looked much bigger than he had a few days ago.

"He's growing. Is he healing also?"

"I said, do not speak of my son!"

Elixyvette lifted a hand and shooed away the handmaiden, who quickly departed with the baby. She turned her murderous glare back to Ciela. "You cannot outwit the god of death and chaos."

"If you'd just *listen*, you'd see there is a way." Ciela hesitated. "And perhaps, if we succeed, we could use the power we create to help Elior also."

The electric queen tightened her lips as she swallowed her anger.

"Speak," she finally replied. The electricity teeming from her flesh shook the air around her.

"I know you have Jasvinder's eyes," Ciela began.

Elixyvette tensed and her breathing quickened, but her expression remained stoic.

Ciela continued, "We need them."

"I don't have them," Elixyvette lied with unnerving conviction.

"Yes, you do."

"I don't. And even if I did, why would I share their power with you? Find your own lost relic."

Ciela shook her head. "The eyes are one part of a whole. We need all nine relics—we think that combining them will create a power as strong as the scepter of alchemy."

Elixyvette's left eyebrow rose.

Ciela's hands clenched into fists. "And we already see how brilliantly the scepter protects the Woodlins from Kólasi. If we had a second source of magic with power that great, maybe we *could* outwit and outlast Him."

"How many of the other relics are accounted for?" Elixyvette asked.

"Are you joining the alliance?"

Elixyvette faltered, then lied again. "I don't have the eyes."

"I know for a fact that you do."

"How?"

"Noelani told me."

"Noelani is dead."

"There is much you do not know, and I will not tell you anything more until you pledge your allegiance to our cause."

"How can we work together when we cannot trust each other?" Elixyvette asked.

"I'm willing to try, but I already gave you a lot of information and have received nothing in return."

"How about a bargain," Elixyvette started. "Once you find and are in possession of the other eight relics, then I'll consider joining your team."

"I thought you didn't have the eyes," Ciela challenged.

"I may be able to find them." Elixyvette remained unrattled. "Plus, I don't think you'll be able to locate and secure the other eight."

"If you helped, maybe we could."

"I don't want to take part in your shoddy plan until I know it's solid. I'd like to keep my hands clean."

"So, you no longer serve Gaia, you serve Kólasi?" Ciela questioned.

"Of course not, but if Kólasi learns of your plan, it's over for anyone involved. I'd rather not face His wrath until I know we can win."

"Your cowardice will follow you into the afterlife."

"I offered you a bargain. Do you accept?"

"Yeah," Ciela conceded. "But make sure you're ready to hand the eyes over as soon as I have the other eight."

"And, assuming I can find them, you will give them back to me immediately after we vanquish Kólasi?"

"Yes."

"Deal," Elixyvette confirmed.

It took all of Ciela's constraint not to roll her eyes.

As she flew out of the open sky light, Adaliah and Lonan followed.

"Are you sure Elixyvette's lying? Noelani was a massive source of trouble during her final days," Adaliah inquired as they flew in aella form to Crystet.

"I am positive," Ciela answered. "Noelani was troubled indeed, but she was never a liar. And Elixyvette has been hiding her magic source from us—it makes sense that it's the eyes."

"She tensed up when you revealed her secret," Lonan added. "She definitely has them."

"For now, let's focus on Gwynessa," Ciela said. "She has the lost relic of Gaia. We need her cooperation."

The trio flew through the icy mist surrounding Crystet, and when they exited the frigid fog, they were greeted by a horrifying sight.

Thousands of mindless Glaziene wandered the land, many of whom swarmed the castle's magic-enforced shield. They waited with undying patience for a break in the defense—a crack to slither through.

"They are not safe here," Ciela noted in horror.

"Will the magic shield hold?" Adaliah asked. "There are droves of mindless pressing against it."

"One slip and they'll barrel through," Lonan added.

"I don't know if it will hold," Ciela confessed as she flew faster toward the castle.

Hovering over the glass ceiling of the solarium, Ciela opened her steel-tipped beak and released a deafening squawk—a war cry for all to hear.

Adaliah and Lonan echoed her urgent sentiment.

It didn't take long for the surviving Glaziene to appear beneath the glass windows. The small group stared up at the fearsome Gasiones as the windows cranked open.

"You are not safe here," Ciela informed them as she lowered into the solarium.

"We're as safe as we can be," Gwynessa replied. A majestic snow owl sat on her shoulder. "Thank you for coming."

"Thousands of the mindless are pressing against your shield."

"We know."

Ario, Jahdo, Tyrus, and Mina stood around Gwynessa.

"Is the magic strong? Will it hold?" Ciela asked.

"It's strong, but not infallible," Gwynessa revealed as she coaxed the snow owl off her shoulder and onto her forearm. The owl hooted before flying off and resettling on top of a glass bookcase in a far corner of the room. "I made a trip to the Wildlands, and when I left, I needed to use the magic to create a shield for myself. I also needed to levitate to travel above the hordes of mindless below. I didn't realize that I was stretching the magic too thin. When I got back, the shield was so fragile and flimsy, the mindless were able to reach their arms through." She lowered her chin. "I put everyone I love in danger."

"But the trip was a success," Ario stated. "You summoned a meeting with the Gasiones, you reached the drakkina, and you learned of Noelani's fate."

"Whoa, back up," Ciela stated.

"Yes, we have a lot to catch you up on."

Adaliah and Lonan lowered to join the conversation.

"But is the shield reinforced and strong now?" Adaliah asked.

Everyone's attention turned to her. Gwynessa crossed her arms and only held eye contact with her for a moment before looking away.

Ario grimaced and rubbed the back of his neck as he answered her question, "Yes, the shield is strong, and we are safe."

Adaliah stepped backward behind Ciela and Lonan, content to disappear from view.

"Where to start," Ciela said.

"Noelani," Gwynessa said, directing the conversation. She motioned an arm to the snow owl, which was now preening beneath its left wing. "Helgi and a few other owls followed the rogue Gasione as far as they could, but had to abort their mission when she dove into Seakkan. I think Noelani might be the key to our survival."

"I agree."

"You do?"

"She visited us, too," Ciela revealed, creases of confliction lined her expression. "She holds a lot of power. I instructed her to pay better attention so she can relay helpful information to us."

"Did she say anything insightful when you saw her? Her mind was stripped before I realized what was going on and could ask the important questions."

"Kólasi knows about the lost relics. Well, He knows about three of them: the lost relic of Gaia, Rúnar's heart, and Jasvinder's eyes."

"Why does He care about the relics?"

"I'm not sure, but it leads me to believe that I might be onto something with the plan I need to share with you."

"Go on," Gwynessa encouraged.

"I think if we combine all the lost relics, we will create a power source that rivals the scepter of alchemy. And with both, maybe we stand a chance against Him."

"I see." Gwynessa was deep in thought. "I have one of the relics. Do you have any idea where the others are?"

"Rúnar is in Seakkan with his heart. Elixyvette has Jasvinder's eyes. I am working on the others."

"Does it have to be Rúnar's heart?" Gwynessa asked.

"No," Ario objected immediately.

"But if it would help …" Gwynessa urged.

Ciela cut in, "It has to be Rúnar's. Each relic, besides the one around your neck, comes from someone who was in power during Gaia's reckoning."

"I see," Gwynessa replied, a hint of relief in her voice. "You can use the lost relic of Gaia when the time comes, but for now, we need it here."

"Of course. Thank you," Ciela said. "Now, tell me about the drakkina."

"I was finally able to reach them."

"How?"

"I can speak telepathically to the animals here. I used to use my heart magic to do it, but it seems I can still do it with my heart in place. I guess it's my connection to nature or Gaia."

"That's impressive. And you were able to reach the drakkina beyond the cosmic border of Namaté?"

"I couldn't reach them from inside the castle, but from the Wildlands, I could. They can't help, though. Gaia is nowhere to be found, and only She can release them from Cruxeus."

"Cruxeus?"

"Gaia's heart. It's beautiful, cozy, and warm, but it's also a prison. It's where she keeps the drakkina and all the doors to her many worlds."

"How do you know all of this?"

"I've been there."

Ciela stalled, struggling to restrain her jealousy and disbelief. "The mother brought you into Her heart?"

"Yes, before She sent the drakkina here. I was tasked as their temporary master."

Ciela clenched her jaw. "Hmph. Well, if they can't return, we can't rely on them to help."

"No, we can't," Gwynessa agreed. "I'll keep trying to find a loophole, but for now, we are on our own."

"I hope we can find all the relics in time."

"Me too. Oh, and have you seen baby Elior of Elecort?"

"I have," Ciela answered. "He is sick."

"Sick? How so?"

"Elixyvette says he has no glow since the drakkina touched him."

Gwynessa furrowed her brow. "Amari said he may be the one to answer our prayers."

"A baby?" Ciela asked.

Gwynessa shrugged. "That's what she said."

"I'll keep a closer eye on him, but it'll take years for him to mature into a man, and we don't have years. We have months, maybe. Our time is quickly running out."

"I will help with the relic hunt."

"For now, just stay alive," Ciela replied. "You have monsters knocking at your door."

"We will survive." Gwynessa smirked. "I am the mother of monsters, after all."

"You've worn that moniker well.

"And I will continue to do so."

"Stay safe, my friends," Ciela offered before she and her comrades pounded their wings and flew out of the solarium's open window.

Gwynessa turned to her family and friends.

"I don't know about these relics, but I have an idea on how to stop the muscas."

Chapter 11

Elecort

"Take him!" Elixyvette screeched, holding her screaming son at arm's length.

Helaine dropped her wire knit project and raced to retrieve Elior. She gently took him from the queen's outstretched arms and cradled him in her own.

He stopped crying immediately.

Elixyvette shrieked. Frustration, fury, heartbreak—nothing else mattered while her only love was crippled. His brokenness was her brokenness, and she could not stomach another moment of this despair.

"That child is not mine," she blathered furiously. "I gave birth to a healthy baby boy!"

"My queen, he suffered a grave injury," Helaine tried to reason with her.

"My son was stolen from me!"

"He will heal," Helaine urged. "Give him time."

"His pain is my pain, and I cannot rule while I am crippled by him." The disgust in her voice sizzled.

Helaine sensed Elixyvette's desperation—a state of being that often turned ruthless.

"Let me care for him," she offered. "Out of sight, out of mind. I will help him heal while you continue to lead and protect our people. And when he is ready, with his neon glow returned, I will bring him home."

Elixyvette silently considered the offer.

After a long stretch of tense silence, she finally agreed. "I want weekly reports on his progress."

"Of course."

Helaine left the throne room, holding Elior close to her chest.

"Zohar," Elixyvette said, summoning her most trusted soldier forward.

"Yes, my queen?"

"Keep an eye on her and Elior." Elixyvette's unkind expression tightened. "Discreetly."

Zohar nodded. He departed, leaving Vukane and three other soldiers-in-training by the queen's side.

"What are your names?" she asked the commoners who had been forced to train as guards.

"Corentin."

"Raiden."

"Torben."

"And what did you do prior to the flood? Prior to this damned fate we now endure?"

"I was a wire welder in District 9," Corentin answered.

"Coil corrector in District 9," Raiden replied.

"Metellyan recruiter, District 8," Torben revealed.

Elixyvette's brow raised. "You were one of three survivors from Opulade."

"We tried to save others, but failed."

"There were only three outlets at the charging station."

Torben nodded. "All the others were underwater."

"I'm curious," she said, her tone taunting as she forced him to relive that horrible day. "I've never had the heart to ask Helaine. How did you decide who plugged in and who died?"

"There was no discussion," he answered. "We got there first."

"Did others fight you for your spot?"

Torben clenched his teeth, flexing the muscles in his cheeks.

"I watched a lot of innocent Voltains die that day," he said.

Elixyvette smirked. "Do I sense a hint of accusation in your voice?"

"Of course not, my queen." Torben bowed his head.

She accepted his submission. "When do you finish your training?"

"At the end of this week."

"Excellent. Starting next week, your focus will be Metellyan reconnaissance. Arjan is cooperating, for now. They are performing well, but the day will come when we need more from them, and I need to make sure they're operating in a state of obedience and compliance when that day comes."

"When do you think that will be?" Torben asked.

"After Kólasi is gone."

"Do you really think we will survive Him?" Vukane asked.

"I do."

"I have faith in your lead," Vukane offered. "We will survive. You will restore Elecort to its former glory, and we will once again experience the blessing of a Boaneres reign through you and Elior."

Elixyvette's brief reprieve from her son vanished and the frown lines around her mouth resumed their usual depths.

The soldiers shared concerned glances before looking back at their queen.

"I need space," she announced, standing from her throne. "Everyone, leave!"

The children and elderly Voltains, who often spent their free time in the throne room with Elixyvette, departed alongside the guards.

Alone again, Elixyvette's thoughts returned to Elior.

Shame, disgrace, humiliation.

The Boaneres name would not live on in infamy with a cripple as the only heir.

Her heartache stewed around the theft of her son's health. His stolen voice, then his stolen glow; one traded for the other.

Without a charge, Elior could never produce or ride lightning bolts, he'd never possess the raw power of electricity that elevated the Voltains above other Namatéans, nor could he produce a suitable heir—voltage was inherited at conception, and Elior had none to share.

A mute Voltain king with a ferocious glow would have been a better fate than a loud king with no electric charge.

But they were forced to endure the latter.

How could she replace Lucien's lost namesake?

How could she love the broken boy again?

She couldn't.

The blessing of Elior's birth was now a burden.

He was a stain she could not wash, a wound she could not heal.

How could she escape the curse of his little life?

Elixyvette festered in her darkening thoughts.

Day in and day out, she spent countless hours sitting on her throne, staring blankly at the wall. Her trance broken only by unpredictable fits of fury.

On the first day of her bereaved solitude, she clawed at the curtains, tearing them from their rods. On the second day, she tore every painting off the wall, tossing them to the floor and shattering their frames. Every statue, large and small, was toppled from its pedestal as she flailed manically about the room.

Every fit of rage ended in tears.

She sobbed into the throne's throw pillows, hoping to muffle the disgusting sound of her sorrow. She cried until her ducts ran dry. Her sizzling tears singed the fabric, leaving bald spots on the pillows, and she was left with raw red circles around her eyes. When there were no tears left to cry, she resumed her silent perch on the throne, where she lost hours staring at the wall once more.

On her third day of isolation, her worst day, she had nothing left in the room to destroy.

All that remained was herself.

When her erratic rage surged, she retrieved the knife from her leg holster and held it to her throat, pressing hard until blood spilled. The droplets tickled as they ran down her neck.

Enraged, disappointed, terrified, she tossed the knife, lobbing it into the back cushion of the throne.

Her tears burned deeper on this evening.

Sleep beckoned, but she fought the urge until her fourth night of solitude. On this evening, she succumbed. Her eyes weren't even closed for an hour before visions of her crippled son plagued her dreams, waking her up in a breathless, sobbing panic.

Sleep held worse nightmares than reality, so she stayed awake, allowing the deprivation to eat away at her sanity.

Her only reprieve from grieving were moments spent reinforcing the shield created by Jasvinder's eyes.

At his own peril, Zohar attempted to enter and offer her comfort on the fifth day, but Elixyvette tossed furious lightning bolts at him every time he tried, effectively forcing him back out of the room.

By day six of her isolation, Zohar surrendered all attempts to speak to the queen.

Elixyvette kept everyone out of the throne room for an entire week.

On the queen's seventh day of isolation, Helaine returned, as promised, with an update on Elior's progress.

She knocked on the door.

"Go away, Zohar!" Elixyvette shouted.

"It's Helaine."

Elixyvette had forgotten about this meeting during her week-long bender of despair.

She sat in her own dread for a moment.

"Come in," she finally replied.

Helaine cracked the door open and slipped through, then closed it behind her.

All the shades were drawn and the room was dark.

Elixyvette paced in front of the dais platform her throne sat upon. Her wild black curls were loose and knotted, the dark circles under her eyes had doubled in size, and her thin body was beginning to look emaciated.

"Let me fetch you water and food," Helaine offered.

"No. Where is the boy?" Elixyvette snapped.

"He's with Zohar."

"Is he better?"

"Not yet, but—"

"Kill him."

Helaine stiffened. "Excuse me?"

"Kill him," Elixyvette repeated, her voice shaking with unhinged rage. "Kill that imposter child."

"It's only been a week—"

"I don't care."

"We are working on a way to return his glow."

"I don't care!"

"Please, give me more time," Helaine begged.

"*I* cannot live while *he* continues to live." Elixyvette's steel-pink eyes sparkled with madness. "I cannot spend another day locked in this room. It's him or me." Elixyvette spat as she paced the room again.

"You aren't thinking clearly. You will regret this."

"Do not pretend to know how I will feel!"

"I can fix him. I just need more time."

"His existence smothers me. Knowing he is out there, alive, tarnishing the Boaneres name—I cannot allow it. I have to begin again, and I cannot do that while he lives."

"Lucien would have never allowed this," Helaine challenged as she fought the tears forming in her eyes.

"You're right." Elixyvette paused her stride to stare down Helaine. "He would have done it himself the moment Rúnar ripped out the child's throat wires. He would have killed the child immediately as an act of kindness. I am weak. I had hope that he might heal. I should have known better. I prolonged the boy's suffering."

The queen's furious pacing resumed.

"He isn't in pain," Helaine argued. "Everything about him, except his electrical storage, is healthy and perfect."

"A Voltain without a charge is unhealthy and weak."

Helaine did not reply.

"The decision is made. The boy must die."

"You do it then," Helaine barked back, challenging the queen.

"I cannot."

"You *are* weak," Helaine said, repeating the queen's self-confessed vulnerability. "You are a coward, too."

Elixyvette narrowed her gaze. "Fine, leave the boy with me."

"No!"

"Be careful, dear handmaiden, or you could find yourself answering to Kólasi instead of me."

The threat was simple and clear—obey or be tossed outside the shield protecting Elecort.

Helaine's furious objection softened.

"I will do it," she said. "I will kill the boy."

Elixyvette laughed. "And in a few years, by some 'miracle,' I'll be forced to face my scorned son again. You can't possibly think I'm that foolish."

Helaine seethed.

"It's settled," Elixyvette commanded. "Bring him to me."

Helaine left without acknowledging the mad queen's request.

Outside the throne room, she went right to Zohar.

"She wanted me to kill him," she revealed in a furious whisper.

"What?" Zohar asked, appalled.

Helaine nodded, tears running down her face.

"She's gone mad," Zohar stated.

"I said no."

"Have *you* gone mad also? If you don't do it, she will have you killed, too."

Helaine shook her head and explained, "She plans to kill Elior herself."

Zohar was rendered speechless.

Helaine continued, "She asked me to bring Elior to her, but I can't." Tears fell down her cheeks.

Years of trauma caused by Elixyvette's rage-fueled whims flashed within Zohar's gaze.

Sparing Helaine the burden by carrying it himself, he offered, "I will do it."

Chapter 12

"You should reconsider," Zohar urged Elixyvette. "Helaine offered to care for the boy until he heals."

Elixyvette extended her arms. "Give him to me."

Zohar obliged.

Elior erupted into a fit of sobs the moment he was back in his mother's arms.

She glared up at her loyal guard. "He will not heal. He is damned." She paused, struggling to ignore her screaming child. "It's my fault, too. I should've told you to hide in the secret passageway. I knew Rúnar couldn't be trusted."

"The only one to carry blame is Rúnar, and he met his fate."

"Death was a kindness," Elixyvette seethed. "I would've made him suffer."

"And your innocent child?"

She glared down at the boy, who violently fought her embrace.

"I will make it quick," she asserted. "I should have killed him when it happened, but I was weak."

"You aren't weak."

"Lucien would have shown the boy mercy."

"Death is not mercy."

"He will not live a full life. He will struggle and suffer. Killing him is a kindness."

"I beg you to reconsider."

"I will not."

Zohar took a step back. "Then I suppose there is nothing more for me to do here."

"I need your assistance."

"With all due respect, I decline. The rest of this burden is yours to carry alone."

Though she wanted to strike him down for his insolence, she couldn't—this was the first time he had ever said no to her, and he was right—this was her burden to bear.

"You can go," she offered.

Zohar exited, making a swift departure before she had a chance to change her mind.

She looked down at the familiar yet foreign baby in her arms.

"I know you, but you aren't mine," she declared in a soft, frantic whisper. "Not anymore."

She yanked the knife from where she had lobbed it into her throne's backrest and held it to Elior's throat.

The boy cried louder.

"You aren't mine," she repeated, sweat beading around her hairline as she pressed the blade into his long-healed wound. The scar broke open, and a droplet of blood trickled out.

Elixyvette panted heavily, trying to muster the fury to finish him off quickly, but couldn't.

I am weak, she thought.

"No, you're not," she replied to herself aloud.

She pressed the blade harder.

The blood fell faster.

Elior screeched louder—his tiny screams of betrayal pierced her heart. A knife of his own, stabbing her repeatedly—a solid attempt to force her guilt to the surface.

He would not succeed.

He could not.

Tiny, helpless, innocent—his wide eyes stared up at her with desperation. He looked so much like Lucien, even in this moment of anguish. A sharp pain seared her heart; her buried guilt protested violently.

Elixyvette closed her eyes, blocking sight of his bright red and tormented face. She could not bear to see him, could not bear to see Lucien within him.

Heart pounding against her coiled rib cage, she focused on the loud drumming of her rage instead of the shame Elior tried so desperately to make her feel.

She pressed the blade deeper. Elior's warm blood dripped down the blade and ran over her fingers.

She did not open her eyes.

She kept them squeezed tight until Elior's crying stopped.

His wretched suffering had turned to silence and his body went limp in her arms. Elixyvette opened her eyes and saw red.

Blood covered everything.

His neck, his body, her hands.

She looked beyond him in her arms—blood soiled her dress, the throne, the floor. The dress could be tossed, the floor could be cleaned, but the fabric covering the throne's seat would forever mark this moment.

Unable to look at her lifeless son again, Elixyvette placed him into his wire-weaved bassinet and fastened the cover.

Out of sight.

Out of mind.

She had set herself free.

The world stood still for a moment as Elixyvette contemplated what she had done.

Was this freedom?

Or would this sin bind her to new unforeseen shackles?

"It had to be done," she said, voice shaking. "He wasn't mine," she stammered to no one, convincing nobody, not even herself.

Driven by her delusions, Elixyvette buried her doubt. She'd never think of it again.

She pressed her hands down the sides of her dress, smearing more of her son's blood onto her skirt. Over and over, she tried to clean herself of the evidence, but the blood remained as stains in the lines of her palms.

"You're gone now!" she screamed deliriously. "Leave me be!"

She continued wiping her hands onto her blood-covered dress, making her hands dirtier each time.

Frantic, she needed to cleanse herself.

As she scanned the room for towels, her sight locked in on the bassinet.

She needed to dispose of the body, only then would she be free.

Holding the handle of Elior's bassinet, she launched herself out of the skylight windows using Jasvinder's eyes. A controlled ejection out of the castle, they arched over the many peaked towers and landed gently in the royal courtyard.

Elixyvette turned her magic back toward the castle and locked every door and window.

No one was allowed to leave.

No one would interrupt her.

The bassinet hung heavy in her grip.

She ignored the weight—this would be over soon.

Vindicta Strait, formed by the recent flood, ran through the northwest corner of the royal grounds. Elixyvette had tried to drain it, tried to cleanse her land of all memory of that shameful day, but every dam she had built caved and every attempt to reroute the water resulted in Voltain deaths. The narrow channel ran through the northern courtyard and former District 7. Connected to the ocean on both sides, there wasn't enough magic or manpower to conquer the strength of the sea.

She knelt beside the raging water and opened the lid of the bassinet.

Sizzling tears burned shallow trails down her cheeks. Though emotion fell, she felt nothing—her heart and mind were numb. The physical manifestation of her sorrow came from a depth she could no longer reach.

"I loved you once," she said, her expression blank. "I'm sure of it."

She stared at the lifeless child. His vacant azure eyes were dull without their electric glow. "You look like him, but it's just an illusion. The drakkina replaced my boy with an imposter."

Her emptiness filled with rage, and her expression scrunched with anger as she recalled all that she had lost.

"You aren't mine," she repeated. "I wanted you to be, but you aren't." Her tears fell faster as she forcefully closed his eyelids.

Elixyvette shut the lid of the wire-weaved bassinet and hooked the latch. She then lifted the solid base of the bassinet and placed it into the rough water. It floated, for now, but the raging current would soon fill it with water. She held it in place while the choppy waves pounded the sides, splashing the bassinet and rocking it violently. Water dripped in where specks of light filtered through.

The boy was dead, and the ocean would cleanse her of this sin.

Free from her burden, Elixyvette watched with an empty heart as the forceful current carried her baby away.

Death for Elior.

Freedom for Elixyvette.

Chapter 13

Cerébrum

The familiar darkness consumed her once more.

Noelani whimpered as she resumed her place in the dark, quiet prison.

Faraway cries broke the silence.

Noelani turned toward the sound and saw a distant flicker of light.

It was the same cries and fire she experienced the last time she was here.

Cool mists and warm fogs passed through Noelani as she tore through the darkness toward the fleeting signs of life. The noise and light were the only hope she had that she was not utterly alone in this dismal purgatory.

As the light grew closer, its faint glow illuminated everything around it.

People.

Creatures.

Living beings she did not recognize.

As the light grew stronger, she realized the warm and cool sensations passing through her had been the minds of the other prisoners. She looked down at her own hands, now glowing in the light, and discovered they were semi-translucent.

"I'm sorry," she called over her shoulder to everyone she had passed through.

Various voices replied to her apology from the darkness.

"You're running toward disappointment."

"And false hope."

"Save yourself the heartache."

"Stay in the dark."

She could not heed their warnings; she had to see for herself. Noelani continued toward the light.

Though it felt like she was running fast, and that the light was so close, it was hard to determine time and distance in this place.

She kept moving, the flame growing bigger ever so slowly, and when she finally reached it, she found it came from a familiar source.

A Boulde.

"You're from Namaté?" Noelani asked as she approached.

"Not *you*." The Boulde's groan carried deep resentment.

"Do I know you?"

"No, probably not. But we *all* know *you*."

Noelani looked past the Boulde creating the light and saw more familiar faces: King Morogh, Rhoco, Valterra, Chesulloth, Azmon. And around them were hundreds of other creatures from Namaté.

"My name is Grette," the Boulde introduced herself. "You really caused us all a lot of trouble."

"An enormous disappointment to the Mother, also," Chesulloth added.

"I was under Kólasi's influence," Noelani explained. "I was among the first who were touched by His darkness."

"As someone who was also touched by His darkness early on, I can vouch that He truly took over," Rhoco chimed in. "I wasn't right in the head during my final days." He looked at Chesulloth. "And it all stemmed from those webs of yours."

Noelani added, "It started for me after healing in your netting also."

"Are you blaming the Bonz for all of this?" Chesulloth asked, her anger rising.

"Of course, not," Rhoco assured her. "But we ought to show Noelani a little grace, considering we are all victims to the same devious god."

Chesulloth crossed her bony arms over her chest. "Hmph. I suppose none of it matters now anyway. Not while we're all trapped here."

"I come and go," Noelani revealed.

"You come and go?" Grette asked, her periwinkle eyes aglow with hope. "How?"

Noelani hesitated, her expression tightening with shame.

"Go on," King Morogh stepped in. "Even if it's bad, it might be our only shot out of here."

"Kólasi uses me as a vessel to spy on Namaté. When he's not using me, he sends me back to this prison. Does anyone even know where we are?"

"It's called Cerébrum. Only your mind is imprisoned here. Your body and soul are still on Namaté."

"But why does He need her mind to occupy her body?" Chesulloth asked. "Why wouldn't He just leave her mind here?"

"Sometimes He asks me questions as we tour around Namaté."

"Do you answer Him?" King Morogh asked, his tone accusatory.

"Everything was confusing for a while—ricocheting between here and there left me fuzzy—but after talking to Ciela, I know now that I need to do better. I need to be a spy for my people, not for Kólasi."

"You spoke to Ciela?" King Morogh asked. "How? When?"

"After He leaves my body, my mind lingers in Namaté for a while. An hour or so, usually." Noelani sighed. "I wish I could just stay there."

"This is incredible!" Grette declared.

"It's actually quite miserable," Noelani mumbled.

"You can relay messages to the survivors."

"You can tell us what's going on at home," Rhoco added.

"I guess so, but what I need to focus on is learning Kólasi's secrets and weaknesses so I can help the survivors outlast Him, or help them find a way to make Him leave."

A baby's cries echoed across the dark space again.

"Where is that coming from?" Noelani asked.

"We aren't sure," Grette answered. "Once I teach some of the other Bouldes how to make fire, we plan to investigate."

Grette blew out her flame, then conjured another.

"How did you learn how to do that?"

"Orso taught me." Grette looked around for her smoky friend, but he wasn't nearby. "I don't know where he went."

Noelani nodded, less interested in Orso and more interested in the company of her fellow Namatéans. "Can I stay with all of you until I'm taken away again?" she asked.

"Of course," Grette offered. "Despite all the conflict and turmoil we inflicted upon each other while alive, it seems in death, we are family."

Noelani hadn't considered that this might be the afterlife.

"Do you really think we are dead?"

The corners of Grette's pretty smile slackened. "What else *could* this be?"

"It sure feels like Hell," King Morogh added.

The others mumbled in agreement.

If this was the case, Noelani's trips back and forth to Namaté were her final connection to life.

While she was grateful to find the minds of her brethren here, she had to find a way to stay with the living.

Chapter 14

Elecort

The Voltains locked in the castle watched Elixyvette's shameful crime from the north tower window. While they shared in mournful horror, Helaine was determined to retrieve the boy—to save him or to honor him with a proper burial, it was too soon to determine. Though Elixyvette had been drenched in blood, Helaine held on to hope that the boy still lived within the bassinet, and that she could reach him before he drowned.

She raced around the castle, trying to find a way out. She bumped into Zohar near the throne room and he followed her as she searched for any door or window unaffected by Elixyvette's spell.

"She locked us in with magic," Zohar tried to explain as Helaine desperately yanked on the door handle leading to the north courtyard.

"I have to help him," she replied, unable to hear reason.

"His fate is with the gods now."

"I can intervene." Helaine kicked the door, but it didn't open. "I can retrieve the bassinet before it reaches the ocean."

"He might already be dead inside that bassinet. You saw the blood she wore … "

"What if he's not dead yet, though?"

"Fine. Let's say he's still alive and you're able to reach him in time … if Elixyvette finds out, she'll kill you."

"Not if I can fix him!" Helaine slammed her body into the unbudging door.

"You'd have to heal him twice. First, from whatever maiming she did to him, and then a second time for his glow."

"I know," Helaine grumbled. "I am sure I can fix the second. The first, I'll have to wait and see."

"You really think you can fix his electrical charge?" Zohar asked.

"Yes. I spent the week talking to some of the Metellyans, who offered to help."

"Did you tell *her* that?"

"Yes! I told her I believed I could heal him. That it would take time, but that it was possible." Helaine jiggled the door handle frantically. "She didn't care. She wanted the problem solved immediately."

"Then I stand by my previous statement—if she finds out you disobeyed her desires, she will kill you."

"Even if I fix her son's glow?"

"I think so."

Helaine growled. "She doesn't deserve our allegiance."

Zohar did not argue.

Helaine kicked the door again, which stood as sturdy as ever, then doubled over to clutch her knee. Pain seared upward into her hip.

"You're going to hurt yourself," Zohar warned.

"I don't care!" she exclaimed as she slammed her body into the door again. This time, it flew open.

Elixyvette's voice echoed through the castle, gleefully announcing her reemergence as queen. The shakiness in her voice was gone and her confidence had returned. She wore murder well.

While Elixyvette returned to her day as if nothing had happened, Helaine raced into the northern courtyard, desperate to save the baby she had grown so fond of.

Zohar did not follow.

Helaine was familiar with Vindicta Strait, as she had to cross its newly built bridge daily to get to her refurbished home in District 8. The current flowed from the north shore into Litrell—former District 7—so she knew which direction the bassinet would be carried.

The streets and buildings of Litrell were mostly underwater, with only a few rooftops and non-functioning pipes sticking out. Vacant fields of overgrown wires separated each district, but here, the dense electrified turf had become the banks for Vindicta Strait.

Helaine followed the water's edge into the wild lands surrounding the submerged district of Litrell. The wires were tall, thick, and tangled, making it hard for her to maintain a fast pace. Her feet kept getting snagged, but she pushed through, tearing the smaller wires and stopping to untangled herself from any of the bigger wires. Eyes glued to the water, ears listening beyond the rushing current, she searched for Elior while battling the wire field.

There was no sight of the bassinet, no familiar cries.

Had she missed her chance? Was she too late? Had Elior already floated out to sea?

She was nearing the end of the channel—the ocean and border shield came into view.

Then, from a few paces ahead, she spotted unnatural movement in the water.

It was the bassinet.

"I'm coming!" Helaine shouted, tripping and stumbling through the wires. The buzz of the protective shield was audible now, and right below, inches from passing through the magic shield and into the sea, sat Elior's bassinet caught on the coiled brush.

The basket was taking in water.

Helaine ran faster.

"I'm coming!" she cried as she hurled her body toward the sinking bassinet.

Helaine snatched the wires of the basket before it was completely submerged and then unlatched the lid—water had filled the bassinet.

Helaine's panic worsened when she realized that the water was red.

She reached into the water and lifted Elior into her arms.

Blood still poured out of his fresh neck wound.

"No, no, no," she stammered as she kicked the bassinet free from the brush. It floated back into the current, and then drifted through the shield and out to sea.

She ripped off her sweater, draped it onto the ground, then placed Elior on top of it. She held the wound shut with one hand and gently pried his eyelids open with the other.

His azure eyes were vacant.

There would be no miracle, no saving this life.

This was the end.

It was time to say goodbye.

Chapter 15

Orewall

Through the portal of Occavas, through the overgrown wildflower field, beyond demolished Amesyte Valley, and back into the mines, Feodras led Carrick and Stennis to the collapsed tunnel he hadn't been to since he was a child. It took a few days, and they had to dodge many mindless Bouldes along the way, but they had finally made it.

The trio stood in front of a blocked entranceway.

"Are you sure Amezite's stone brain is down there?" Stennis asked.

"Pretty sure," Feodras answered.

"How are we supposed to get to it?" Carrick inquired. "The tunnel is completely caved in."

Feodras reached into his pocket and pulled out a glowing green stone.

"With help from Occavas," he revealed. He closed his eyes and channeled his desire. Moments later, invisible heat carved a perfectly arched pathway through the rubble.

"Is it safe?" Stennis asked.

Feodras assessed the smoothed stone, which was still hot to the touch.

"It feels solid. Just stay near me. I'll have my stone at the ready in case."

Feodras crossed the threshold into the tunnel that had not been traveled in centuries. As a child, Feodras had worked on a neighboring tunnel and was told horrible stories from older Murks who were alive during the time of this tunnel's collapse. Hundreds of Murks and Fused died that day.

As they trekked further into the tunnel, ancient Boulde bones appeared in the newly welded archway. Ribs, arms, legs, skulls—all melded into the melted stone.

The further they traveled, the more bones they saw, and it began feeling like a disturbed burial ground. By the time they reached the first fork in the path, the archway was all bones and no stones.

"We are in a graveyard," Stennis noted.

"We've interrupted their eternal slumber," Carrick added.

"We shouldn't be here."

Feodras huffed. "Don't get superstitious on me now. The dead cannot reach us."

"But what if they can?" Carrick challenged. "This tragic site has remained untouched for centuries. That's plenty of time for the deceased to fester and infiltrate the living world."

"This place reeks of death," Stennis said.

"Of course, it does," Feodras replied. "Many Bouldes lost their lives here. And I doubt they'll be upset that we bothered their slumber in an attempt to save our own lives."

Carrick and Stennis weren't convinced.

Feodras added, "Don't let the ghosts get the best of you."

The fearful duo reluctantly continued following their Murk king—partially because they trusted him, but mainly because it was too late to turn back now. They were too far into the mine shaft. If they turned around and something went wrong, they wouldn't have Feodras's magic stone to assist.

"What makes you think the brain is here?" Stennis asked, breaking the silence.

"I've never seen the stone brain, but I heard about it as a kid. Older Murks told me about it. When this tunnel collapsed, not only did it kill many Bouldes, but it also buried an ancient treasure room. One that Queen Amezite herself used, as well as the royal generation after her."

"Why hasn't anyone ever tried to clear this tunnel out if there is lost treasure here?"

"It collapsed during King Rupes's rule, and though he tried to clear out the tunnel many times, hundreds of Bouldes died during each attempt—the tunnel kept collapsing on their digs—and they never got very far. His son, Cairn, also tried during his rule, but had the same results. During King Cairn's last attempt, ocean water began leaking into the tunnel. After that, it was deemed impossible and the room was slowly forgotten about."

"Ocean water?" Stennis asked.

"This tunnel runs beneath the sea. That's also probably why it's so unstable."

"Great..."

"I will keep us safe," Feodras promised.

"I'm surprised King Alun didn't use the scepter to access the treasure room," Carrick noted.

"I don't think he remembered it was here. But if he had possessed the scepter a little longer, I'm sure it would've happened eventually."

Carrick and Stennis shuddered.

"Better us than him," Carrick stated.

"Indeed," Feodras agreed as he held his Occavas stone with one hand and traced the sides of the tunnel with the other.

The air turned moist and salty.

They were close.

He slowed, closed his eyes, and gently rapped against the wall as he progressed. When the knocking shifted from solid to hollow, he paused.

"I think I found it."

Feodras faced the solid wall of bones and took a deep breath. He squeezed the Occavas stone tighter and manifested his desires.

An invisible laser seared an eight-foot-tall rectangle into the wall. As the magic finished, the bones disintegrated into dust, leaving a pile of Boulde ash at the doorway's threshold.

The entrance had just enough height for Carrick and Stennis to fit through. The width was slender, and all three Bouldes had to shimmy through sideways.

The saltwater in the air was potent, thick, and dense. It temporarily masked the stench of death.

"Almost feels like I'm outside again," Carrick noted.

"I can't see anything," Stennis grumbled as he stayed close to the wall to keep his bearings.

Feodras summoned a beacon of light from the Occavas stone, and as the green light illuminated the blue stone walls, piles of ancient treasure became visible.

Mounds of gold, silver, and copper coins. Stacks of dusty books containing valuable lost knowledge. Buckets filled with Woodlin seeds—the only way to grow a new Woodlin tree. Corked vials bubbling with acidic swamp water from Vapore. Dimly glowing lightning conductor rods from Elecort. Sand from the original terrain of Soylé in glass bottles. Bonz bone jewelry and Metellyan precious metals adorned with local gemstones.

"We really used to rule the world," Stennis said in awe.

Feodras and Carrick wore similar expressions of amazement.

"Most of this stuff is from before the reckoning," Carrick noted.

"It seems we might own a big part of the blame for the reckoning," Feodras added.

"It wasn't just us," Stennis argued. "I bet every land has a room filled with ancient artifacts like this one."

Feodras shook his head, unsure, and began his search for Amezite's stone brain. The misdeeds of the past were not his burden to bear. Especially not now, while the fate of every Boulde's survival depended on them defeating Kólasi.

The future was the focus, not the past.

Feodras sifted through the heaps of objects from days long lost. Carrick and Stennis followed his lead.

They moved with care, as many of the items were fragile from age.

Carrick examined a necklace made of gold coils, Bonz fangs, and emeralds.

"Rubi would have loved to have jewelry like this," he commented. As he traced the coils, they radiated a smoldering golden light. "Does all jewelry glow?"

Feodras turned his attention to Carrick.

"No, it shouldn't."

Feodras lifted his Occavas stone to the necklace.

It blazed brighter.

"I think those are Barzilai's finger coils," Feodras explained. "Another lost relic."

"And look at this!" Stennis exclaimed, lifting an impeccably carved amethyst box. A large object rested inside its semi-opaque walls.

Stennis placed the box on top of a pile of books, carefully unlatched the lock, and lifted the lid.

Inside sat Amezite's stone brain. Small cracks in the amethyst stone sparkled with light.

"We found it," Stennis exclaimed.

"We found two!" Carrick corrected, lifting up the necklace.

A wide smile stretched across Feodras's face.

"There is hope."

"Those don't belong to you," a slithering voice echoed through the chamber.

Stennis spun in a terrified circle, searching for the source, while Feodras and Carrick clung tightly to the relics they had found.

"Put them back."

"Who was that?" Stennis asked.

"It was no one," Feodras answered. "Just ghosts."

"Ghosts?" Stennis tensed.

Carrick took a few steps backward toward the cavern's threshold, still clutching the necklace to his chest. "I thought ghosts weren't real.

"They aren't," Feodras rationalized, clarifying what he meant. "The voice is some kind of curse cast upon this place to stop looters."

"So, we can't leave?" Stennis asked.

Carrick screamed.

Stennis and Feodras turned their attention to Carrick, who was halfway through the door frame and set ablaze. The arm and leg that had made it through were swallowed by blue flames. Stennis yanked Carrick's unaffected arm and pulled him back into the room.

He writhed on the floor, hollering in pain.

Feodras tossed sheet after sheet of luxury fabrics from Fibril onto Carrick to smother the flames. The fire did not diminish, it simply turned the fabric to ash.

"You cannot leave with the relics."

The room shuddered, causing cracks in the ceiling. Salt water dripped through.

"If you try again, you will not leave at all."

Stennis dragged Carrick under the dripping water, positioning him so the droplets landed on the flames. It gave Carrick no relief—the fire was unnatural; it was immune to water.

"What do we do?" Stennis asked.

Feodras didn't answer, instead he walked to the doorway and peered through.

Carrick had dropped the necklace on the other side. It was safely out of the treasure room.

Feodras put the brain relic down and then touched his finger to the threshold.

No fire, no flames.

Encouraged, Feodras lifted the box with the brain inside, took a few steps back, placed the box back onto the ground, and then shoved it forcefully at the doorway. It slid across the floor, perfectly aimed at the exit, but when it reached the threshold, instead of passing through, it bounced back.

"Argh!" Feodras growled, increasingly frustrated. He tried to toss the box through, but it ricocheted again.

The relics could only pass through while being held, which brutally maimed the holder.

"Can *we* pass through without the relics?" Stennis asked, holding Carrick's uninjured hand.

Feodras pressed his finger to the invisible threshold once more.

No fire, no injury.

"I think so," he answered.

"Then we have to leave the relics behind," Stennis said. Carrick squeezed Stennis's hand so hard, Stennis felt the pressure.

"Yes. We will come up with a plan and return," Feodras agreed.

"You will never return," the voice hissed. The crack in the ceiling widened and more water poured through.

The more water that landed on Carrick, the taller the flames engulfing his body grew. Each droplet fueled the fire.

He screamed in agony.

Stennis grabbed his ankle, Feodras grabbed his wrist, and they dragged him out of reach of the water.

"Use me," Carrick said, his voice strained.

"What do you mean?"

"I'm already injured." He panted. "I'll carry the brain through."

"No," Feodras objected.

"You can't," Stennis agreed. "You won't survive another injury."

"I'm not going to survive *this* one."

"We will carry you out."

"We will will come back for the relics," Feodras added.

Carrick shook his head and spoke through gritted teeth. "No, you'll take them now. I'm going to die either way. Let my death mean something."

Using his good arm and leg, he crawled across the floor, dragging the deadweight of his flaming injured half toward the threshold. When he reached it, he paused and extended his uninjured arm. "Give me the brain."

Stennis lowered his head as Feodras retrieved the box and gave it to Carrick.

Carrick wrapped his fingers around the side handle and then pushed his body upright. It took him a minute to get to his feet, but once he did, he wobbled precariously within the flames.

He glanced over his shoulder. "You both need to exit first."

Feodras and Stennis agreed and exited the room with no problems. They stood on the other side of the threshold, ruefully awaiting their friend's sacrifice.

"I'm sorry," Feodras offered, struggling to contain his emotion.

Carrick shook his head. "I'd rather go out this way than at the hands of Kólasi. I'll go to Gaia's nirvana. I'll get to see my girls again," he said, thinking of Rubi and Claramae, his voice shaking from pain and sorrow.

The flames consuming him had burned through five layers of sediment. Weakened, the weight of his own body had become too heavy to hold upright. Carrick lurched forward and fell through the doorway.

The box holding the brain fell through with him.

He crumbled to the ground, unmoving, as blue flames incinerated the rest of his body to dust.

There was no time to mourn—the ceiling of the treasure room split open and the ocean surged through.

Feodras grabbed the box and started running.

Stennis lifted the necklace, but the moment it touched his stone fingers, he yelped.

"It's on fire!" he shouted, shocked that he could feel it, but Feodras was too far ahead to hear.

Stennis ripped off his shirt and grabbed the necklace again, this time running as he did so. He used the cloth to toss the necklace from hand to hand, never holding it long enough to feel its searing heat.

A swell of sea water chased him down the tunnel.

He wasn't faster than the pressured flow of water, and death grew nearer with every racing step forward.

He wanted to use the relic's magic to stop the wave, but not only was he unsure how to use the necklace, he couldn't even hold it long enough to garner its magic.

Stennis charged forward, fueled by sheer determination.

Carrick's sacrifice would not be in vain—he had to get the necklace out of this mine.

"You're almost there!"

He couldn't see Feodras, but he heard him. His voice reinvigorated him to run faster.

The tunnel grew brighter.

Outside light filtered in.

As the wave caught Stennis's heels, he raced out of the tunnel and into the daylight.

The water did not follow. The magic ceased at the cave's threshold, causing the water to rise against an invisible wall.

Feodras and Stennis watched the water rise to the top of the entranceway, linger there for a while, then slowly recede.

"Where is it going?" Stennis asked.

Feodras shook his head. "That wasn't the ocean, that was cursed magic."

The adrenaline from the chase and near death had distracted Stennis from the necklace—its touch no longer burned.

"The cost was too high." Stennis glanced up at Feodras, who wore the same forlorn expression.

"Yes, too high, but invaluable," Feodras considered. "His sacrifice might end up saving us all."

Chapter 16

Cerébrum

Crying resonated through the dark space.

"Is it coming from the mind of a baby?" Morogh asked, cramming his fingers into his ears. The sound continued to resonate through the figment of his mind.

"I suppose that's possible," Grette replied.

"But why is it echoing?" Chesulloth asked. "Our voices don't carry across the vast nothingness. Why does the baby sound like it's crying from the heavens?"

Nobody knew the answer.

As the distant wails continued to ricochet through the darkness, Noelani felt a deep shiver.

"He's coming for me," she whispered.

Only Grette heard her.

"Kólasi?" Grette asked.

Noelani nodded, then remembered, "I need to pray to Gaia's progenies."

"Why?"

"It's the only thing I haven't tried yet."

"If she can't hear us, why would they?"

Noelani shrugged, then searched for the nearest Glaziene. Exton was huddled near a flame created by a large Obsidian Boulde, but before she could speak to him, the crying ceased and her shiver intensified.

"It'll happen soon," Noelani warned in a whisper only Grette could hear.

While the other Namatéans debated the source of the crying, and how it came and went so sporadically, Grette's focus shifted to Noelani's forthcoming departure.

Orso snuck up on them.

"Maybe she can take you with her," he whispered into Grette's ear.

Her hopes heightened, constricting so tightly she feared the figment of her mind's heart might implode.

"Is there any way to take me with you?" Grette asked Noelani in a low voice, not wanting the others to overhear.

"I don't see how I could."

"There must be a way."

"It's worth a try," Orso suggested.

Grette turned to him. "You've been here a long time. Have you ever encountered a mind that comes and goes like Noelani's? Someone who Kólasi repeatedly removes from this prison?"

"I haven't," Orso confirmed.

"Exactly!" Grette declared, her hope dangerously inflated. "We have to try."

"Your fate is a blessing, indeed," Orso encouraged.

"Is it really a blessing, though?" Noelani asked.

"Of course, it is!" Grette challenged.

"This is risky," Noelani grumbled to herself. "What if He catches us?"

Plumes of eager black smoke exited Orso's nostrils and ears as he watched their banter with morbid fascination.

"Better than being stuck here," Grette answered. "This might be the only way."

Rhoco barreled over to them.

"Only way for what?" he asked.

"Shh!" Grette demanded.

"Must be a way for what?" he repeated in a whisper.

Grette groaned, annoyed that another had joined their conversation.

Noelani answered, "A way to leave with me."

Rhoco's eyes widened. "Is there?"

"I don't think so."

"You should try," Orso encouraged Rhoco.

Noelani shivered again. This time, her whole body shook.

"Is He near?" Grette asked.

Noelani nodded, her eyes glimmering with tears.

"He's coming for me," she repeated as her body convulsed.

Orso gave Rhoco an elbow nudge. "If you don't do it, I will."

Desperate, Rhoco lurched toward Noelani and firmly grabbed her shoulders.

"Let me go!" Noelani squawked, unable to break free.

"How do I do this?" he asked Orso, who shrugged in reply.

"A merging of minds," Rhoco grumbled to himself before pressing his forehead into Noelani's. Their figmented bodies began to meld.

"No!" she cried, terrified that she'd be punished for his actions.

Grette and Orso gasped, watching in horrified awe as Rhoco made this incredibly impulsive decision. The other creatures of Namaté turned their attention to the frantic scene unfolding.

Rhoco scrambled desperately, clinging to Noelani as she tried to push him off.

"I'm sorry," Rhoco offered, unwilling to let go.

"Get out!"

"Let me try," he begged.

"You'll get us both in trouble!" Noelani argued.

"I'm willing to die for this."

"I'm not!"

"Don't you want to save the others?" he asked. "This might be the only way. And I'm willing to risk my life being the test dummy."

Noelani grumbled, still combatting his efforts.

Rhoco continued, "Plus, we don't know how many more times you'll come back and forth. For all we know, our chances are running out."

He was right—there was no telling how much longer Kólasi would use Noelani as a spy.

She hadn't considered this.

Her fight against Rhoco softened and she allowed the merge.

She wanted to save the others, too, and this might be the only way.

As the final granules of Rhoco and Noelani's minds joined, Kólasi swept through as a humid breeze and took them away.

Noelani vanished.

So did Rhoco.

"It worked?" Orso asked, mouth agape and eyes beaming with wonder.

"He's gone," Grette confirmed, shining her light around to make sure it was true. "He did it."

Orso's lips curled upward.

"I'm next," King Morogh declared.

"No, me!" Valterra countered.

"Do you think she could conceal more than one mind at a time?" Chesulloth asked.

The cacophony of minds asserting their desire to go home next and hypothesizing possibilities was deafening.

"Don't be so quick to volunteer next," Orso warned them all, bringing the murmuring to a halt. "We still need to learn the fate of the stone brute. Did Kolasi sense his presence? Was his mind ejected with no host to claim? Did he fully perish upon leaving this place?"

Everyone quieted.

"He's right," Exton of Crystet said. "We won't know those answers until the winged woman returns."

"*If* she returns," Grette noted.

Chesulloth nodded. "If Kólasi senses Rhoco tagging along, He might punish them both."

"Or decide not to use Noelani as a spy anymore," Azmon added.

"Or look deeper into his possession of Noelani's body and realize that her mind lingers in Namaté before coming back here," Grette considered.

"A lot of things could go wrong," Azmon agreed.

"Let's hope the Mother is on our side," Chesulloth said.

Princess Valterra snorted. "The Mother doesn't even know we are here. Most of us were decent mortals—we should have been granted access to Gaia's nirvana in death. And for the bad among us, Kólasi's abyss. Instead, we were cursed to this mind-numbing purgatory—one of Kólasi's forgotten prisons. We are on our own."

As much as Grette and the others wanted to hold on to hope, it was hard to challenge Valterra's logic.

Orso chimed in, "Don't let my warning impede hope. Progress is rarely delivered without a renegade."

"Chaos strewn is progess sewn," Exton said, eyeing Orso cautiously. To which Orso replied with a devilish smirk.

"I like it."

"You know it?" Exton asked.

"Never heard it before."

Exton grunted.

The group accepted Valterra's cynicism, while still clutching tightly to Orso's encouragement, aware that the answers to all their questions were contingent on Noelani's return.

Chapter 17

Kólasi's Abyss

Kólasi—in full form—lounged in the comfort of His abyss. Tribal markings etched in gold covered His onyx-black flesh—small shapes, lines, and ancient symbols commemorating each of His nefarious achievements. One leg draped over an armrest, torso leaning over the other, His hulking, chiseled body draped across His oversized throne.

His illuminated golden eyes blazed with eternal fire that starkly contrasted His darkness.

<<*Feed me!*>> He bellowed, hungry for a snack.

His chamber serpents slithered and fetched a terrified mortal soul from one of the adjacent pens. Six fanged mouths latched to the unlucky soul, who screamed as they dragged it to His throne.

Kólasi watched, amused, as the soul writhed at His feet, begging for mercy.

"Please. Not again."

Kólasi sniffed the air above the soul. <<*Ah, yes, I have tasted you before. Smoked ham and russet potatoes,*>> He mused before spearing the soul with one of His daggered fingernails and popping it into His mouth. Kólasi nodded as He chewed, then noted between bites, <<*Same flavor.*>>

He swallowed.

The soul rematerialized back in the pen, shaking furiously from the trauma of being devoured, digested, and disposed.

<<*Another!*>>

The serpents fetched a second desperate soul for Kólasi to consume. He ate His second snack, then shooed His chamber serpents away to enjoy the depravity of His home in solitude.

Golden specks of fire floated around His lavish throne room like fireflies, their glow shedding a dim light on the suffering beyond.

Eternal screams of agony, ripping fresh throats raw. These souls screamed perpetually despite the continual blood spewing from their mouths.

Ceaseless cries of desolation, draining souls dry. They cried incessantly despite the debilitating dehydration crumbling them to dust.

Infinite pleas for mercy from those too stubborn to secede. They begged persistently despite the crippling delusion nibbling on their sanity.

Everlasting pain for those doomed to this fate.

The orchestra of despair echoing into His chamber delighted Kólasi. It brought Him great joy. It reinvigorated His spirit.

He enjoyed the relaxing discord, unbothered and unconcerned by the depraved chaos.

His sons, the filii diaboli, managed the various sections of His abyss. They kept the chaos in order so that He could come and go, wreaking havoc elsewhere whenever He pleased.

But His sons were elsewhere now—they were on Namaté with the task of sending every creature there to Cerébrum, His purgatory prison for mortal minds.

Kólasi stood from His lush throne of black velvet smoke and faced His wall of black holes—portals to every corner of the universe.

<<*Time to check on Namaté,*>> He thought to Himself.

He could not leave the abyss. Without His filii diaboli present, His abyss operated with a skeleton crew of devil guards and He needed to stay nearby in case of emergency.

So He split.

He reached into His ear and separated a fragment of His divine being. Same size, but semitranslucent and far more feeble, Kólasi's split stood tall beside Him.

<<You have a direct tether to me. I'll be with you the whole time,>> Kólasi telepathically informed His split—He had to give this speech every time as His splits never remembered. *<<But you must enter Noelani's body fast. Without a host, you'll snap back to me.>>*

I understand.

<<I'll be looking through you, talking through you. Once you're in the vessel, I will guide the mission.>>

His split nodded and then dove through the portal to Cerébrum.

Kólasi hated His dependance on the mortals, but He was divinely forbidden from directly interfering with His sibling's mortal realms. This loophole—possessing a mortal—allowed Him more freedom to spy and interact with the mortals. It was also easier to maneuver undetected this way, a sneaky way to stay off His siblings' radars.

Noelani clutched her mind's stomach as she hurtled through time and space in Kólasi's grip. Neon colors swirled and passed in a blur as they tore through cosmic blackholes.

He moved at light speed. Countless galaxies, countless stars and planets—the long trip passed in a few blinks.

When Namaté came into view, Noelani panicked.

Rhoco's groggy mind was still nestled inside of hers.

Wake up! she urged. *I know the journey is exhausting, but you need to wake up.*

Kólasi dove into Namaté, entering over Elecort.

Rhoco stirred.

Leave! Noelani urged.

<<*Where has your body wandered off to?*>> Kólasi wondered as He scoured the land.

Noelani squirmed in His grip, trying to shake Rhoco free.

Where are we? Rhoco asked, his voice a tired croak.

Home! You have to let go.

I'm very disoriented.

Let go of me! Noelani urged in a frantic thought whisper. *Before He senses you here.*

Rhoco finally obeyed and his mind slipped out of hers.

Noelani was alone with Kólasi.

She scanned the area for Rhoco, aware she was searching for a ghost. Where did he go? Would he survive?

<<*Ah!*>> Kólasi proclaimed. <<*I see you.*>>

Noelani had no time to wonder about Rhoco, she had to worry about herself now.

Kólasi soared toward the shores of Elecort, where hundreds of mindless bodies stood patiently outside the shield Elixyvette had created. Noelani stood among them, her eyes empty and expression vacant.

Every other time, she had been too disoriented to see how He had possessed her body, but this time she was paying attention.

Kólasi summoned her body into the air. It met them where they hovered. He then pressed the figment of Noelani's mind into her left ear, while simultaneously slithering Himself into her right.

Noelani opened her eyes at Kólasi's command.

He was in control.

Though He steered her vessel, she remained alert and focused. They were so intertwined, she felt everything He felt.

His many emotions crisscrossed with potency: enthusiasm to learn the muscas's progress, frustration because of His dependency on Noelani, anger after recalling His primordial siblings.

None of this was helpful. Not yet, at least.

He shifted Noelani into an aella and hovered above the shield, over the Voltain castle. He zoomed His vision through the throne room skylight to spy on Elixyvette. The Voltain queen paced the room while spinning the glowing eyeballs in one hand.

<<*I need to find the others,*>> Kólasi thought to Himself.

He dove into the ocean to make sure Rúnar's heart was still possessed by His mindless cronies.

It was.

Kólasi directed His attention inward.

<<*Noelani,*>> He coaxed. <<*Speak to me.*>>

Yes, my lord?

<<*Tell me about the other lost relics.*>>

I only know about the eyes and the heart.

Her mind quivered.

<<*Are you lying to me?*>>

No, I swear. Why do You need the other relics?

<<*They are very powerful when combined,*>> He revealed.

Why do You need more power?

I don't.

Kólasi pushed Noelani's mind down, burying her in the messy recesses as He rocketed out of Seakkan.

<<*Think harder while you're down there,*>> Kólasi commanded of Noelani. <<*You will either volunteer the information or I will pry it out of you.*>>

Noelani shuddered.

Kólasi tore toward His edifice erected over top of Fibril, flying circles around it and examining its fresh cracks. When He reached the top, He exited aella form and perched atop the highest peak. From His high perch, He observed this world.

There were as many mortal minds here now as there were the last time He visited.

No progress had been made.

Kólasi lifted Noelani's arms and summoned His sons to join Him.

It only took a moment before thousands of golden flies swarmed the lighthouse.

"Lucifer!" Kólasi shouted through Noelani's vocal chords.

One of the muscas flew to the front of the pack.

"Yes, Father?"

"Did I not leave you with enough power last time to finish this assignment?"

"There's nothing more we can do here. Not while their shields are in place. It's a standoff. We wait around, hoping that one of them will make a mistake. Our services would be better utilized elsewhere."

"Where?"

"In our assigned Hells."

"I need to wipe this planet clean," Kólasi stated. **"I left Earth too soon, and they recuperated. I am not making that same mistake here."**

"Or, you could leave Matrigaia and Her planets alone and focus on your own," Lucifer suggested.

Kólasi swung Noelani's hand through the air and swatted Lucifer away. The impact rocketed His devil son through the sky and out of sight.

Kólasi turned to the rest, who buzzed in nervous unison. **"If you have an assigned netherworld within my abyss, you may depart and return,"** Kólasi informed them. **"The rest of you will stay here to control the mindless and repair this lighthouse. Something is slowly eating away at it—find out what it is."**

The devils with netherworlds departed, while the others remained in Namaté as golden muscas and got to work on sealing every crack in the edifice with liquid gold.

Kólasi circled the working flies, surveying their progress. **"Without my edifice, all the work I've accomplished here will be squandered,"** He reminded them.

"Can't you build another?" one of His sons inquired without breaking his focus on the crack he filled.

"You are young," Kólasi noted. **"You don't know the time or sacrifice it takes to grow an edifice. They are like trees—they are alive with roots connected to my divinity. For mortals, my edifices are gateways to the afterlife, portals that lead directly to their fate."** Kólasi's energy lightened as He reveled in this teaching moment with His younger sons. **"For me, each edifice is a direct connection to the world it is rooted in and the mortals living there. For proper balance—life and death—I have at least one edifice, if not more, on all of Matrigaia's planets. It facilitates the inevitable transport of deceased mortal souls."**

"Then why did you have to rebuild an edifice here? Shouldn't one already be here?"

"Matrigaia demolished my edifice in Namaté eons ago when She stripped the mortals here of their magic. It took over one thousand years to regrow the edifice standing before us now."

"Why did She demolish it?"

"She blamed me for their bloodlust and greed." Kólasi smirked—Noelani's lip beneath her steel-tipped beak curled upward. **"She might have been right, I might have lent a hand, but I wasn't solely to blame, and She knows that. And if She wants to believe the worst in me, then I'll show Her the worst. As retribution, this time, my edifice is an *active* source of chaos and destruction. Anyone who enters its light goes directly to Cerébrum. Bad souls and good souls alike—no abyss or nirvana. No choice for rebirth for the good souls either. Straight to prison for them all."**

"What would happen if this one falls, too?"

Kólasi paused in thought. **"Besides forcing me to regrow another edifice from scratch? I'd fail my mission here. The diseased roots would wither and die; they'd no longer be infectious to the surviving mortals. And the mindless bodies still roaming this world would drop dead, once and for all. It would take another thousand years to regrow an edifice for Namaté—the mortals here would repopulate, and I'd have to start from scratch."**

"We understand," His son declared on behalf of himself and all the others. "We will keep this edifice healthy and alive."

"And I will return in full form to finish what I started here. This mission is almost complete."

Perched atop the lighthouse, Kólasi's split exited Noelani's body. His translucent form touched her forehead with two fingers as He muttered, *Mittere ad Cerébrum.*

Kólasi rocketed into the atmosphere, leaving her body surrounded by golden muscas.

Noelani quickly filled her lungs with a helium concoction gathered from the depths of her gaseous gut and lifted herself a few centimeters off the top of the lighthouse. Touching it for too long would surely shorten her stay in Namaté.

Safely hovering above the lighthouse, she tried to control her panic—she had never been so aware during Kólasi's departure.

Though He had said an incantation to send her back to Cerébrum, her mind remained in Namaté. Did He always do that before leaving? Did it always take a while to work?

She had a wealth of new information, but she was trapped. If the muscas sensed her awareness, they'd attack. Or worse, report back to Kólasi. She had to move cautiously, or not move at all.

The choice was critical—the fate of the survivors depended on her.

Noelani did not want her newfound purpose to end before she got a chance to right all her old wrongs.

Chapter 18

Elecort

Helaine carried Elior's lifeless body to her refurbished home in District 8. She did her best to suppress her grief, but the red rings around her emerald eyes gave her away.

Opulade village was one of the first to be rebuilt after the flood and the coil-stoned streets glowed with their former grandiosity.

Though the villages were repaired, they were primarily occupied by Metellyans—most of the surviving Voltains had relocated to live within the castle. She kept Elior hidden under her sweater as she raced toward her illuminated brownstone.

Her neighbor, a quirky Metellyan named Paz, sat outside on his front stoop. He sang one of his many folk songs as he tinkered with coils and wires.

"Slaves to sparks, we endure the neon cage.
Metal heartbreak, this fate we must obey.
Everything I earned was taken away,
replaced again by the fist of electric rage.
Despite the waves of freedom calling my name,
I choose to stay.
I choose to stay."

"That's a pretty melody," Helaine offered as she passed by.

Paz looked up, startled by her arrival and failing to notice the sadness in her voice. He shifted nervously.

"Oh, thank you, Miss Helaine. You're quite kind."

"How old is that song?"

"I just wrote it actually." His fingers tangled knots into the coils. "How much of it did you hear?"

"Just the melody from afar, and then the last few lines as I got closer."

He nodded, then noticed the sorrow she wore on her face. "Are you okay?"

"Do you know any songs about grief?"

"Many."

"I might ask to hear them soon."

"Any time."

She hurried inside where it was safe to cry.

Helaine placed baby Elior onto a cradle of blankets on her couch and then burst into tears.

The bleeding had stopped, and she traced her finger along the open wound. The quickest way to kill a Voltain was by ripping their neck wires, which connected their brains to the rest of their bodies, and Elior had suffered this injury twice.

The first time—by King Rúnar—which had cost him his voice. His wires were repaired, but not his vocal cords, and when the Drakkina gave him his voice back, it cost Elior his electrical charge.

This time—by his mother.

This time, the injury was fatal.

Tears poured from Helaine's eyes. A cruel and unfair fate, though she supposed the same miracle could not be gifted twice.

This poor child lived and died knowing only conditional love.

Though he was dead, she aimed to honor his short life. She had to stitch him up. She had to make him whole.

She needed help.

Then she thought of Paz, who still sat outside singing to himself and fiddling with a small wire project.

Helaine returned to the front door, scanned the area to make sure there was no one else around, and then called out to him.

"Hey, Paz!"

He redirected his silver sheened eyes to her.

She continued, "I was wondering if you might help me with something."

"I can try."

"Come here."

Helaine waved him over and Paz obliged.

"What do you need help with?" he asked as he reached the front door.

"Before I let you in, you must commit to discretion. You cannot tell anyone what transpires here today."

"Am I in danger?"

"Possibly."

"Is it for the greater good?"

Helaine considered this, then replied, "It's the right thing to do."

Paz nodded. "Then I will help. Your secrets will be safe with me."

Helaine hesitantly accepted his promise—mainly because she had no one else to turn to—and led him into the living room.

The bloody prince lay motionless on her couch.

"Who is that?" he asked, paralyzed in place.

"Prince Elior, son to Queen Elixyvette."

"Who did that to him?"

"She did," Helaine seethed.

"His mother?"

"Yes."

Paz gulped. "I can't bring him back to life."

"I know that. I'm hoping you can help me clean and stitch him up." Helaine fidgeted. "I can do it alone, if it's too much to ask."

"No, I can help. You don't need to do this alone."

Paz stepped closer to the lifeless baby, then touched his tin fingers to the exposed wires. The moment he made contact, flecks of amber in Elior's eyes sparked.

Paz removed his hand to check the edges of the incision and the amber light faded.

"Did you see that?" Helaine asked, voice animated with deranged hope.

"See what?" Paz asked.

"His eyes."

"No. I was looking at his neck."

"Touch the exposed wires again."

Paz did as she asked, this time looking at the boy's eyes as he made contact.

Faint sparks of amber flickered in their depths.

Paz glanced up cautiously at Helaine. "What does it mean?"

"I think it means we need to repair him as if he were still alive. Can you do that?"

He nodded. "Fixing wires is my specialty."

As Paz got to work, a knock sounded from the door.

Helaine tensed.

She tiptoed to the door and peered through the peep hole.

It was Torben.

She opened the door just wide enough for him to slip through then hastily closed it behind him.

"Why are you acting shifty?" he asked, trying to get a better look at her. "Have you been crying?"

Helaine grabbed his hand and led him inside.

"Why is there a Metellyan in here?" Torben asked.

"She invited me here," Paz immediately declared in his defense.

"I needed his help," Helaine said in a hushed and urgent voice.

Torben froze as he saw the small prince laying on their couch.

"Why is he here?" Torben asked.

"I couldn't let him drift off to sea all alone." Helaine sniffled.

"He's dead."

"Maybe."

Torben furrowed his brow. "Are you kidding? Look at all this blood."

Helaine buried her face into her hands. "I know."

"He's dead, Helaine."

"His eyes lit up when Paz touched his exposed neck wires."

Torben crossed his arms over his chest. "So, what is your plan, then?"

Helaine shrugged and took a deep breath. "I know he's probably dead, but Paz is going to repair his wires before we stitch him up, just in case. We'll give it a few days, and if he doesn't return to us, we will say goodbye."

"They are holding a funeral and memorial service for him at the royal grounds tomorrow," Torben informed her.

"What will they bury?" Helaine asked, her voice laced with venom. "Elixyvette took his life and left his body to the mercy of the ocean! She cannot honor his memory."

"Yes. I'm just letting you know what's happening. His official funeral is tomorrow."

"More like an official charade." Helaine's eyes blazed with anger. "We will give him a proper ceremony."

"I just need you to promise me that you will let this go after we bury him."

"I will never forgive her." Helaine glared at him. "I won't forget either."

"Fine, but you must let it go."

"I can't make any promises."

Torben sighed.

"All done," Paz announced.

Elior's wires were reconnected and his neck wound was stitched up.

"Thank you, Paz," Helaine said, her tone softer than that which she had spoke to Torben with.

Paz looked down at his blood-covered hands. "I need to go home."

"Yes, sorry, I will take care of the clean up."

Paz nodded. "Let me know if he wakes up."

"I will."

Paz left, and Helaine and Torben were alone with the dead prince.

"Have you gone mad?" Torben asked her.

"I had to save him." She shook her head. "I had to try."

"You didn't *have* to do anything." Torben massaged his temples as he paced the room. "Elixyvette will kill you if she ever finds out."

"I won't tell anyone."

"You've already told the neighbor!"

"Paz swore to secrecy. And if he ever breaks that promise, I'll deny it."

Torben stopped pacing. "We have to get rid of the body."

"No!"

"It's him or us."

"You can leave if you don't want to help."

"I'm not abandoning you. Not now, not ever."

"Then you need to wait this out with me. If he doesn't revive soon, we will bury him."

Torben grumbled and shifted uneasily, his dark blue glow surging as he considered their other options.

"This can't be our end." He grabbed her hands and held them against his chest. "We've survived too much. I can't lose you now."

"You won't. Please trust me." Her tone was fierce and resolute.

They held each other's gaze in silence for a few moments before Torben conceded.

"I do."

"Thank you." Her emerald green eyes lifted to meet his sympathetic cyan gaze.

He kissed her hands. "I am with you until the end."

Helaine nodded, her tears of sorrow were now filled with love. She leaned in and kissed Torben, then let go of his hands and looked down at Elior.

He lay as still as ever—only the amber twinkle buried in the depths of his blue eyes moved.

Helaine's hopes weren't high, and though she'd known many blessings in her lifetime, she feared she might have used up her allotment of miracles.

Still, she prayed for one more.

Chapter 19

Where is my body? Rhoco wondered to himself as he floated around Namaté as a mind ghost.

The world was quiet.

Most lands were eerily empty.

Rhoco walked on air, letting the wind carry him faster as he traveled.

Soylé, Wicker, Orewall, and Coppel were devoid of life. Not a single being walked the visible terrain of those lands except a few rogue mindless. Rhoco wondered—hoped—that survivors hid below in Occavas.

Fibril had no signs of life either, only the golden flies and Noelani hovering above the edifice that had overtaken the land. Rhoco floated toward her to tell her that he hadn't died, that the transport had worked, but she couldn't see or hear him in his current state. She was in trouble, too. She was surrounded by Kólasi's sons and unable to do too much without risking the reveal of her active mind.

Rhoco couldn't help her as a mind ghost—he had to find his body.

He continued his search and learned that the majority of mindless bodies were congregated around the shield protecting Elecort and scattered throughout Crystet.

He visited Elecort first and observed a small, private memorial service being held on the coiled castle grounds. Elixyvette stood in front of a very small coffin. In her arms she held a batch of blue wires tied together by a blue ribbon.

A Voltain guard standing beside her opened the lid of the coffin and she placed the wires inside. A small crowd of Voltains watched, their expressions as vacant as Elixyvette's.

There were no tears, no words about lost love. Just a rigid ritual performed with little emotion.

Rhoco left the off-putting memorial and searched for his body around the perimeter of Elecort. He circled the shield ten times before concluding that he was not there.

He redirected his hovering trek north to search Crystet. The mindless were scattered all over the land. He started at Jökull Cliff, checking the area thoroughly before moving east into the villages. After conducting systematic scans of every mindless mob, Rhoco determined that his body wasn't in Crystet either.

He let the wind carry him to the castle before departing. The thin purple dome of protective magic that shielded the royal grounds flickered unsteadily at random intervals.

It was a dangerous flaw in their defense with so many mindless waiting for a glitch to break through.

Rhoco floated overtop of the castle, peering through the glass ceilings until he found who he was looking for.

Gwynessa was alone in the solarium practicing elemental magic with the lost relic of Gaia.

No wonder their shield was faltering—she was stretching the magic too thin.

Streams of fire and ice swirled around her head. Though the origin of these elements was unclear, their intensity was unquestionable. They brought with them a violent wind that whipped Gwynessa's long white hair in all directions. Her slender muscles were ripped and engaged as she tried to control the fierce magic she had summoned.

You're jeopardizing your shield! Rhoco shouted, but he had no voice as a mind ghost.

He had to find his body. He had to help Noelani and warn Gwynessa.

The only place left to check was Vapore.

Why would I be there? he wondered.

Rhoco floated toward Vapore, using the wind as an accelerator. He somersaulted between the clouds, floating freely and happily toward his destination. The serenity of this space between alive and dead was divine—a far better purgatory than Cerébrum. If repossessing his body didn't work, living an eternity in this half state might not be so bad.

When he reached Vapore, he tumbled through the breeze and through the foggy protective chemicals of the dome. He drifted over Captivus River—most of the cages dangling above the bubbling acidic water were occupied by a mindless prisoner.

Poor chumps, Rhoco thought. *Didn't stand a chance against the flies.*

When he reached the giant cypress tree, about twenty mindless came into view.

His body stood among them.

Rhoco felt delight until reality set in—how was he supposed to reinhabit his body while it was surrounded by other mindless? If they sensed his mind was back, they'd attack and send him back to Cerébrum.

He waited, watching for any sign of movement or indications of departure, but their standoff with the Gasione warriors perched among the high treetops endured. Empty fog-ridden eyes staring upward, angry orange gazes glaring back.

Neither side was budging.

Rhoco hesitated—would it even work? Could he really reattach his mind to his brain? Could he resume his life?

Drifting through the world as a mind ghost wasn't the worst fate. Maybe it was safer to stay this way.

Then he thought of Noelani and Gwynessa, and then of all the other trapped souls in Cerébrum. He took this risk to save them all. He had to see it through.

It was now or never.

Rhoco tried slamming his mind into his body.

Didn't work.

He tried pressing his mind's forehead into his body's forehead.

Didn't work.

He needed to get into his skull; he needed his mind to reach his brain.

His mouth, nostrils, and ears were the fastest routes there, so Rhoco slithered into his ear.

It worked—he was able to crawl into the dark cavity of his skull.

A golden mucus sack was latched to his stone brain. Rhoco tried to rip it off, but his hands scraped right through. He couldn't make contact. He reattached every tendril of his mind to his zombified brain.

He sunk his tendrils deeper.

Nothing happened. Everything remained dark. He could not see out of his eyes or control his body.

Come on, Rhoco pled.

Tendrils wrapped tighter, he hoped the roots of his consciousness would take.

No progress.

As Rhoco feared the worst, a sliver of light sliced through the darkness.

Then another.

Rhoco moved his eyelids first, blinking away the fog.

As the color returned, so did the sulfuric scent of Vapore.

Life had resumed. The transfer had worked. The gold mucus sack still latched to his brain, but he was back and there was hope for everyone trapped in Cerébrum.

The mindless around him were motionless besides occasional twitches of restlessness. Little jolts, little spasms to keep them awake.

Rhoco remained as still as possible. He tried to catch the eye of the Gasione warriors sitting in the treetops, but their watch over the mindless wasn't as laser focused as it had seemed.

No one noticed that color had returned to his flesh and irises. No one noticed the beads of sweat forming around his mossy hairline. No one noticed that his statuesque stance had turned wobbly.

No one noticed except the mindless Mudling standing beside him.

Rhoco tried to hold his breath, but the Mudling was now sniffing the air wildly.

Rhoco glanced over and recognized the Mudling—it was Horlach, the nasty little mud goblin he had met when he first left Orewall so many moons ago.

"Hey buddy, you know me," Rhoco said, trying to talk reason to the salivating Mudling, but the moment he spoke, Horlach's foggy eyes lit up with gold light.

"Oh no," Rhoco said as Horlach pounced.

As Rhoco tried to shake the small muddy body off of him, the other mindless turned their attention and attacked.

"Help!" Rhoco shouted up to the Gasiones. "My mind is back! I have news! Help me!"

The Gasiones stirred, observing at first.

Rhoco was single handedly combating a large group of mindless Mudlings and Bouldes. As he shook and swatted them from his arms and legs, more emerged to take their place. They tried to drag, push, and pull him toward the nearby bramble of infected vines.

One touch would send him back to Cerébrum.

After a few exchanges of heated squawks, Adaliah left the safety of the treetop to help Rhoco.

She dove down, snagged Rhoco by his stone shoulders, and removed him from the fight. Two Mudlings clung to his legs as he was lifted into the air. Rhoco kicked them off, sending them plummeting back down into the sizzling swamp below.

The stench of Adaliah's living mind hit Rhoco like a wall.

Attack! a voice declared.

Terrified, Rhoco searched for the source. The breeze of her flight kept him in the wake of her potent mind odor.

Kill her!

It was only him, Adaliah, and her scent now, soaring high above the swamp of Vapore.

Bring her to the vines!

The voice lived inside Rhoco's mind.

It was the muscas, the devil latched to his brain.

You must obey.

His hands shook as they reached for her.

Stop! Rhoco demanded in thought, silencing the voice and burying it deep beneath his consciousness.

He lowered his arms and tightly gripped the sides of his trousers.

"Explain," Adaliah demanded.

"Explain what?" Rhoco asked, terrified to let her know that he was still bound to the muscas.

"You died, then you were mindless. Explain how you're back."

Unsure where exactly to start, he blurted out, "Noelani brought my mind back."

"Of all the minds lost, she chose to bring *you* back first?"

"Well, she didn't exactly *choose* me. I sort of forced it."

"Typical Boulde."

"There was no guarantee it would work. Better me than someone more important," he tried to rationalize. "I'm just a test dummy. But it *did* work, and we need to tell Noelani. She needs to know it was a success and that she can bring others back next time."

Adaliah sighed. "Where is she?"

"On top of Kólasi's lighthouse."

"On top of it?"

"I guess that's where He left her."

Adaliah released an ear-splitting whistle, summoning Ciela and a few of her fellow warriors to join.

Kill them all.

Rhoco shook his head, ignoring the devil.

"Noelani is back," Adaliah advised Ciela. "She's on top of Kólasi's lighthouse."

"Deliver him to the Bouldes in Occavas, then join us," Ciela instructed Adaliah.

Adaliah dove toward the green pond portal while the others left for Fibril.

"Do you think it'll last?" Adaliah asked Rhoco as she entered Occavas and soared toward Radix de Orewall.

"What do you mean?"

"Do you think your mind will stay in that dense skull of yours?" she asked, clarifying her question.

"Why wouldn't it?"

"Noelani's mind comes and goes. Maybe yours will, too."

With the devil's constant chatter and evil demands ringing through his head, Rhoco wondered if she was right. Maybe this second chance at life was temporary; or maybe it wasn't a second chance at all. Maybe it was a fluke, an accident, an oversight. If the golden mucus sack stayed attached to his brain, he'd remain a prisoner of Kólasi.

His thoughts of doom shifted to wonder.

Or maybe he had scored himself a massive dose of luck. Even with the devil in his head, he was back in his body, and figuring out how to rid himself of the devil was far preferable to the dark, endless purgatory of Cerébrum.

"Time will tell," Rhoco replied.

"Does it scare you?"

"No," Rhoco replied. "I believe the universe is on my side."

Adaliah carried him over Radix de Wicker, which no longer had roots dangling from the sky, and the land was encased in an impenetrable shield of light.

She sensed his curiosity.

"They have the scepter of alchemy," she informed Rhoco. "The light covering them is celestial—no gods or mortals can pass through."

"Why don't they use it to shield all the lands in Occavas?"

"We don't know. We haven't been able to talk to them since they enacted that shield." Adaliah's tone held deep resentment. "They left the rest of us to perish."

"Surely, they have a good reason for only protecting themselves."

"It's hard to imagine any reason that's justifiable."

"Drop me there."

"Where?"

"In Wicker."

"The shield is impassable."

Rhoco was determined. "I'll find a way in."

"Not today," Adaliah advised as she carried him away from the blinding light of Radix de Wicker. "What you do after I deliver you home is your own business, but I'm not babysitting you while you test fate. And if you are smart, you won't do foolish things that will risk this second chance you've been given."

"It's not foolish if I succeed," Rhoco countered.

"I see your density hasn't improved," Adaliah said with a scoff. "Let's hope your durability remains."

With the same incredible strength she used to carry Rhoco's stone body, she swung and tossed him toward the shield covering Radix de Orewall.

His massive body flew through the air. An awful lurching feeling twisted his gut as he fell.

Adaliah didn't wait to watch his landing. She departed immediately, missing the momentary pause in Rhoco's fall.

Directly above the shield, his free fall stopped, leaving him dangling over the shield.

The golden orb inside his head swelled painfully.

"It's me," he said through gritted teeth. The pulsating burn radiated between his temples.

Though there was no reply, he sensed the question the shield wished to ask.

"I am in control," he added.

Another brief moment passed before his free fall resumed and his body plunged through the shield.

When he finally landed, his heavy stone limbs hit the terrain with such great force they created a crater.

Rhoco scanned the area—neon cacti and shimmering dust. The desert of Radix de Orewall welcomed him home.

Chapter 20

Kólasi's Edifice, Fibril

Noelani was running out of time.

Still perched atop the lighthouse, trapped by the swarm of golden flies tending to repairs, she waited for a miracle.

Mother, please hear me. I beg of You. Let me stay here. Deliver me home, once and for all, Noelani prayed.

But her prayers were not heard.

"To the progenies—the drakkina, the Vorso—whoever may hear me: please help. In return, I offer my undying allegiance. In the name of the mother, Her children, and their profound holiness, I vow."

Her prayers remained unheard.

Instead, a small swarm of darkness approached from the west.

Anyone but Kólasi, she thought.

He had never repossessed her while her mind still lingered in Namaté, but there was a first time for everything.

Noelani braced herself for His cold inhabitation.

Eyes closed, muscles tensed, she waited.

He never came.

She peeked through her long eyelashes and found familiar faces barreling toward her.

Ciela. Lovise. Lonan. Dasan. Haizea. Mazin.

They came for her.

Gaseous tears swelled in her eyes as her brethren used a potent paralytic blend to stun the golden muscas with their breath.

Ciela broke away from the Gasione warriors to retrieve Noelani.

"The progenies answered my prayer!"

Ciela thought of Rhoco—who had told them Noelani's whereabouts—and donned an incredulous frown. Doubtful, but there was no time to investigate this particular claim.

"Is it still you?" Ciela asked, her urgency apparent.

"It's me," Noelani sobbed. "For how much longer, I'm not sure."

"Do you have news?"

Noelani nodded and wiped the tears off her cheeks.

"Tell me," Ciela urged.

"Can we leave here first?"

"We don't know how long you have," Ciela reminded her.

Noelani began to cry again.

Ciela swooped in closer, cradled Noelani in her arms, and flew away carrying her.

"Talk to me," Ciela urged.

"I asked why He cares so much about the lost relics, and He said that they have a lot of power when they're combined. Then I asked why He needs more power, and He said that He doesn't." Noelani shook her head. "It made no sense."

Ciela's eyes widened with realization.

"*He* doesn't need more power, but He doesn't want *us* to have that power. He wants the relics to stop *us* from getting them."

"Oh," Noelani said, the realization hitting her like a wave.

"Does He know about the others?" Ciela asked.

"No. He asked me about the other relics, but I lied and said I didn't know. He sensed I was lying."

"That's okay. Stand firm. It's for the greater good. What else did you learn?"

"The prison planet is called Cerébrum. It's one of three prison planets ruled by Kólasi. Cerébrum imprisons minds, the other two imprison souls and bodies."

"All the minds are there?"

"Yes—the minds of anyone who was alive before the edifice arrived."

"You died prior."

Noelani considered this. "You're right, I did. Maybe I went to Cerébrum instead of Incarna because Kolasi had been using me as a pawn prior to revealing His arrival here?"

"Perhaps. If that's the case, there might be others like you, too."

Noelani convulsed in Ciela's arms.

Ciela took a sharp turn toward Coppel. Being abandoned and free from the infected due to the lack of mortal minds, it was the nearest and safest place to land.

As she touched down, she placed Noelani's shaking body onto the aluminum-coated cobblestone of the abandoned market.

Ciela paced, prepared to take off if Noelani reemerged from this seizure mindless, but hopeful to have a few more moments with her to acquire more knowledge.

The convulsing lessened and eventually stopped.

Noelani groaned.

"Is it still you?" Ciela asked.

"Yes," Noelani answered, "but not for much longer. That always happens before I am sent back."

"Tell me more. Start with the most important."

"The edifice," Noelani revealed. "That's the key to weakening Him."

"We need to demolish it?"

"Yes."

"Is that even possible?"

"It must be. He's very concerned about its health. Something is already slowly chiseling away at it, which is why the muscas are there doing repairs."

"I wonder who or what is causing the damage currently," Ciela thought aloud.

Noelani's spine tingled.

"When the edifice falls, so will all of the mindless."

"This is brilliant news. Noelani, you've done a wonderful job."

The tingling turned into a tremor.

"He's coming back," Noelani warned as she trembled violently. "In full form. Placate Him. He has to keep using me as a spy." Tears fell from her eyes. "We have to find a way for me to stay here."

"I will try my best to find a way," Ciela offered.

Noelani nodded as the fog of mindlessness covered her fiery irises.

She was gone.

Ciela quickly stepped away to observe Noelani's transformation from a safe distance.

Her body thrashed, her head jerking at unnatural angles to take in her new setting. When her foggy eyes landed on Ciela, her disjointed movements turned swift and feral. She lunged at the Gasione Queen, who rocketed into the sky and out of reach.

Noelani released a guttural scream as Ciela disappeared beyond the cloud, stranding Noelani's body in Coppel.

Chapter 21

Radix de Orewall

Rhoco landed in the luminescent desert. A cloud of radiant dust rose from where his heavy body left a crater.

"Little sludge?"

Rhoco coughed and swatted at the plume surrounding him.

"Cybelle?" he called out.

The neon dust settled.

Cybelle stood near a giant boulder in the distance.

Rhoco clambered to his knees, achy from the fall and moving slow.

"Stop!" Cybelle shouted.

Steady with one knee and one foot on the ground, Rhoco halted.

"It's me," he promised.

"How?"

"Noelani brought me back."

"How?" Cybelle repeated.

"My mind was trapped in one of Kólasi's prisons. Noelani showed up—apparently, she comes and goes at Kólasi's command. When He came for her again, I merged my mind into hers and hijacked a ride home."

Cybelle took a cautious step toward him.

"Is it really you?"

"Yes!"

She hobbled toward him. He matched her hobble with an achy limp and met her halfway.

Cybelle opened her arms and Rhoco fell into her embrace. He was bigger than her, but she cradled him like a child.

The potent scent of Cybelle's vibrant mind choked Rhoco.

Seize her! the devil still latched to Rhoco's brain demanded.

Rhoco shook his head, ignoring and suppressing the evil voice.

"I'm finally home," he said.

Cybelle leaned back, held his face, and examined him closely. "Will you stay?"

"I want to."

"Can you?"

Rhoco sighed. "I'm not sure how this works exactly."

Cybelle's expression tightened as she nodded. "Let's hope for the best then."

The strong aroma of her mind hung stagnant in the air around them.

Kill her, a voice inside Rhoco's mind commanded.

"No," he replied.

"What?" Cybelle asked.

Bring her to the edifice.

Rhoco shook his head. "A devil is still latched to my brain. It speaks to me. I couldn't remove it when I reentered my body."

"What does it say?"

"It doesn't matter. I am in control."

Cybelle eyed him cautiously. "Are you sure?"

"If I ever sense that I am not, I will leave. I won't put anyone I care about in danger."

"Can it hear what you hear? Does it report back to Kólasi?"

"I think I am one of many brains it is latched to, and so far, it only speaks when it smells living minds nearby. So I think it only smells what I smell."

"Okay," Cybelle conceded, unable to do anything but trust her longtime friend.

"Don't tell the others, please," Rhoco begged. "They won't believe me."

"Your secret is safe with me, so long as you're acting right."

"Thank you." Rhoco released a sigh of relief before asking. "What have I missed?"

"We've been using Occavas magic to keep Kólasi's infected roots at bay. It works, but it's exhausting. Everyone has to help. There is a strict schedule and rotation. It works, but it isn't sustainable. Feodras, Carrick, and Stennis went on a mission to find Orewall's lost relic."

"Amezite's stone brain?"

"Yes. If they can find it, we'll have a stronger and steadier source of magic to create a defense."

"The brain hasn't been seen in eons."

"Feodras had an idea of where it might be."

Rhoco glanced upward at the very thin veil of magic shielding them.

"I hope they find it."

As the words left his mouth, the veil shuddered aggressively before disappearing.

Terrorized screams echoed from all directions.

"I don't want to go back," Rhoco stated, unable to calm his fear.

Cybelle extended a hand, which Rhoco took. He trembled as they prepared for the worst.

Two shadowed figures lurked in the distance.

"Do you think it's the mindless?" Rhoco asked.

"I hope not. They hadn't found their way into Occavas yet."

"If it is, I can probably fight off two or three," Rhoco declared. "But if more come, I'll need help."

Cybelle squinted her eyes, narrowing her vision. She let go of Rhoco's hand and took a few steps toward the approaching figures.

"What are you doing?" Rhoco asked.

The lines on Cybelle's worried face softened, and her lips ticked upward into a smile.

"I know that walk," she said of the figure in the middle. "It's Feodras."

She skipped into a fast-paced hobble toward the duo.

"What if they turned mindless during their travels?" Rhoco called after her.

Cybelle didn't stop, so Rhoco followed in a heavy slow jog, remaining a safe distance behind her.

Feodras and Stennis came into view.

"Are you yourselves?" Cybelle called out.

"We are!" Feodras shouted in reply.

Cybelle hobbled faster toward them, while Rhoco slowed down, creating more distance. His ankles and knees were shot from the fall.

"The shield is down," Cybelle warned.

"A better shield took its place," Feodras reassured her. He tapped the bottom of his knapsack. "We have the brain."

"And Barzilai's coils," Stennis added. Despite their success, their shared mood was sullen.

Cybelle noticed the missing member of their crew.

"Where's Carrick?"

"He didn't make it," Feodras answered, chin tucked.

"What happened?" she asked.

"The mines were cursed; we entered a trap. He sacrificed himself so that we could leave with the relics."

"He died a hero," Stennis added.

"He deserved to see the other side of this nightmare," Cybelle softly wept.

"He will see Gaia's nirvana," Feodras assured her.

She nodded. "A better fate than mindlessness."

"Which may be the fate awaiting the rest of us."

Stennis looked past Cybelle and saw another hulking figure walking toward them. "Is that Rhoco?"

"Sure is," Cybelle answered.

"How?"

"Apparently Noelani brought him back."

"I thought we lost him." He paused. "I thought we lost her, too."

"So did I."

Feodras furrowed his brow. "Does he seem like himself?"

"He's a little off, but I think he'll be okay. I'm choosing to trust him."

Rhoco was in earshot now.

"Did you find it?" he shouted.

"We did," Feodras replied, running to greet Rhoco. He threw an arm around him and gave him a side hug. "I thought I'd never see you again."

The forceful scent of Feodras's mind riled the devil inside of Rhoco, but Rhoco kept Him contained.

"It's great to have you back," Stennis added.

"We missed you," Feodras confessed.

Though Rhoco was elated to be surrounded by his friends, he noticed that one was missing.

"Where is Carrick?" he asked.

Feodras bit his lip, then shook his head and replied, "He didn't survive the trip."

"Why not?"

"He got injured, then sacrificed himself for the greater good."

Rhoco fought back tears. "That sounds like him."

"He quite likely saved all of our lives. Not yet, but in time."

Emotion swelled inside of Rhoco as his best friends told him this terrible news.

"He deserved to live," Rhoco said through clenched teeth.

Feodras and Stennis buried him and Cybelle, who he always viewed like a mother, in a group hug.

Their combined scent was too strong and the devil reemerged.

Bring them to Kólasi's roots beyond the border shield.

Rhoco shoved his trembling hands into his pockets as he pulled out of the hug. He thought of Cerébrum and how Carrick was spared from that torturous purgatory.

"He will know peace," Rhoco professed, holding back stubborn tears.

The voice vanished.

"We're happy to have you back," Feodras encouraged. He exited the group hug, as did the others. "And we want to hear all about what happened, but we have to finish this mission first. I need to update Ciela."

"I'll join," Rhoco insisted. "I need to know if they relayed my return to Noelani."

"Why does she need to know?" Cybelle asked.

"So that she knows its safe to bring others next time. I also have to make a trip to Crystet to warn Gwynessa that she is stretching her magic too thin."

"What do you mean? How do you know that?"

"While I was searching for my body as a mind ghost—"

"A what?"

"I know, it's strange. We'll come back to that—but I saw Gwynessa in her castle practicing elemental magic. A violent storm of fire and ice swirled around her. It was terrifying and mesmerizing."

"She conjured the elements through the lost relic of Gaia?" Feodras asked.

"Yes, and it weakened the shield around Crystet."

"I wonder why she was doing that. We will visit her also—to warn her and gather information. Sounds like she might know something that we don't know."

"I'll stay behind," Cybelle announced. "I've had enough excitement for one day."

"Take the coils," Feodras insisted. Stennis stepped forward and handed Barzilai's finger coils to Cybelle. Feodras continued, "The coils are creating the shield around our land. They need to stay here."

"They won't leave my sight," Cybelle promised as she wrapped and wore them around her fingers. She staggered off, leaving the trio to their mission.

"How will we get there?" Rhoco asked.

"Oh, wait till you see what the brain can do," Feodras answered. "Occavas magic is wonderful but limited. These relics are the real deal."

"The brain magic was easier to navigate than the coils," Stennis added.

"Yeah," Feodras cut in. "It took a while to figure out how to create a shield with the coils. We managed, but accessing its magic was like solving a puzzle. The brain was much easier. It transported us from the mines to this desert without any trouble at all."

"I wonder why?" Rhoco asked.

Feodras hypothesized, "I think the brain is easier to use because it's from a Boulde. We are inherently connected."

Feodras retrieved the stone brain from his knapsack and cradled it in his palms.

Rhoco and Stennis placed their hands on the jagged amethyst dome.

A chilly surge of power coursed through their fingertips and up their arms. A clear protective veil formed around them.

"Ascend," Feodras commanded, and the trio was lifted into the air. Though they traveled slowly, they were safe. No golden flies or mindless could access them.

Feodras steered the brain with slight movements of his wrist.

From high above, they were granted a bird's eye view of the ocean below. The sun beamed through the lapping black waves, catching the foggy white glares of the mindless ocaemons below.

None were spared.

Every monster of Seakkan had been stripped of their minds and tasked to serve Kólasi.

"I was with King Morogh in Cerébrum," Rhoco revealed.

"Where is Cerébrum?" Stennis asked. Feodras listened intently.

"I don't know *where* it is, only *what* it is—it's a prison for mortal minds. Anyone who is mindless here is trapped over there."

"Even those that died centuries ago?" Stennis asked.

Rhoco thought hard about this before answering. "No, I don't think so. I didn't see Rúnar or any other ancients while I was there."

"What was the prison like?"

"It's awful. Until I found the others, I was isolated in pitch black silence. I had no concept of time or space. I had no control over my spiraling thoughts. For a while, I thought that was going to be my eternal fate."

"Noelani brought you back?" Feodras asked, confirming what Cybelle had told him earlier.

"Yes. Kólasi brings Noelani back and forth and inhabits her body to monitor us."

"Why doesn't He leave her mind in the prison?"

"He needs her mind for insider information."

"I hope she isn't revealing anything that will make it easier for Him to defeat us," Stennis said.

"According to her, she hasn't been very lucid during the possessions until recently. And since talking to Ciela, she knows how important it is for her to help the survivors."

The trio lowered through the thick gaseous shield of Vapore.

Rhoco knew this land well—the acidic air, the stench of swamp water, the noxious sizzle of Captivus River.

The captives in the cages hanging over the bubbling river were now mindless, and scattered throughout the marshlands were free-roaming mindless.

"This is where I found my body," Rhoco disclosed, then added, "I don't know why I was here."

"Because there are fresh minds here," Feodras answered, motioning toward the giant cypress tree inhabited by Gasiones. "The mindless gather where there are minds to take. That's why you won't find any in Coppel, Soylé, Wicker, or Fibril. And there are very few in Orewall. They sense us living beneath their feet in Radix de Orewall, so some still linger above, trying to find us, but most have vacated."

Ciela's arrival startled the trio.

"What is this?" she squawked, motioning toward the odd sight of Bouldes flying.

"We found the brain," Feodras announced.

Ciela's brash greeting morphed into delight.

"This is great news!" she exclaimed.

"We also found Barzilai's finger coils," Feodras added. "They are being used to maintain a sturdier shield in Radix de Orewall."

"You really pulled through. Great work," she commended. "Only five relics left to collect."

"What's left?" Stennis asked.

"Brixton's rooted rib cage, King Dagmar's clay lungs, Bozrah's skull, Rúnar's heart, and of course, Elzaphan's black feathers."

"You don't know where the feathers are?" Feodras asked.

Ciela shook her head. "I wish I did. My warriors have been searching, but haven't found them yet."

"Where are all of your kings and queens buried?" Rhoco asked.

"There are no Gasione kings," Ciela corrected him. "Only queens. And we turn to stardust upon death."

"No ancient burial grounds or memorial sites?" Rhoco pressed.

"You don't think I checked there already?" Ciela snapped. "There was one queen between Elzaphan and I—Alizé—and she left no record of the feathers' whereabouts."

Everyone stewed for a moment in contemplative silence before Rhoco asked another question.

"Where did Elzaphan die?"

Ciela's orange gaze blazed like fire. "The Holy Three were in Wicker when they sacrificed themselves for the greater good."

She thought of all the times she had visited the impenetrable shield surrounding Radix de Wicker, and how the Woodlins always replied to her pleas for help by pointing up. "I think the feathers are in Wicker."

"Do you know *where* in Wicker?" Rhoco asked, thinking of the thick, massive forest they'd have to search.

"All the trees are gone," she reminded him. "The Woodlins replanted their roots in Occavas." Ciela summoned her warriors with an earsplitting whistle.

Like a fleet of starlings, they blanketed the dim daylight of Occavas as they circled their queen overhead.

"To Wicker!" she commanded. The armada of darkness circled upward before nosediving toward the portal in Occavas.

"Come with us," Ciela requested of the Bouldes.

"Did you tell Noelani that I survived the trip?" he asked.

"I didn't get the chance. Her mind was stripped before I could say much. I retrieved a lot of helpful information from her, though. Acquiring all the relics is imperative. Kólasi is searching for them, too."

"Why does He want them?" Feodras asked.

"Because He doesn't want *us* to have them. We were correct to assume that combining their magic will help us."

Stennis, who normally kept quiet during meetings with other Namatéans, blurted out his concerns. "I'm fine with trying—it's better than sitting around in defeat—but this relic hunt is extensive. Even if we find them all, will it really be strong enough to defeat a god?"

"No, it won't be enough to defeat Kólasi, but it should be enough to demolish His infectious edifice."

Constricted expressions of confusion lined the Bouldes' faces.

Ciela explained, "From what I understand, destroying the edifice also destroys Kólasi's stronghold over Namaté."

The Bouldes' narrowed their glares with determination.

"Let's find those relics then." Stennis grinded his stone knuckles into his palm. "I'm ready to smash stuff."

Chapter 22

Elecort

The night passed without Elior's revival.

Helaine and Torben woke up to an unmoving infant on their couch. She leaned in close to make sure the amber in his eyes still glimmered.

It did.

"Let's give him time."

She recruited Paz to check in on the child throughout the day, then she and Torben trekked to the royal grounds to attend the child's false memorial.

The callous sham of a funeral only deepened Helaine's anger.

The only way to stomach Elixyvette's theatrical remorse during the prayers was to disassociate.

Helaine scanned the crowd and found that everyone wore vacant expressions—their apathetic attention was hollow and glazed over.

Their shared repulsion gave Helaine some comfort.

After Elixyvette finished her weepy, tearless monologue, they buried a few wires, none of which belonged to Elior. The pallbearers braided the buried wires into the elaborate terrain wires, and Elixyvette turned her back to the proceedings. Not from grief or guilt, but relief. She clapped her hands together, took a deep breath like her mission was complete, and a sick smile of liberation stretched across her face.

"We must carry on," she declared. "Brighter days await!"

Elixyvette marched away with a skip in her step, leaving her woefully loyal subjects to process the aftermath of her destruction on their own.

The air buzzed with the spark of rebellion, the surviving Voltains had had enough, but a revolt was not in the making. Not while Elixyvette possessed ancient magic.

Helaine grabbed Torben's hand and led him away from the dispersing crowd.

"Let's go home," she urged.

They needed to get back to Elior.

The weight of Helaine's growing fear made the trek feel longer than usual. Torben sensed her unease and squeezed her hand. Helaine leaned on his sturdy presence while navigating her tangled grief and hope.

Paz sat on their stoop, awaiting their return. He caught Helaine's eye and shook his head.

Tears poured down her face as she let go of Torben's hand and raced inside.

She ran into the living room and fell to her knees beside the couch where Elior lay in his nest of blankets.

"I'm so sorry," she sobbed. "I prayed, I hoped, I tried."

Torben came inside and knelt beside her. "You did all that you could." He kissed the side of her head. "It's time to say goodbye."

Helaine nodded.

Torben continued, "Where do you want to bury him?"

"In our backyard. That way I can visit him."

Torben gave her a small, sad smile. "I'll get the site ready."

He gave her another kiss and then left.

Paz stood near the kitchen. "Can I do anything to help?"

"Stay with us while we bury him," she requested. Paz's friendship had become another source of strength as she grieved.

"Of course."

Helaine lifted Elior. His flesh was still slightly damp from the drowning, but dry enough now to return him to the terrain.

She carried him outside, and Paz followed. They stopped in front of the shallow grave Torben had dug.

Proper burials in Elecort consisted of removing the top layer of soil and placing the dead body on to the exposed terrain wires. In the first few hours, the smaller terrain wires would branch off the main coils and slowly wrap and merge into the corpse. In a few days, the corpse would naturally decompose, remineralize, and become one with the land.

Helaine placed Elior's small body onto the spot Torben created for him.

"You were loved," Helaine said to Elior. "By me and so many others. Though this life robbed you of time, I know your soul will return and be avenged."

Torben put his arm around her from the left, and Paz grabbed her right hand.

The trio spent a moment of silence huddled around the grave site. Time stretched beautifully as their quiet love blanketed Elior where he lay.

Smaller underbranches were already growing and stretching toward Elior. They climbed up his body from all sides, inching slowly across. By morning, the boy prince would be fully ensnared.

"I'm going to head home," Paz said after an hour of shared grieving.

"Thank you for being a friend," Helaine said.

"Always."

Paz departed, but Helaine wasn't ready to leave yet. Torben stayed by her side.

An hour later, the first moon began to rise. Torben softly squeezed Helaine's shoulder.

"We ought to get some sleep."

She nodded and let him lead her inside.

The process of getting ready for sleep passed in a blur, and Helaine operated in a trance until she heard the sound of a baby crying. Startled, she sat up, surprised to learn she was already in bed. She glanced at the clock to see she had been sleeping for five hours already.

Elior's nightmarish cries echoed in her mind.

Heart racing, she took a deep breath to calm her panic.

Torben rustled awake.

"I'm sorry. Go back to bed," Helaine encouraged him. "I was just having a nightmare."

"A nightmare?" he asked, groggy but concerned.

"I thought I heard Elior crying, but it was just a bad dream."

"No," Torben said, jumping out of bed. "I hear it, too."

He raced out of the room, followed closely by Helaine. They dashed into the backyard, where Paz was already kneeling beside the crying prince and attempting to sever the wires wrapped around him. Helaine and Torben joined, frantically cutting the wires to release Elior from the terrain's grip.

The wires snapped back and recoiled, and once every connection to Elior was cut, Helaine snatched him off the ground and held him tight to her chest. She rocked him in her embrace and whispered sweet words to him until he calmed down.

"How is this possible?" Torben asked.

"I'm not sure," Paz replied, searching for any logical explanation. "My metallic touch had sparked something in him." Paz massaged his brow. "Maybe he just needed to dry out. He was quite waterlogged."

"Over a day without a heartbeat or oxygen," Torben considered out loud. "How?"

"Just how Paz explained," Helaine cut in, unwilling to let anyone complicate this blessing. She took a deep, calculated breath. "Miracles aren't meant to be questioned, just accepted."

Her curt reply ended their wonder.

Elior was back, and that was all that mattered.

Chapter 23

Crystet

Using the lost relic of Gaia, Gwynessa harnessed fire from the sun and ice from the moon. She encased herself in an elemental whirlwind—a feat she had to master if she wished to rid Namaté of the muscas, and greater yet, save her brother.

Flames ripped at her dress as they swirled around her body. Tiny ice blades pricked her delicate glass flesh as they encircled her. Though she was closer than ever to mastering the art of harnessing elemental magic, she still lacked full control.

The fire singed her hair, blistered her tongue, and scorched her hands. Its smoke choked the air she breathed; the heat left her dehydrated.

The ice numbed her nerves, hazed her vision, and induced a deep, internal shiver. Its cold temperature froze her muscles, making it difficult to move.

Burned by both the heat and frost, she exited each whirlwind with charred and raw flesh wounds.

The kiln room door had an eye slit through which Ario and Tyrus observed. They waited for her to reemerge so they could help her tend to her newest injuries.

Gwynessa wasn't ready to give up, though. Not yet. Her command of the elemental storm was tightening and her authority strengthening. Soon, she would be in complete control.

Among the whirring icicles and crackling flames emerged a hiss.

This was new—she had reached a new level of connection to the elements.

The hiss turned into a chant.

::The boy.::

::The boy.::

::Bring us the boy.::

She recognized the voices; they belonged to the drakkina.

::The boy.::

::The boy.::

::Bring us the boy.::

The boy? Which boy? Bring him where?

Distracted by the unexpected presence of the drakkina, Gwynessa's grip loosened. The perfectly circular rotations of the fire and ice turned lopsided and violent. Sharp shards of ice flew haphazardly in all directions, piercing the walls. Tiny fireball flecks ricocheted in all directions, burning holes through everything in the way.

::How?:: Gwynessa thought as she lost control.

::Add earth, add air.::

::Extremes from the four elements combined.::

::He is the answer. The boy will save us all.::

Their voices sounded farther away.

::Which boy? Where am I bringing him?:: she thought.

There was no reply. The connection was lost.

It was time to give up, time to surrender for the day.

As Gwynessa lessened the power surging through the relic, the whirlwind dwindled to a stop.

Snow flurries and glowing embers floated in the aftermath, hovering until they fell to the floor and dissipated.

Gwynessa collapsed to the ground.

Ario and Tyrus raced into the room.

Tyrus grabbed the lost relic from Gwynessa's loose grip and immediately strengthened the shield around Crystet.

"Are you okay?" Ario asked, kneeling beside her and cradling her head. Tyrus placed the relic beside his queen and then circled the room slowly, examining the aftermath of her chaos.

"I heard the drakkina," she revealed between heavy breaths.

"How?" Ario asked.

"Why are you doing this?" Tyrus cut in before Gwynessa could reply to Ario's question.

"It's the only way to get rid of the muscas."

"You're hurting yourself and risking our shield," Tyrus challenged.

"I have to do this," Gwynessa argued, her composure rattled. "It's the only way to help Calix."

"Getting rid of the muscas won't bring Calix back," Ario gently reminded her.

"I need to rid his mind of the devils for when he *does* come back."

Ario pulled her in tighter, his embrace one of deep understanding.

"It's for the greater good," Gwynessa insisted. "It will help all of the mindless. I'm so close. I'll get it on the next try."

"This will end in disaster," Tyrus grumbled.

"His warning is fair," Ario said as he helped Gwynessa to her feet.

"If the drakkina hadn't distracted me, I think I would have mastered the fire and ice this time." Gwynessa brushed the charred specks off her dress.

"What did they say?" Ario asked.

"To 'bring the boy' to them."

"Which boy?"

"I'm not sure."

"Luckily, there aren't many people left," Tyrus quipped. "Even less children. Shouldn't be hard to narrow it down."

Gwynessa thought hard, recalling all the drakkina had mentioned to her during their recent chats.

"Amari once mentioned Elior of Elecort, but Ciela told me that he is very sick."

Tyrus shrugged.

Gwynessa huffed and shook her head. "I need to focus on one task at a time. Freeing the mindless from the muscas is my focus for now."

"Can you kill the flies?"

"No—they are gods in fly form—but I can banish them."

"Will banishing them harm the mindless?" Ario asked. "They are tethered to each other; the flies have inhabited their minds. You can see the gold behind their foggy eyes."

"I hope not … I just want to sever that bind. I hope to set the mindless free. Without the devils' influence, they'll be less violent."

"That would lessen the burden on our shield."

"We might not even need the shield anymore." Gwynessa looked to Tyrus, her steadfast guard. "This is why I'm so determined. I want to live freely; I want to lessen our reliance on that shield."

"The shield keeps Kólasi out, too," Tyrus reminded them.

The castle shook, sending a quaking tremor across the lands and giant fissures up the glass walls. Tyrus joined Ario and Gwynessa where they crouched together with their heads covered.

When the tremor stopped, they shared worried glances.

"Was it the shield?" Ario asked.

Gwynessa clutched the lost relic of Gaia and closed her eyes. She felt the power of the shield resonating through the relic.

"No, the shield is fine."

"Then what was that?"

An ethereal voice echoed through the sky

<<OBEY OR PERISH!>>

Chapter 24

Gwynessa, Ario, and Tyrus raced to the nearest window.

The sky swirled with black clouds. Streaks of gold lightning cracked and sparkled across the darkness every time the thunderous voice spoke.

<<*Gaia has forsaken you!*>> the ethereal voice declared, His voice carried by the wind. Thunder rumbled around His words, followed shortly by lightning. <<*Come to my edifice for salvation! A special oasis awaits you in the abyss.*>>

"It's Kólasi," Gwynessa realized. "This is a trap."

"Of course, it's a trap," Tyrus replied. His voice held deep terror. "Calix had felt the abyss. He sang its grave warnings daily. There are no safe spaces there."

"We have to warn the others not to obey," Ario urged.

Without the possession of a mortal, Kólasi could only interact from a distance. In full form, but hidden from view, He watched the mortals panic from the heavens of Namaté. Some squirmed uncomfortably, staring up at the dark sky, awaiting further instructions. Others ran about, conversing and contemplating what they should do. But most remained defiant.

<<*If you stay here you will die as a fateless,*>> Kólasi warned, His bellowing voice carried with it a storm of massive proportions.

Thunder, lightning, high winds, hail, and torrential rain—a sunny day turned violent.

The threat of fatelessness stirred an extra level of motivation among the mortals in Crystet, Elecort, and Radix de Orewall, but the Woodlins protected beneath the scepter of alchemy did not budge.

Beaumont stood in the middle of a forest of Woodlins.

They awaited his direction.

"Do not fear," Beaumont began. "He cannot touch any mortal living here."

"How about up there?" Bolivar inquired, thinking of those living beyond the protection of the scepter. "Should they beware? Should we extend our magic to them? Is it time to share?"

"They will be fine. Primordial gods cannot directly interfere with mortals who don't belong to them. That is why Kólasi sent the flies, His golden devils."

"And why He needs the mortal vessel."

"He cannot touch us, He cannot force our hands," Bohdan, second in command after Beaumont, repeated. "Only Gaia can directly control the fate of mortals—Kólasi's power resides in death. He has no real control until we draw our last living breath."

"Isn't His edifice a direct attack on our fate?" Bolivar asked. "Its mere presence is an interference."

"It is still our choice to avoid His infestation. We have free will to reject His invitation."

"Do our neighbors know that His false warnings are just a ploy for compliance? Should we warn them? Should we aid their defiance?"

Beaumont considered this. "You may be right. They may need our help. Though we cannot abandon our mission here, sharing a bit of magic is more than fair."

The scepter of alchemy was lodged into the soil beside him. Its magic radiated into the terrain, creating roots of light that extended all the way to Radix de Fibril. There, the tendrils of light knotted with Kólasi's diseased edifice roots and slowly disinfected the roots, destroying the lighthouse from the inside out.

Bolivar gripped the scepter and separated a sliver of magic. It unfurled as ribbons of luminosity before weaving itself into an orb of divine light.

"Bravery, confidence, and faith. Keep our neighbors safe."

Bolivar tossed the orb into the air, and it dispersed in all directions, sending a wave of light through their protective dome and into the world beyond Occavas.

A nuclear blast of divine light encased the lands of Namaté, turning all chaos into serene confidence. Everyone ceased their frenzied planning and returned their curiosity to the sky.

Kólasi fumed.

<<Do not test my patience,>> He warned. *<<My kindness will expire.>>*

His threat did not sway the stubborn mortals below.

<<Be warned. In seven days, the red moon will rise, and this offer will end. The blood of your ancestors will rain from the heavens and drown anyone who still lingers here.>>

Cannon blasts of thunder rolled across the sky, shaking the world beneath. Chaos incarnated—each raucous boom carried currents of Kólasi's essence. Delivered to the mortals as tremors beneath their feet, His message was clear and resolute.

Submit to His demands, or endure a fateless afterlife. No nirvana, no abyss, no opportunity for reincarnation—your soul's story ends permanently.

On the Namaté side of Wicker, the Bouldes and Gasiones had paused their mission to receive Kólasi's ultimatum.

The sky raged above. They stood on the shoreline, the black seawater lapping their ankles with each wave.

"Do you think it's true?" Adaliah asked. "Do you think Gaia has abandoned us?"

"No," Ciela answered confidently.

"I agree," Feodras added. "I think His lies about Gaia are a manipulation tactic to get us to surrender. And if we don't," Feodras paused, "the threat of a fateless death might be imminent."

"Unless we can destroy the edifice first," Rhoco said, encouraging optimism among his friends and allies.

"Yes," Ciela agreed. "Perhaps we can outrun this fate."

"Better get to work then," Rhoco urged, ignoring the buzzing devil in his head.

Chapter 25

Wicker

The dense and lush forestry of Wicker was gone.

No more tree line—the vast unknown hidden within the dark forest was exposed. Barren and wide open, only broken branches, dusty soil, dead tree trunks, and fallen leaves covered the terrain.

The Bouldes and Gasiones could see far across the landscape. Though the hunt for the relics from the Holy Three should be easier with less woodland to search, there was still massive ground to cover.

They fanned out and walked the eastern side of the wasteland at synchronized speeds, hoping to find Brixton's rooted rib cage, Bozrah's skull, and Elzaphan's black feathers. They did not have enough bodies to cover the width of the island, so if they could not find the relics on this pass, they would have to walk back on the western side and try again.

"Ready," Feodras shouted after thoroughly checking his area for the relics. Soon after, everyone echoed him, announcing that they were ready to move forward.

Ciela gave the order, and the line moved forward three large steps. They searched their respective areas before repeating the process.

"Ready!"

The line progressed forward.

Next in line to Rhoco was Stennis.

After ten hours of repeating this monotonous action, Stennis fell behind.

Rhoco glanced over his shoulder and saw Stennis doubled over and convulsing.

"Are you okay?" Rhoco asked, ready to abandon his spot in line, but Stennis held up a hand.

Rhoco stayed put.

Stennis caught his breath, then stood tall and marched confidently back to his spot.

"What happened?" Rhoco asked. Though they were next to each other in line, they were spaced far apart.

Stennis shook his head, kept his gaze down, and shooed away Rhoco's concern.

"Onward!" Ciela shouted, pushing the line forward.

Half an hour later, and halfway across the island, Adaliah halted while the rest of the line moved forward.

"Onward," Ciela repeated while glancing over her shoulder at Adaliah.

"I think I found something."

"Say more," Ciela instructed impatiently, motioning for everyone else to stay where they were.

"There's a dim light coming from beneath the leaves and soil."

Adaliah fell to her knees and raked her sharp fingernails into the ground. She dug until she reached an old, rotted tree stump. The center was hollow.

With the dirt and bark removed, the glow beamed brighter through the stump's rotted center. Adaliah stuck her face into the light and gasped.

"What do you see?" Ciela shouted.

"It's a portal."

"To where?"

"It's hard to tell."

Adaliah's body slithered into the tree stump and she disappeared.

The silent line of Bouldes and Gasiones watched in terrified wonder, stifling their breath while hoping for the best.

Stennis bounced impatiently on the tips of his toes.

When she remerged an hour later, she was carrying a Bonz skull and a set of Gasione wings.

"Stay where you are," Ciela ordered the others before rushing to meet Adaliah.

"Where did you go?"

Adaliah's orange eyes sparkled with enchantment. "At first, it was a looking glass—I could see everything happening in Occavas all at once. I could zoom in, zoom out. After I stepped through, I could *go* anywhere I wanted."

"Anywhere within Occavas?"

"Occavas or Namaté."

"So this is how the Woodlins kept tabs on the rest of us all these years."

"The view was omniscient," Adaliah revealed. "It's a testament to the Woodlins discipline—they could have intervened and taken control at any time if they had wanted to, but they never did."

"They never sought power, only peace," Ciela said, understanding more clearly why the Woodlins were Gaia's favorite.

"Anyway, I chose to go where the relics were hidden," Adaliah explained.

"And where were they?"

Adaliah shook her head. "I think I was inside of a tree. They were hanging on wooden hooks, alongside other strange items. I only found these two relics, though. When I tried to travel to the wooden ribs, I bounced back here."

"Did you at least see where they are?"

"They're in Radix de Wicker. I couldn't cross through the shield."

"At least we have these now. We are two relics closer to freedom. Can I see the wings?"

Adaliah placed the giant black feathered wings into Ciela's extended arms.

"I thought Elzaphan's relic was a few feathers, not her wings in their entirety."

"Me too."

"And Bozrah's skull," Ciela said, shifting her focus to where it sat in Adaliah's hands.

"It came with the drakkina skull that the Bonz wear for armor, but the Bonz skull within is the true relic," Adaliah explained as she lifted the smaller skull out of the larger one.

The Bonz skull had three empty eye sockets on each side, fanged teeth, and delicate etchings carved into the bone marking achievements, losses, and triumphs only known to Elzaphan. A thin layer of gossamer threads still laced the skull, creating a shimmering sheen that smoldered in the faintest of light.

Stennis glanced over his shoulder at Rhoco. His solid black eyes now had tiny gold pupils.

"You shouldn't be here," Stennis said. The threat was accompanied by a wicked smile.

"Huh?"

"Curious, indeed." He pointed at Rhoco's head. **"You still belong to me, though."**

"Who are you?"

"Shh."

Stennis turned back around and marched toward the Gasiones.

Rhoco tried to chase after him, but the muscas orb attached to his brain suddenly swelled and throbbed, sending him to one knee. A sharp ring filled his head, making it impossible to hear anything happening around him. He fell to the ground, convulsing wildly.

Feodras and Cybelle raced to his side, but the pain intensified and the only sounds Rhoco could make were grunts and groans of agony.

"They're beautiful," Stennis said as he approached.

"Stop where you are," Ciela commanded. Stennis obeyed. "Why did you leave the line?"

Stennis pointed back at Rhoco, who thrashed in pain.

"What happened to him?" Ciela asked.

"We don't know. I need one of the relics to help him."

He extended his hands to the Gasiones, neither of whom budged.

"Please," he begged.

"*I* can use it to help him," Ciela offered.

"You don't understand Boulde anatomy as well as me."

"Do you?" Adaliah asked her queen in a hushed voice so Stennis couldn't hear.

Ciela shook her head. "I don't."

Rhoco released an unhinged howl that echoed across all of Wicker.

"Please, hurry."

"Can we trust him?" Adaliah asked, voice soft and out of Stennis's earshot.

"I suppose we must. He is an ally, after all."

Ciela took a step closer with Elzaphan's wings extended toward Stennis.

He extended his arms to accept the offering, his gluttonous gaze locked on the relic.

Ciela paused.

"Your eyes look different," she noticed.

"They are the same."

"No, I don't think so," she wondered aloud, struggling to pinpoint the change.

"Give me the relic!" Stennis had lost his patience.

"Excuse me?"

"Now!" he growled, motioning toward Rhoco, trying to cover his outburst. **"We are running out of time."**

Ciela took a step back and clutched the wings to her chest. "Who are you?"

"Give me the relic!"

"Absolutely not!"

Stennis unleashed an ethereal roar.

Unable to directly interfere and take the relic from her, Kólasi's mission through Stennis had failed. She had to give it to Him voluntarily; it had to be free will.

Kólasi exited Stennis's body, leaving him to crumple to a heap on the ground, and rocketed toward the clouds.

"It was Kólasi!" Ciela shouted to the others. Everyone abannonced their positions to join Ciela, except Feodras, Cybelle, and Rhoco.

With Kólasi's departure came relief for Rhoco. The pain ceased, and his body stopped thrashing. He laid still, appreciating each deep breath. Finally, he spoke.

"Kólasi," he mumbled. "He's in Stennis."

"He was," Feodras corrected. "He's gone now."

Rhoco opened his eyes a little wider and tapped a finger to the side of his head. "He did this to me."

Cybelle gently wiped the sweat off Rhoco's forehead.

"Yes, it appears so," she said.

"Is Stennis okay?" Rhoco asked.

"Are *you* okay?"

Rhoco pushed himself up into a sitting position and lovingly swatted Cybelle's doting hands away.

"I'm fine," he grunted. He repositioned to his knees, then slowly stood. He hobbled toward where the fleet of Gasiones hovered around Stennis. Feodras and Cybelle followed.

The sky darkened as Adaliah and Lonan helped Stennis to his feet.

Ciela glanced up. "Looks like we aren't clear of Him yet."

Lightning seared from the sky, hitting a dead tree stump with force and setting it on fire.

The heavenly inferno spread at unnatural speed. Whips of fire flayed in all directions.

"Watch out!" Feodras shouted as the flames rose and lashed Adaliah's back.

She screamed and fell to her knees. The Bonz skull rolled out of her hands and across the ground.

While the Gasiones threw dirt onto her wings to extinguish the flames, Feodras spotted the rolling skull.

He chased after it.

The fire chased him.

Feodras was small, but mighty. He would not let Kólasi's firestorm strip a relic from them.

The skull rolled into a pile of dead leaves. Sparks sizzled the edges of the undergrowth, but they hadn't caught fire yet.

Feodras snatched the skull and held it tight as the brush burst into flames.

Crisis averted.

Another bolt of celestial lightning rocketed through the sky and hit a second area of Wicker.

The fire moved faster, and from all directions, now.

Feodras raced back to where everyone had gathered. Thick black smoked encased them.

"We have to get out of here!" Ciela shouted.

Feodras held out Amezite's stone brain. "Let's see what happens when we combine the three relics we have."

They worked quickly.

The stone brain fit perfectly inside the Bonz skull, and there was a notch at the base to attach the wings.

"I think the wings will be sturdier once they're attached to the spine of the wooden rib cage," Ciela noted as she hooked the wings to the base of the skull.

While they fussed with the relics, Kólasi's furious flames had reached them. The blaze rose to terrifying heights as it encircled the group.

As the flames hammered down, the relics connected and an intense surge of energy emanated from the united relics.

A ring of protection formed around them—a shield the fire could not pass through.

They were safe.

"Did you will forth a shield?" Ciela asked Feodras, who shook his head.

"I did," Cybelle said from where she knelt, one finger on a feather. "The fire was getting too close."

"Good work."

"What now?" Cybelle asked.

"We leave this fiery hellscape," Ciela answered. "Everyone, link up."

Thunder rumbled as the group disappeared and reemerged in Coppel.

Kólasi's storm clouds could be seen in the distance, and His thunder heard, but He did not follow them.

Ciela and Feodras placed the relic onto the ground, and the group disconnected from one another.

Lonan, Lovise, and Dasan tended to Adaliah's wound. She had a nasty flesh burn and the fire had singed many of her feathers, but it wasn't enough to stop her from flying.

"I'll be okay," she insisted.

"Are we safe?" Cybelle asked.

"If He wanted to resume His fire fight against us, He'd already be here," Feodras rationalized.

"Yes," Ciela agreed. "He knows it's a waste of time. We'll just make another shield. We are safe, for now."

"I'm sure He's watching, though," Stennis said with a shudder. Though he was back to normal, his nerves were shot.

"He's always watching," Rhoco warned.

The combined relics lifted off the ground and pulsated with tangible energy that tickled their ankles.

Everyone, except Feodras, took a step backward.

Feodras stepped closer to the levitating relics and traced his fingers along the skull's forehead etchings. He closed his eyes and felt the relic's energy.

"Conexus," he said.

"What is that?" Ciela asked, stepping closer.

"The relic after all of the lands contribute their piece."

Together, they placed their hands on the combined relic to feel its full power.

Silent tears streamed down their faces as they were filled with a profound ethereal love they had never experienced before.

The other Gasione warriors and Bouldes observed in curious awe.

"We are meant to live a connected life," Ciela said, her tone serene and joyous. "Not one of division and disharmony."

Ciela and Feodras reached out their hands so the others could connect.

"Do you feel it?" Feodras asked. "Do you feel the quiet serenity? Do you feel the peace?"

Nods, mumbles, and sighs of relief came in reply.

Inspired, empowered, and uplifted—this half-powered relic filled everyone in observance with renewed hope.

A loud explosion boomed from the north, jolting them out of their bliss.

Crystet.

"Did we do that?" Feodras asked, yanking his hand off the skull.

"How could we have?"

"I didn't wish harm upon Crystet."

"Neither did I."

"We have to help them," Feodras insisted.

"Is everyone connected?" Ciela asked of the Gasiones and Bouldes, to which she received unanimous confirmation.

Unified, Feodras and Ciela used the Conexus relic to teleport their small militia to Crystet.

Chapter 26

Crystet

The shield over the castle was down.

Mindless swarmed the royal grounds.

Glaziene survivors hid within the castle while Gwynessa single handedly battled the mindless with a magic-fueled fire and ice whirlwind. She hovered a safe distance above the ground, controlling her tornado from the sky.

There was no sign of Calix in Crystet. A blessing, as Gwynessa had not yet mastered this elemental magic and her cohorts were maiming every mindless in sight.

Tyrus, Ario, Jahdo, and Perce stood on the castle rooftop, shooting glass arrows at any mindless who managed to sneak past Gywnessa's elemental tornado.

"Aim for the legs," Tyrus reminded Perce after he accidentally shot a mindless in the head. "They can't return to a dead body."

"Right," Perce mumbled. He didn't have much practice with a bow and arrow.

Though they did their best to debilitate the mindless before they could enter the castle, they couldn't stop them all.

"They're in the castle!" Ario shouted over the whistling winds to Gwynessa.

She looked over her shoulder and saw that she was failing. She had been trying to spare their bodies—killing their bodies meant their minds would not have a body to come home to, but in her conservatism, the mindless were rampaging past her.

She couldn't get to the muscas inside their heads without harming their bodies.

To save her living loved ones, she was going to have to kill the mindless.

She tried not to think of Calix as she considered those who still lived.

A mindless Glaziene man covered in fresh fissures raced toward the castle. Aware now that she had no other choice, she directed her tornado to tear through him, leaving his body shattered.

Gwynessa set her elemental whirlwind on a path toward a large group of approaching mindless before lowering herself and kneeling beside the demolished man to examine the mess of glass and gore. Among the mushy brains of the obliterated Glaziene were tiny golden pearls. So small, Gwynessa would not have noticed them if she hadn't been poking through the fleshy mess.

Ario shouted down to her from the roof, "What's going on?"

"There's no fly in here," she answered.

"I thought they were inside their heads."

Gwynessa shook her head. "Looks like the tether is some kind of pearl." She poked one of the small golden orbs with the end of her scepter. It popped and oozed goo. "Or maybe they're little eggs."

"Where are the flies then?"

Gwynessa stood tall and turned her attention to the sky.

As she searched for the golden muscas, she noticed an unnatural ripple tearing through the clouds.

Terrified by the unknown, she wrangled her elemental twister and prepared to strike the anomaly.

"Wait!" a familiar voice shouted from the nothingness.

The sky ripped open and a small fleet of Gasiones and Bouldes barreled through.

"Rebuild the shield!" Ciela commanded.

"I can't. Not yet. This is the best elemental whirlwind I've been able to create. I can't let it fizzle out until I complete my mission."

"What's your mission?"

"Banishing the muscas."

"Okay, fine," Ciela grumbled as she lowered herself and her caravan to the ground. Once everyone disconnected, she used the Conexus relic to create a new shield around the castle.

"Thanks," Gwynessa began, "but now there are mindless trapped inside the castle with the Glaziene survivors."

Ciela grumbled as she split the magic and directed a stream into the castle. It slithered and divided, searching and snagging every mindless deviant by the ankles. They were promptly dragged out of the castle and ejected through the new shield.

"How will this tornado banish the muscas?" Ciela asked now that the castle was once again a safe place for the survivors.

"Fire from the sun, ice from the moon. Elements in their most extreme forms," Gwynessa explained as she lassoed the twister and redirected it away from the mindless pressing against their new shield. There was no need to kill any more of them—she and the other survivors were safe within the new shield, and she had time to find a new plan without losing this perfect whirlwind. She continued, "I thought I could lure the flies out of their heads, but it seems they aren't in there at all."

"How are they controlling them then?" Ciela asked, shocked.

"They planted little golden eggs, or pearls, inside their brains."

Rhoco stepped forward into the conversation. "Do you really think you can free the mindless of their muscas tethers?"

"Yes," Gwynessa answered. "I know I can."

He wore a look a conflicted consideration.

"What aren't you telling us?" Ciela demanded.

"They aren't eggs or pearls," Rhoco confessed. "It's a mucus sack of little ethereal radio beads." Rhoco tapped his temple. "Mine is still attached. Whichever devil I'm attached to is constantly chattering, but it's pretty easy to ignore with my full consciousness intact."

"Can it hear what you hear?" Ciela asked, appalled.

"No. The tether must be latched to the part of my brain that controls my nose because the devil only speaks when I smell living minds. It's never activated by noise."

"What if you're wrong?"

"I'm not," Rhoco replied confidently. "The devil doesn't even sense the return of my mind. He would've left the edifice to fetch me and force me back to the edifice if He knew."

"He's probably linked to a multitude of mindless all at once," Feodras speculated. "Probably sends blanketed commands to all when a scent is detected."

Rhoco nodded.

"Is that where they all are? The edifice?" Gwynessa asked Rhoco. "I need to attack them directly. I need to eliminate the cause to free the afflicted."

"Yes. They're fixing the edifice in Fibril," Rhoco answered.

Everyone turned to look at him.

"How are you so sure?" Ciela quipped.

"I saw them with my own two eyes." He paused. "Well, my mind's eyes. I was there, but also wasn't. It's complicated."

"You're *sure*?" Gwynessa asked, her tone urgent. "I can't waste any time."

"Positive."

It was her only lead.

“Hold the shield,” Gwynessa requested of the visiting Gasiones and Bouldes.

Ciela and Feodras nodded, indicating their allegiance.

They used the Conexus relic and the lost relic of Gaia to hold off the mindless while Gwynessa rode the winds of her elemental storm to Fibril.

Sea water misted her bare glass feet, soaking the bottom of her long skirt. The sensation stirred distant, yet familiar memories. While heartless, she abused this mode of travel, tearing across the sea using magic to ravage and torment neighboring lands.

That version of herself felt like a stranger now.

The majority of her adult life replayed like a foggy dream within her memory. Though the details from that time were now faded and unclear, the residual trauma lived loudly in every nerve of her body.

Whispers and visions haunted her daily. Every morning when she woke, every night while trying to sleep. The whispers turned to screams when life was too quiet. The visions turned to nightmares when she closed her eyes to dream. Uninvited, and seemingly unprovoked, she could not escape the terror of who she once was.

It was a battle she fought daily.

It was a battle she’d never surrender.

Her fate was her own fault, and she would fight to avenge herself, her loved ones, and her homeland until the day she died.

Though she currently possessed a comparable level of power and capability for violence through the lost relic of Gaia, her purpose was noble and her intentions pure. Her heart was full and her mind was clear.

She would banish the muscas.

She would bring the Namatéan survivors one step closer to safety.

The edifice came into view.

Thousands of gold muscas shrouded the ethereal lighthouse. They worked diligently on the cracks forming from within, spackling and filling each fissure with liquid gold.

Gwynessa raised her arms and unleashed her elemental whirlwind, sending it on a fast path toward the edifice.

The muscas noticed and tried to scatter, but it was too late. The sweeping force of the magic-fueled tornado sucked them into its swirl. The sun fire and moon ice obliterated the celestial flies, turning their bodies into gold dust and sending their essences back to Kólasi's abyss, where they would return to their normal forms.

The flies were gone.

Gwynessa released her grip on the whirlwind, letting it dissipate, but as she surrendered control of the tornado, she also unintentionally surrendered control of herself. Energy drained, muscles fatigued—without the force of the wind to keep her lifted, she plummeted toward the ocean.

Too tired to scream, she fell silently toward the sea.

Far enough away to avoid detection, but close enough to help, Ciela, Adaliah, Lonan, and Dasan hovered in waiting, observing Gwynessa's mission.

As the whirring tornado dispersed, Gwynessa's freefall became the only sight in the sky.

The Gasione's tore toward her, manipulating the air with warrior speed.

Despite her injury, Adaliah reached her first. She extended her arms and caught the glass queen moments before her fragile body shattered against the hard surface of the sea.

Though saved from a shatter, Gwynessa's body still cracked and fissured where it made contact with Adaliah.

Body limp but intact, Gwynessa groaned. "Am I alive?"

"You are," Adaliah answered.

Gwynessa peered up at her through a squinted gaze. Old animosity cast aside, a tear of genuine gratitude spilled down her glassy cheek.

"Thank you," she offered.

Adaliah nodded, choosing not to further complicate this interaction.

They returned to Crystet with Ciela, Lonan, and Dasan tailing them downwind. Adaliah lowered Gwynessa's body carefully onto the castle roof, and once she was safely on the ground, Ario raced to embrace her.

The Gasiones respectfully stepped back.

"She's has a few new cracks to attend to," Adaliah informed them.

"We can take care of that," Ario assured them as he kissed Gwynessa's forehead.

"It's a good thing we followed," Ciela announced. "We almost lost her."

"Thank you," Ario expressed, making eye contact with Adaliah as well. "What happened?"

"I didn't realize how much energy I was expending on the whirlwind. When I released it, I fell," Gwynessa explained, her voice soft and strained.

"Are the muscas gone?"

She nodded.

Jahdo shuffled his old, fissured body to the edge of the roof and lifted a pair of glass binoculars to assess the state of the mindless.

"They're calm," he announced. "They're still foggy-eyed, but they've stop battling the shield."

Tyrus peered over Jahdo's shoulder. "He's right. We should keep the shield up, just in case, but it seems that the mindless have lost focus, or motivation, without the muscas here."

"How about Rhoco? Is he freed from the devil in his head?" Gwynessa asked.

Jahdo shifted his crystal binoculars to where Rhoco stood on the royal grounds with the other Bouldes. Feodras and Stennis wore celebratory expressions as Rhoco held the sides of his head and beamed with delight.

Tyrus bellowed over the roof's edge, "What's your status?"

Rhoco raised a giant stone thumbs-up. "I'm free!"

Gwynessa heard the declaration and relaxed in Ario's arms. "Mission complete."

Chapter 27

Elecort

Elior raced around Helaine's small apartment, holding a wire-coiled toy bird and pretending to make it fly as he ran.

"Be careful!" Helaine shouted as Elior nearly knocked over a porcelain vase.

Elior giggled but continued to soar the toy bird around the room.

Helaine finished putting the breakfast plates away, then sat beside Torben at the dining table.

His expression was forlorn as he watched the rapidly growing child play in their home.

"He's growing too fast," he said in a quiet voice to Helaine. "He's the size of a five-year-old now."

"I don't understand it either."

"I thought we had more time to hide him, to search for a cure, but if he keeps growing at this rate, it will become impossible to conceal his survival."

"I know—"

"Not only does he have the same piercing azure eyes and handsome face as Lucien, but he's also the only Voltain without a glow," Torben rationalized. "Elixyvette will know it's her son."

"Paz thinks he's close to figuring out a cure."

"We don't have as much time as we originally thought. We need it now."

Torben stood and stormed so furiously past Elior, the force of his strides knocked the child to his bum. Elior immediately started wailing.

Helaine raced to scoop him into her arms as Torben stormed out the front door.

"Shh," Helaine hushed Elior as she cradled him with love. "He's just scared. I'm scared, too," she confessed to the child. "You're growing very fast, my little spark. We need you to slow down."

Through his tears, Elior looked up at her with his big, beautiful azure eyes. Flickers of amber blazed within the blue. His crying ceased, but his lip continued to quiver.

"I'm sorry," Helaine offered, "You must be scared, too."

She kissed his forehead.

Elior giggled as the voltage in her lips sent tiny, tickling emerald lightning bolts across his forehead. The sensation faded quickly.

Helaine wished she could fix his electric charge with a kiss. She wished she could transfer her charge into him and heal him. But it wasn't that simple—Elior had to create a current on his own for it to be long-lasting.

"Do you remember Paz?"

Elior's expression did not change.

"The silly Metellyan who sings funny songs and does funny dances."

Elior smiled and clapped his hands as he hummed one of Paz's happier melodies.

"Yes! He is coming over again today to check on you." Helaine gently traced the gruesome scar across Elior's neck.

"I won't let anyone hurt you ever again."

Elior lifted his little hand and touched his scar. The glimmer in his eyes conveyed deep hurt.

"I know you can't speak yet, but I hope you can understand everything that I say to you," Helaine said. "You are safe with me."

She placed Elior onto his feet. Instead of returning to his playtime, he grabbed Helaine's hands and kissed them.

The tears she had been holding back fell.

He understood her, and he was thankful.

"Go play," Helaine insisted, hoping to lighten the mood.

Elior smiled and ran off to find a new toy to play with.

The front door creaked open.

"Anyone home?" Paz called out.

"Come in!" Helaine replied, clearing off the table and laying down a clean sheet. "Elior! Paz is here for your checkup."

A loud crash and the cracking tinkling of glass came from the back bedroom, followed by Elior racing down the hallway holding a long, jagged shard of glass.

"No!" Helaine shouted, running toward the child, hoping to snag the broken electron tube before any accidents happened, but she wasn't fast enough. Elior tripped before she reached him.

He tumbled forward, landing neck first on the glass spike.

No cries or screams left his mouth, only streams of dark sparkling blood.

"No!" Helaine shouted again as she fell to her knees beside the young boy. She lifted the child into her arms and cradled him.

"Oh, dear," Paz said to himself, stunned into inaction.

"Help him!" Helaine screeched.

Paz grimaced as he scanned the brutal wound from afar.

"This is much worse than his previous injury." Paz gulped. "I don't think I can fix that."

"You have to try!" Helaine sobbed harder.

Paz leaned in and pressed Elior's neck flesh back together. As soon as he released, it separated and poured blood again.

Helaine's chest rose and fell with terror.

Paz tried again, pressing both sides of the wound together to stop the bleeding. Sweat dripped from his tin forehead and his hands shook from panic.

"Even if I stop the bleeding, his wires beneath are severed."

"Then fix the wires first!"

"The blood is pouring out too fast," Paz stammered, fumbling as he continued to examine the wound. "He'll bleed out if I don't keep the wound shut."

Too much blood had collected beneath Paz's hands and it began to seep out of the corners of the wound.

Paz let go.

Blood gushed down the sides of Elior's neck.

"No!" Helaine cried.

Paz used the sheet on the table to clean the wound the best he could, then hunched over the boy and began tinkering with the wires. The blood was flowing too fast, and the wires were too slick to hold.

"They're impossible to hold with all this blood." Paz panicked. "The wires are too tiny, I need a solid grip to twist them back together."

Helaine used the sheet to try to help clean the blood as it gushed, but the boy was bleeding out.

"I'm so sorry," Paz offered, continuing to try, but aware that his attempts were futile. His breathing deepened as his hands slowed. He cautiously glanced up at Helaine.

"He's gone."

Helaine shook her head, tears falling. "No, he can't be."

"I'm so sorry."

"He's not dead!"

Paz exhaled deeply, holding back his own emotion.

"I'm sorry," he said again.

Helaine swallowed her sorrow and squeezed a few final tears from her eyes. She placed Elior onto the sheet and left the room. When she returned, she was carrying a fresh sheet and a towel.

Silently, she cleaned up the excess blood with the towel, then wrapped Elior's body in the clean white sheet.

She stroked Elior's covered head, quiet tears brimming her eyes.

"Are you okay?" Paz asked warily.

Helaine did not reply.

"What will you do with his body?" Paz asked.

She wiped the tears off her cheek, smearing Elior's blood all over her face. "I'll wait until Torben gets home to decide."

Paz nodded, relieved to get an answer out of her.

Helaine said no more. She simply stared vacantly at the wrapped body laying on her dining room table, which was starting to bleed through the clean white sheet.

"I need to be alone with him."

"Are you sure?" Paz asked.

"Yes." Helaine's voice fell flat. "I will be okay," she assured him.

"Okay," Paz agreed, his hesitance abundant. "I'll be right outside if you need anything."

She nodded and Paz scuttled out the front door.

Helaine sat in an armchair that faced the dining room, keeping the sheet-wrapped prince in view. The blood stains grew with each passing second, as did the darkness of the room.

Adrift in a trance, Helaine lost track of time. She sat in silence, staring at the blood-stained sheet concealing the dead child—her dead child—until nightfall turned the room black.

Hours had passed.

When she noticed that night had consumed her, she tried to strengthen her spark to add light to the room, but her grief weighed too heavily. A soft green glow was all she could muster.

As she stood to turn on a lamp, the front door opened. Torben raced inside.

"Paz told me what happened," he blurted out as he charged toward Helaine.

Helaine nodded solemnly as Torben pulled her into a tight embrace.

"After everything he survived."

"I know. I'm so sorry," Torben offered.

"I loved him like he was my own."

"I loved him, too."

Helaine sniffled into his shoulder, then glanced over to where Elior lay dead, wrapped in his blood. "He deserved better than this. Better than all the horrors he endured."

"His was a cruel fate," Torben agreed. "Surely Incarna will reward his soul for its suffering here. Perhaps his next life will be abundantly blessed."

"I hope so."

Hand in hand, they walked over to Elior.

Torben grabbed the edge of the sheet and Helaine looked away.

The sheet lifted and Torben gasped.

Elior's bright azure eyes were wide open and glimmering up at him.

"Helaine, look."

"I can't," she objected, holding back another round of tears.

Torben lowered the sheet in disbelief, gathered his wits, then lifted it again.

This time, Elior giggled.

Helaine whipped around.

"How?" she asked, confused tears falling. She examined Elior's healed wound while planting furious kisses all over his face. Torben held Elior's hand as he fell to one knee beside the table.

Elior giggled harder as they showered him with love.

"I swear, he was lifeless a few hours ago."

"I see all the blood. I believe you."

Helaine traced her fingers over the spot of the wound—it was smooth and scarred, blending in with the scars from his infancy.

"Is he immortal?" Helaine asked Torben in a low whisper.

His breathing was deep and slow. "It appears so."

Chapter 28

Cerébrum

"She's back!" Grette announced as Noelani reappeared in Cerébrum. Every Boulde mind cupped a flame, creating enough light to illuminate the area where the Namatéans gathered.

Noelani was greeted by a barrage of desperate curiosity.

"What happened?"

"Tell us!"

"Did Rhoco survive?"

Noelani buried her face in her hands. "I don't know."

The interrogation continued.

"You don't know?"

"Why not?"

"Weren't you there?"

Noelani lowered her hands and stood tall.

"Stop!" she demanded.

The furious chatter ceased.

"I carried Rhoco all the way to Namaté. He had to vacate my mind before Kólasi possessed my mindless body." She shook her head. "I don't know what happened to Rhoco after he let go."

The crowd of minds wondered silently.

Grette finally spoke. "He either dissipated immediately, reentered his body, or is floating around Namaté as a ghost."

The Namatéans considered this.

"Better than being stuck here," Orso urged. His reappearance caught Grette off guard—though time was impossible to determine here, it felt like days since she had last seen him.

"He's right," Grette declared, to which everyone exited their silent contemplation to agree.

"Much better."

"I'd rather dissipate than be stuck here."

"Floating around Namaté as a ghost sounds nice."

"I'd choose any of those options over this place."

Noelani shuddered. An icy chill raced through her mind's figment.

How much time had passed?

"Did Kólasi sense Rhoco inside of you?" Grette asked.

"I don't think so."

She shivered again.

Only Grette noticed.

"Is He coming?" Grette asked in a whisper.

Noelani nodded.

"Do you want to bring others back with you?"

"We don't know if it works yet."

"Sounds like they're willing to take the risk."

"Fine, but they're too desperate. If they know I'm about to leave again, they'll swarm. Too many will latch on." Noelani shook her head. "Kólasi will sense them, and I will pay the price."

"I will help you," Grette offered.

"Don't you want to leave?"

"Of course, I do, but I'll have other opportunities."

Noelani gave Grette a small smile of appreciation.

Grette continued, "Who should leave next?"

"Azmon and Chesulloth," Noelani answered confidently. "I will try two minds and see how that goes."

"Excellent. I'll inform them, discreetly."

Grette left and returned not only with the giant, regal Bonz, but also five hulking Bouldes.

The nearby Namatéans were too busy squabbling about their theories to notice.

"Stein, Carraig, Gedeon, Cloch, and Feldspar will stand guard to ensure that the others don't surround you and latch on once they realize you're leaving again."

The quintet of Hematites and Obsidians nodded to confirm their allegiance.

"Thank you," Noelani offered.

"No," Chesulloth interjected. "Thank *you*."

"It's a risk," Noelani warned. "We don't know if it works yet."

"We are aware, but it's a worthy gamble, and we appreciate you choosing us.

Noelani nodded curtly. "I don't know how many trips I've got left, and there are no Bonz left in Namaté." She extended a hand to Chesulloth. "The Bonz deserve to live."

Chesulloth shook her hand and Noelani yanked her into a tight embrace.

"Press your forehead into mine," Noelani instructed.

Chesulloth did as she was told, and their minds merged.

Noelani extended her hand to Azmon.

"Hey!" King Morogh shouted. "What are you two doing?"

Heads whipped in Noelani's direction, and the nearby Namatéans clambered closer.

Azmon took Noelani's hand and pressed his forehead into hers.

His mind disappeared into hers.

"It should be a group decision!" Morogh barked.

"Does anyone object to Chesulloth and Azmon going first?" Grette shouted in reply.

Nobody challenged the choice.

Grette smiled at Morogh, "Seems like we are all in agreement."

Morogh grumbled. "Forced agreement. Can we have a group chat *before* the decision is made next time?"

Grette left the small group surrounding Noelani and marched to Morogh. Once close enough, she spoke in a softer voice. "This place reeks of desperation. Do you really think a collective decision could be made? Or do you just want to strong arm your way into going next?"

Morogh smirked. "I just want a chance."

"Everyone will get a chance."

"Will we?" he challenged. "How many trips do you really think she has left? And she's only willing to take two minds at a time?" Morogh shook his head. "Most of us will get left behind."

"Have patience," Grette urged. "If two minds work, she may be willing to try more next time."

Noelani shook violently behind the wall of Bouldes.

"Is she leaving again?" Exton of Crystet asked.

"Take us with you!" Keane, a different Glaziene begged.

The crowd erupted into a frenzy, pushing toward Noelani and challenging the Bouldes standing guard.

The giant Hematites and Obsidians easily swatted the smaller minds away, while Grette climbed up Feldspar's body, stood on his shoulders, and shouted orders of composure and peace to the chaotic mob.

"Stand down!"

Nobody listened.

They were determined to go home.

As the crowd pushed forward, Noelani convulsed and then vanished.

She was gone.

Kólasi had taken her away again.

The desperate Namatéans erupted into furious chatter.

"We missed our chance!"

"What if she doesn't come back?"

"This isn't fair!"

"What do I have to do to be next?"

"Enough!" Grette shouted from Feldspar's shoulders. The jabbering turned into soft whispers as they turned their anger toward Grette. "We need organization and order."

"I want to be next!" King Morogh declared.

This revived the loud and incessant squabbling among the minds.

"No, me!"

"I'm next!"

"Stop!" Grette shouted. When they quieted, she continued. "I know it's hard, but we must practice patience. She cannot take all of us at once."

"How will we decide who goes next?" Exton asked.

"There isn't a single mind here that is more important than the rest. The only fair way is to let Noelani decide. She is the only one who sees firsthand the state of Namaté. We have to trust her judgment."

Though their energy was dissident, nobody challenged her.

All they could do now was wait and hope that Noelani returned.

Kólasi's split carried Noelani's mind back to Namaté.

As they crossed through the planet's outermost atmosphere and plummeted through the clouds, Noelani urged Azmon and Chesulloth to let go.

They obeyed without hesitation, releasing their tight clutch of Noelani's cognizance.

She was alone with Kólasi.

His divine energy was manic, His course around Namaté sporadic. Noelani's body was nowhere to be found.

<<*Where is your body?*>> He asked.

I don't know.

He rerouted His path to cover the uninhabited lands and located Noelani in Coppel.

<<*Why is your body here?*>> He asked.

I don't know, she repeated. *I can't see what happens when I'm not here.*

Kólasi ignored her and rocketed into her body. The transition was hasty and harsh— Kólasi was on a tear.

<<*Your incompetence forced me to possess the living.*>> He shuddered with disgust as He recalled the interaction. <<*Vile, suffocating, revolting.*>>

Why do You need me if You can use them?

<<*Because there are time restraints with the living. I can possess your dead vessel for however long I choose. The living vessels … if I stay inside them too long, they die.*>> Kólasi rolled His eyes. <<*Forbidden technicalities. I'm not allowed to kill mortals belonging to my siblings. Not so directly, at least.*>>

I see. Can't You eavesdrop on them from the heavens?

<<*I can observe from afar, but I can't hear every conversation from afar. That's why I've needed* you*—for your memory, your ears, and your ability to not be seen.*>> He scoffed. <<*Only your invisibility has been useful thus far.*>>

His manic energy had Him babbling; He was divulging more than usual. Noelani's curiosity piqued. His most recent interaction with the Namatéan mortals had severely rattled Him.

<<I am realizing now that your mind is useless,>> He said before shoving Noelani's mind deeper into the recesses of her body, silencing her before she could object. *<<I only need your body.>>*

Though she was smothered beneath His presence within her own body, she still heard His faraway thoughts as He dashed around Namaté without clear purpose.

<<They defied me,>> He thought to Himself. *<<A direct attack, a declaration of insolence.>>*

Noelani could not see what He was referring to, but she felt His almighty rage. Every breath He breathed through her mouth came with a shudder of fury. Every flap of her wings trembled beneath His rampage. Every sight He saw through her eyes was blurred by His wrath.

Noelani happily stayed where He had pushed her—she was too terrified to try to sneak a peek beyond.

After a few hours of hiding from His holy temper, He abruptly discarded her in the ruins of Wicker.

Senses returned, Noelani waited until she was sure He had left before moving from where she lay.

The wind ceased, the sky cleared, and voices shouted her name.

"Noelani!"

It was a man.

"Noelani! Is it you?"

It was a woman.

Noelani lifted her head slightly to find a vision of stone and glass jogging toward her—Gwynessa and Rhoco.

He had survived.

Gratitude, hope, terror, confusion—Noelani's scrambled emotions left her speechless.

"Is it you?" Gwynessa repeated, stopping a few paces away from her. Rhoco followed her lead.

"It's me." She sat up. "I think He's gone."

"*Think?*" Rhoco asked, taking a step back.

"What did you do?" Noelani asked, her tears of terror finally falling.

"What do you mean?" Gwynessa asked.

"He was *furious*. He's never been like that before. Chaotic, spiraling, driven by rage. Something someone did upset Him greatly."

Gwynessa smirked.

"Why are you smiling?"

"I can't tell you."

"Why not?"

"Too risky," Gwynessa stated. "The less you know the better."

Noelani nodded. "You're right." She paused in thought. "In fact, whatever progress you all are making on the relics and edifice, keep it hidden. Kólasi uses my body to spy, and He often shifts into aella form to eavesdrop."

"We figured as much after He busted into our relic search party via Stennis," Rhoco said.

"He can see from afar, but He cannot hear from afar," Noelani said, sharing this new piece of information.

"Do you think He'll start possessing the living more often?" Gwynessa asked.

"Only if He observes a quick and easy way to disrupt a relic acquisition. He can't possess a living body for very long without killing it," she explained, "which would break primordial rules."

"Interesting," Gwynessa mused.

"Hypothetically, can He hop in and out of our bodies to eavesdrop or steer conversations?" Rhoco asked.

"Yes, but I don't know if He will. His emotion was intense disgust while recalling His time spent in Stennis's body. I don't think He likes being inside the living."

"That's good news, I guess."

"Yes. So just be careful when you talk about sensitive matters."

"I will use the relic to check for hidden listeners moving forward, thank you," Gwynessa said.

"Tell Ciela and the others, too."

"I will," Gwynessa promised, then asked, "Did you bring anyone back this time?"

"Azmon and Chesulloth."

"Excellent choices," Rhoco applauded.

Gwynessa looked upset.

"I hope they make it back to their bodies," Noelani expressed.

"If I survived, so will they," Rhoco assured her.

"I hope so. I'm going to try to bring back more minds next time."

"And you're sure Kólasi doesn't notice? He made a strange remark to me while possessing Stennis."

"What did He say?"

"That I shouldn't be here. I wasn't sure if He meant I should be dead or back in Cerébrum."

Noelani's shoulders slouched. "That's terrible news. Even the chance of Him knowing is dangerous. What do I do?"

"Keep trying until you can't anymore," Gwynessa urged. "You have to save as many as you can."

"If he finds out, we may face a fate worse than Cerébrum."

Gwynessa fidgeted where she stood. "Have you seen my brother there?"

"Calix?"

Gwynessa nodded.

"I haven't," Noelani revealed, understanding Gwynessa's fear. "I'm sorry."

"If you do, will you please bring him home?"

"I will try."

"Thank you."

"You better hurry back," Gwynessa urged Noelani. "You're running out of time."

"Kólasi said the same. Why, though?"

"Everything ends in a week."

"Ends?"

"Either we reclaim our home, or we die as fateless."

"Kólasi can't kill you. He's not allowed to directly interfere with living mortals."

"Correct, but He can send a bloodstorm that will indirectly drown us."

Noelani shuddered. "Is that what He plans to do?"

Gwynessa nodded. "In a week."

"I see." Noelani rubbed her forehead. "I *am* running out of time."

"Do the best you can," Gwynessa encouraged.

"Happy to have been the test dummy," Rhoco said.

Noelani shot him a glare. "While I'm glad that you survived, it could've been the end for both of us."

"But it wasn't."

“Might still be for me.” Noelani exhaled deeply, trying to release all her pent-up fear and frustration.

Rhoco bit his lip. “I’m sorry.”

“It’s okay. I’d rather go out swinging.”

A tremor shot up through Noelani’s heels and into the back of her head. She squeezed her eyes shut until the intense pain subsided.

“Are you okay?”

As Noelani peered through her eyelashes, a second tremor shook her to the core. She closed them again

The pain disappeared.

So did the subtle sounds of Namaté.

Noelani opened her eyes to eternal darkness.

“It worked,” she shouted loud for all the minds in Cerébrum to hear. “I can bring you home.”

Chapter 29

Wicker

Without the muscas attached to her brain, Noelani's energy was docile. Her foggy eyes stared past Gwynessa and Rhoco, empty and apathetic. Stationary, with no motivation to move, Noelani was not a threat to them in this state.

Gwynessa grumbled impatiently, itching her freshly fused fissures with one hand while holding Bozrah's skull under her other arm. They had divied up the relics after banishing the muscas—the Glaziene had the lost relic of Gaia, the Bouldes had the brain and the finger coils, and the Gasiones had the wings.

"What's taking Ciela so long?" she asked.

"Maybe they're having a hard time figuring out how to create a shield in Vapore using Elzaphan's wings," Rhoco answered.

"Shields aren't as essential anymore, not with the muscas gone." Gwynessa motioned to where Noelani stood swaying in place. "She is proof. Shields are the lesser priority now. We need to collect all the relics and destroy the edifice."

"We will."

"We're running out of time," Gwynessa warned.

Rhoco grunted in agreement. "That seems to be the theme."

Ciela circled overhead, shifting out of aella form to greet her allies.

"I could've done this alone," she squawked.

"The Woodlins know me," Gwynessa explained. "I have a long history with them."

"They know me, too," Rhoco added. "I sacrificed my life to save them from the Mudlings." Rhoco paused. "Granted, it was *after* the Mudlings had already sent Brynmor to the pits, and it *was* my fault they did that in the first place." Rhoco smiled. "But I think I left on good terms."

Gwynessa grimaced. "Maybe you *shouldn't* come."

"No, no. It will be fine. I want to help. I am your protection."

"Why didn't your glass guards join?" Ciela asked.

"They're too close to me. They care too much. And there are certain parts of my past I'd like to keep to myself."

"I see. Well, I don't think you'll need protection, but it's good to have the stone brute by your side in case."

"You said you could show us an easier way to reach the Woodlins," Gwynessa reminded her.

"I did." Ciela raised a brow at Gwynessa. "Despite your nightmarish reign, I do believe you have the best interest of Namaté at heart."

"I do."

"And Feodras promised that I could trust you," Ciela said to Rhoco.

"You can."

Ciela exhaled deeply. "We discovered a Woodlin secret while searching for the relics of the Holy Three. Follow me."

The ground was covered in leaves, branches, and broken tree trunks.

"There," Ciela said, pointing to a short tree trunk. At first glance, it looked like all the others, but once Ciela brushed a thick layer of dirt and leaves off, a light beamed out of its center.

"It's a looking glass portal," she explained. "You can see anywhere in Namaté or Occavas. And if you enter, you can *go* anywhere you want."

Gwynessa stepped closer, the silver sheen in her eyes glimmered with fascination. "This is how they always knew my secrets."

"And mine," Rhoco added.

"They knew all of our secrets," Ciela confirmed.

"Yet they never used them against us, or to claim power," Gwynessa marveled.

Ciela nodded. "A testament to their benevolence."

"Their secret is safe with me."

"And me," Rhoco chimed in.

Ciela continued, "Adaliah said the shield over Radix de Wicker bounced her back when she tried to go there, but we have to try again."

"They will let me in," Gwynessa stated.

"If they wouldn't let you in prior, why would they now?"

"I never tried prior; I couldn't leave Crystet without taking the lost relic of Gaia with me and disarming the shield around the castle." Gwynessa huffed. "I could hardly get to the Wildlands without risking the lives of all the Glaziene survivors."

"I could have brought you."

"You never offered," Gwynessa countered.

"I didn't know the Woodlins might listen to you over me."

"Enough!" Rhoco intervened. "This isn't helpful."

"You're right," Ciela agreed, ruffling her feathers as she regained her regal composure. "The timing of the universe is divine." She took a deep breath. "It was meant to happen now."

Gwynessa dropped her defenses as well. "Wish us luck."

"You don't need it," Ciela confessed begrudgingly. "You have Gaia on your side. You always have."

Gwynessa offered her a half smile before dipping her head into the hollow center of the old tree stump. The light gleamed bright as her body slithered into the hole.

Inside the looking glass portal, Gwynessa floated in front of a glass orb that was suspended in space. Light from the outside world was gone and only the colorful glow of the globe lit this space.

She moved closer.

An incredible bird's eye view of Namaté existed within the orb. She could see everywhere all at once, as well as the movements of every living being in real time. It took a moment to orient herself to this overwhelming view, but once the wobbly feeling of dizziness passed, she investigated the logistics of this portal.

A quick counter-clockwise spin of the orb rewound time, and while she could look into the past, spinning the orb clockwise only brought her back to present day—she could not see into the future.

Orb set to the present, she touched it with two fingers and zoomed into Wicker—the glass orb expanded and projected her desired location all around her. Then she went to where Ciela and Rhoco still stood beside the tree trunk portal. The closer she got, the more she could hear, and once she zoomed in enough, it was like she was standing there with them.

"What are you waiting for?" Ciela squawked at Rhoco. Her voice was clear, yet distant—it echoed through the portal like a dream.

"I'm too big," Rhoco replied. "I won't fit."

"If the Woodlins fit, so will you."

"Maybe they only reach a hand in or something."

Ciela crossed her arms over her chest. "Really?"

A look of nostalgia softened Rhoco's stone-cold expression.

"She doesn't need me. She can do it alone."

"Yes, she can, yet she allowed you to join," Ciela said. "She needs a friend."

"Maybe you should go instead."

Ciela shook her head. "She chose you."

The harsh lines on Rhoco's face softened again, and his pretty pale green eyes illuminated with long held reverence. It only lasted a moment before his usual stubborn demeanor returned.

"You're going to quit on her now?" Ciela asked.

"I never give up."

"Good. Now, go."

He nodded hastily before dipping his face into the tree light.

While his shoulders were much larger than the width of the tree trunk, the portal still managed to draw him in.

He landed beside Gwynessa into the looking glass version of Wicker.

"Huh?" he stated, confused to be back in the place he had just left.

Gwynessa pushed her arms outward in front of her and the world around them tore away.

Rhoco heaved and covered his mouth with one hand while shielding his eyes with the other, hoping to soothe his sudden nausea.

Gwynessa stopped when the world was a small glass orb floating in front of them again.

"You can uncover your eyes."

Rhoco peered between two fingers to make sure everything had stopped moving before he lowered his hand. He noticed the orb in front of them.

"Is that the looking glass?"

"Yes, but right now it's showing us Namaté. I need to figure out how to switch it to Occavas."

"Try the portal in Amesyte Valley. It's hidden beneath the wildflower field."

While they hovered in place, Gwynessa zoomed in to Orewall. She tapped the portal hidden within the flowers, but her finger merely passed in and out of the veil. It did not take her through the portal and grant her visual access to Radix de Orewall.

She zoomed back out.

"I don't know where all the portals are."

"Try Vapore. Near Captivus River and the black-moss willow throne, there's a bright green lake. It's one of their portals."

Gwynessa zoomed into Vapore and found the lake. Instead of tapping through, she closed her eyes and tried to will her desire into existence, like she had done many times with the lost relic of Gaia.

It didn't work.

She opened her eyes and sighed. "This magic is not like the relics. I don't know how to work this place."

As she was about to try again, Rhoco held out a hand.

"Stop," he requested.

She paused her furious attempts.

He continued, "I think we're looking at it wrong."

"What do you mean?"

"Occavas is the flip side of Namaté—pristine, corrupt; original, copy; right, wrong."

"I don't get it."

"We are looking at it right side up," he explained as he waved his arms through the hollow space, attempting to shift his body. "Maybe we need to look at it upside down."

Gwynessa gasped—it made sense.

She joined him in flipping her body until it was overturned.

The orb, and the room, shifted. They were now looking at Occavas through the glass, and no longer felt like they were hanging upside down.

"It worked," Gwynessa said.

Rhoco smiled proudly.

Gwynessa side-eyed him, seeing him clearly for the first time since they had met. He was simple, but well intended. Brutish, but sensitive. He had done so much for her over the years, only to receive harsh irrelevance from her.

"I'm sorry," she offered abruptly.

"For what?"

"For treating you like you don't matter."

"Oh."

"You do matter. Without you, I'd still be shattered at the base of Jökull cliff. Without you, Feodras might have never found his confidence." She smiled. "I can only imagine how many other crucial fates you have assisted."

"Hmm," he replied, unable to access his emotions in this moment. "I just try to do what's right, or what I think is right. I still mess up sometimes, though."

"We all do."

"I'm not sure I've done enough," he confessed. "I worry where I'll end up when my life ends."

"I suspect you'll end up wherever you feel at peace."

Rhoco grinned. "That would be nice."

"Okay, let's get to work."

Gwynessa touched the orb, and the room filled with views of the world around Radix de Wicker. They hovered in front of the fierce shield surrounding the echoland. Through it, they could see the Woodlins.

"Help!" Gwynessa shouted.

"I think we are only looking at them," Rhoco noted. "I don't think we're actually there."

"You're right. How does this orb turn into a portal?"

Rhoco reached out his hand while concentrating on his desire. The air turned solid under his touch.

"Desire it," he told Gwynessa.

Rhoco parted the air like a curtain and peered through.

Gwynessa did the same.

They could see into real-world Occavas.

"If we step out, we will fall into the ocean below," Rhoco warned. "We can't float there like we do here."

Gwynessa lifted Bozrah's skull, which hung from the belt around her long dress.

"Place a hand on the skull," she instructed Rhoco.

He did as she said.

Magic lifted and carried them out of the looking-glass portal. They floated in front of the shield protecting Radix de Wicker.

"Beaumont! Bolivar! Anyone!" Gwynessa shouted to the Woodlins.

This time, they heard her.

A Woodlin she did not recognize rerouted his roots and slowly trekked to the shield. He was much younger than the Woodlins she knew, but he moved with the same painfully slow steps. When he reached the spot where Gwynessa and Rhoco hovered, he stopped. A solid wall of magic stood between them.

"We need your help," Gwynessa shouted.

He shook his head.

"Why not?"

The young Woodlin tapped the side of his face where his ear was carved into his trunk.

"I don't think he can hear us," Rhoco suggested.

She lifted her wrist to show him the tree shaped stain on her wrist.

"Baldric," she said loudly, exaggerating the movement of her lips so he could read them. "Baldric gave this mark to me. He was my friend."

The Woodlin narrowed his bark brow before departing.

"Where is he going?" Rhoco asked.

Gwynessa groaned. "I don't know."

When the Woodlin returned, Beaumont was with him.

A smile crossed his face at the sight of Gwynessa, and when he noticed Bozrah's skull, his brown eyes became alight with awe.

He reached his lanky wooden arm through the shield, seized Gwynessa and Rhoco where they hovered, and pulled them into Radix de Wicker.

"Don't mind Bohdan, he's still learning the difference between an enemy and a friend."

The young Woodlin smiled sheepishly at them. "Sorry, didn't mean to offend."

"It's okay. Thank you for allowing us a chance to speak to you. There's so much to tell you, so much to do," Gwynessa began.

Beaumont's eyes were stuck on Rhoco. "You've brought a ghost with you."

"A ghost?"

"A ghost made of stone. A sight I've never seen before."

"I'm not a ghost," Rhoco countered.

"Hmm," Beaumont's eyes shifted from Rhoco back to Gwynessa. "Your heart has finally found its home."

"I have the Woodlins unwavering friendship to thank." Gywnessa smiled softly.

"We did nothing."

"You believed in me."

"It all happened in a blink," Beaumont said. "A child, a monster, a woman. Your destiny is greater than you think."

"That's what I'm here about, actually. You hold the key to my fate."

"Anything to help a friend."

"We need Brixton's ribs."

"I see you found Bozrah's skull." Beaumont's branches contemplatively swayed. "And we felt someone take Elzaphan's wings as well. Why do you need more? What are you hoping for?"

"We plan to combine them all."

"Combine? Why?"

"To make a super relic. When we combined the skull, feathers, and brain, their magic was stronger. Surely, the power will be even greater with all nine relics merged."

"Very clever. Brilliant, really. You might create a power that rivals the scepter of alchemy."

"That's the hope."

"To what end?"

"Destruction of Kólasi's edifice."

"A shared goal—we've been working on that, too." Beaumont's sap-filled eyes twinkled with mischief. "We've been healing the edifice's diseased roots."

"The cracks in the lighthouse," Rhoco said, rejoining the conversation. "That was you?"

"I hope so. Hard to tell if it's working. We heal the roots, then soon after, new golden puss oozes."

"That will stop," Gwynessa assured him. "The muscas are finally gone—they were repairing the cracks as you created them."

"I see." Beaumont's branch fingers scratched his brow. "We were working against a force that did not want us to succeed."

"But they're gone now. Keep doing what you're doing. You will weaken the edifice from the inside, and once we have all the relics, we will finish it from the outside."

"Teamwork," Beaumont mused. "United, together. Later than yesterday, but better than never."

"Is that why you could not share the scepter with the rest of us?" Gwynessa asked.

"Indeed. I imagine it seemed selfish to you, but it was for the greater good."

"I knew there was a good reason."

"Did the others?"

"They thought you had forsaken us."

Beaumont sighed. "They still lack faith in the Mother."

"According to the Drakkina, Gaia *has* kind of forsaken us."

"Has She? Or are we looking for Her in all the wrong places? She is in you. She is in me. She is in every action we take, every decision we make. She is with us always."

Gwynessa nodded. "I feel her with me, often. I guess I needed that reminder."

"Do not lose faith. Your destiny is linked to a brighter day."

"So, can we take the ribs with us?" Gwynessa asked.

"Yes, of course," Beaumont said. "Send the relic!" His voice boomed across the land.

Instead of walking to get it, which would have taken a lot of time with how slow the Woodlins moved, long wooden arms reached over the treetops and passed their relic from the center of Radix de Wicker all the way to where Beaumont stood rooted near the border.

Bodhan handed the ribs to Beaumont, who held them in front of Gwynessa and Rhoco still sitting in his giant palm.

"They're much bigger than you," Beaumont noticed aloud. "How will you carry something so huge?"

Gwynessa lifted Bozrah's skull, which was large, but manageable. When it hovered near the top of the rib cage, the rib cage shrunk to a palm size. She then did the same with the skull.

"I didn't know I could do that." She placed the relics into her waistband pouch and pulled the strings tight. "Much easier to carry them this way."

"Before you go, I must inquire … have you heard the baby crying?"

"No," Gwynessa answered.

"I have," Rhoco interjected. "In Cerébrum."

"Peculiar, but expected considering your state of being." Beaumont shuddered, his leaves shaking. "Here, then gone, now back again; the child's celestial tears belong to the heavens."

"I keep hearing that a boy plays a role in our salvation, I just don't know who or how."

"The boy with lightning in his veins—you know his name."

"Prince Elior?"

Beaumont smiled.

Gwynessa objected, "He's just a baby! A sick one, too, from what I've been told."

"Go to him, you may be surprised," Beaumont encouraged. "Intuition never lies."

Chapter 30

"Thanks for your help," Gwynessa offered from where she and Rhoco still sat on Beaumont's hand.

"Anything for a friend."

Beaumont reached his arm out of the shield and delivered the duo back into Occavas. He watched them through the shield, patiently waiting for them to vacate his palm.

Gwynessa retrieved the shrunken skull and rib cage from her pouch and placed the skull into Rhoco's large stone hand.

"Be careful with it," she cautioned.

Rhoco accepted the relic hesitantly. "It's so tiny."

"I'll make it bigger," she offered and used the power of the ribs to enlarge the skull. "Better?"

"Yeah, maybe I won't accidentally crush it now." Rhoco paused. "How do I use it?"

"Feel it—similar to how you did in the looking glass portal."

"Desiring and feeling are very far apart for a Boulde."

"Focus your thoughts on what you want, and the relic will turn your thoughts into reality. Watch." Gwynessa lifted off of Beaumont's hand and into the air. "My thoughts and intentions are set on flying, therefore, I am flying," she explained.

Rhoco took a deep breath while cradling the skull in both of his palms.

"I want to fly," he said to himself in a low voice.

Nothing happened.

Beaumont's big eyes stared at him through the shield.

"Feel the desire deep within your soul," Gwynessa encouraged.

Rhoco groaned and reiterated, "Feeling things is not my specialty."

"Try."

Rhoco closed his eyes and imagined himself flying. He held on to the vision and rerouted the desire to his chest. Breathing in and out, he let the small feeling take hold and grow. When he opened his eyes, Beaumont's hand was gone and he was floating midair.

"I'm doing it!"

"Excellent," Gwynessa said. "Do you want to go back to Radix de Orewall? Or do you want to go to Elecort with me? I need to find Elior."

"I should go back home, but I think your quest to recruit Elior might be futile. While I was a mind ghost, I saw a memorial for a baby in Elecort. Elixyvette placed baby wires into a coffin."

"You think he's dead?"

"That's the impression I got."

"We have to check for ourselves."

"You can use the portal in Radix de Orewall," Rhoco offered. "It's closer to Elecort than Crystet."

They soared to the echoland of Orewall and found the surviving Bouldes existing beneath a sturdy shield and relaxing for the first time since Kólasi's invasion.

Gwynessa and Rhoco landed in the valley where the majority of Bouldes now rested. Purebreds, Fused, and Murks, all existing in unified harmony.

Gwynessa handed Rhoco the netted sling hanging from her waistband, and he secured the skull and hung it from his belt.

"Little sludge!" Cybelle cried out in greeting. "You're back!"

"I'm back. Again."

Stennis jogged toward him and threw an arm around his shoulder. "Happy to see ya buddy. What happened after we split ways?"

Rhoco smiled—it was so nice to have the devil's voice removed from his head, so nice not to smell their minds anymore.

"Where's Feodras?" Rhoco asked.

"He can't rest," Cybelle answered. "He walks the perimeter of the shield every few hours to make sure it's holding."

"But the mindless aren't a threat with the muscas gone."

"He's worried about Kólasi. He wants a strong shield to stop any tricks or meddling from the nefarious god."

"Fair enough." Rhoco said, his unease apparent. "So, we got the ribs."

"Were they in Radix de Wicker?" Stennis asked.

"Yes."

"How did you get them?"

"The Woodlins gave them to us."

"They've ostracized and neglected us since the start of this madness," Cybelle griped. "Why are they helping now?"

Rhoco lifted an arm toward Gwynessa. "They like her."

Gwynessa added, "While we were there, we also learned *why* the Woodlins have been hoarding the scepter of alchemy. They've been repairing the infected roots of the edifice with it, which has caused cracks in the structure above. Now that the muscas are gone and no longer undoing their work, the Woodlins can keep weakening the structure until we can destroy it with the super relic."

"Do we even need the super relic if the Woodlins can destroy it from within?" Cybelle asked.

"I don't think they'll be able to collapse it in time. It's a slow process."

Cybelle sighed. "So, the hunt for relics continues."

"All we need now are Dagmar's clay lungs and Rúnar's heart."

"Rúnar's heart will be easy to retrieve now that the mindless Oceamons don't have any muscas controlling them," Gwynessa said to the Bouldes.

"Bouldes can't swim," Stennis reminded her.

"But I can speak to the sea animals," Gwynessa reminded him. "I can get the heart, but I need to go to Elecort also."

"What for?" Cybelle asked. "We already know that Elixyvette has Jasvinder's eyes. She said she'd help once we had all the other relics."

"I need her son."

"Her son? Why?"

"I'm honestly not sure why, but I keep receiving tips that he's important, so I need to figure out why."

"We will work on finding Dagmar's lungs while you get the heart and figure out Elior's role in all of this," Rhoco said.

Gwynessa nodded. "We will reconvene soon, I hope, with all the pieces in place to destroy that edifice once and for all."

Gwynessa departed, leaving the Bouldes behind with their new task. Between the skull, the brain, and the finger coils, they had enough power to succeed.

The magic of Brixton's ribs carried her to Elecort.

Hovering high above the shield, Gwynessa assessed the land before entering.

Metellyans inhabited the districts while the few surviving Voltains lived inside the castle. Gwynessa dove through the shield and into the open skylight window of the throne room.

The Voltains scattered to the edges of the room, startled by the ice queen's jarring arrival.

"Why are you here?" Elixyvette barked. Her sunken eyes were bloodshot and circled by darkness, and though she wore an air of terror, her petite frame seemed ready to break.

"You look unwell," Gwynessa countered.

Elixyvette clenched her jaw.

"Why are you here?" the Voltain queen repeated.

"Where is your son?"

A collective gasp hushed the room.

"Excuse me?"

"Elior, your son. Where is he?"

"He's dead."

"How did he die?"

"Who do you think you are coming in here, asking questions that are none of your business."

"But you see, it *is* my business. Our fates are somehow intertwined."

Elixyvette scoffed. "Then perhaps you too will be dead soon."

Gwynessa narrowed her glare on Elixyvette, examining her harsh and calloused demeanor.

"You seem unmoved, uncaring. Don't you want to know why?"

"Why would I waste energy on the dead?"

"You don't want to know the greatness your son was destined for?"

"He was ill since birth, thanks to Rúnar—*your* ancestor. No glow, no strength. He wasn't destined for anything except death."

"But what if he was?" Gwynessa countered.

"I guess we will never know." Elixyvette's tone was laced with venom and her guilt spilled through her stone cold façade.

"Did *you* kill him?" Gwynessa inquired.

"Leave!"

Gwynessa's eyes widened in horror.

"Corentin, Raiden—seize her!"

"Your sins know no bounds," Gwynessa shouted as the guards dragged her out of the room. They shoved her into the corridor and closed the throne room doors.

She was alone in the Voltain castle.

She could have used the relic to force the soldiers off of her, but it wasn't worth the fight. Not with Elior dead.

This short mission failed, at least she had tried.

It was time to refocus and acquire Rúnar's heart.

Gwynessa walked to the end of the corridor and opened the window. Shrunken ribs hanging from her belt, she climbed out, both legs dangling as she sat on the ledge.

The door to the throne room opened and closed.

"Wait!"

Gwynessa looked over her shoulder to see Zohar and another guard racing toward her.

"You don't have what I need," she replied, moving farther out the window.

"Just wait," the younger guard insisted. "I think we can help."

"How?"

Zohar scanned the corridor.

"Not here," he urged, extending a hand to her.

"I have a relic," Gwynessa warned. "If at any point I feel like I'm being led into a trap, I will use it."

"Understood."

She took the younger guard's hand.

"I'm Torben," he said. "Seems you already know Zohar. If what you said in the throne room is true, you'll want to come with us."

Gwynessa took Torben's hand and followed them out of the castle. They traversed the royal grounds, which was buzzing with electricity, crossed the newly constructed bridge over Vindicta Strait, and toward the coiled gate leading into District 8.

They walked down a long road of shoddily repaired row homes. Near the end of the street, Torben stopped.

"This is my home," he announced.

"Okay," Gwynessa said, confused.

"Before you enter, I need you to promise that you will not tell Elixyvette about our involvement. We'd be stoned and sent to the ocean for treason."

"I won't tell her anything. She and I are not friends."

Torben exhaled dramatically before leading Zohar and Gwynessa inside.

A beautiful Voltain woman stood near the kitchen window watching a young boy play by himself in the backyard.

"This is Helaine," Torben said, introducing them.

Helaine wore a look of grave concern, but trusted Torben enough to greet Gwynessa kindly.

"Welcome," Helaine offered.

"Thank you."

"I wasn't expecting company, certainly none from Crystet."

"I'm still not sure why I am here either."

"And that," Torben continued, motioning to the grown boy playing outside, "is Elior."

"I thought the prince was a baby," Gwynessa challenged.

Torben shrugged. "We can't make sense of it either."

"He's been growing at an unnatural rate," Helaine explained.

"His body *and* his brain?" Gwynessa asked.

"We aren't sure about his mind. He looks to be about ten years old, but he doesn't speak. Not yet. He makes noise—laughter and crying—but no words." Helaine sighed. "He is a very sweet boy."

"You said your fates are intertwined," Zohar said.

"Both the drakkina and the Woodlins have told me that Elior is the key to our survival. I don't know how he plays a role, but I came here to see if I could figure it out."

Helaine shot Torben and Zohar a knowing glance before divulging.

"He can't be killed," she revealed.

"Elior is immortal?"

"It seems so."

"How do you know?"

"Elixyvette tried to kill him. She slit his throat and sent him down the river to drown. I thought he was dead when I found him—his bassinet was completely flooded with water and blood. We prepared a proper burial for him … but he recovered. He started crying as the land tried to reclaim his body. I assumed it was something to do with Paz's metallic touch and how he stitched the wounds."

Torben added, "But then he had another accident."

"Yes," Helaine continued, "a few days ago he fell neck first on a glass spike." She shook her head, eyes welling with sparkling tears. "I thought I lost him. Again. The spike severed two of his artery cords. I held him as he bled out." Helaine took a deep breath. "But after a few hours, the bleeding stopped and the wound started to mend itself. The rate at which he healed was as unnatural as the rate at which he's been growing."

"Immortal," Gwynessa repeated to herself.

"Or at least partially," Helaine clarified. "I'm not saying he's a god, but he's certainly been blessed by the divine."

"Can I meet him?"

"Of course, but he can't talk," Helaine reminded her.

"That's alright."

Torben retrieved Elior from the backyard and guided him into the kitchen. Upon sight of Gwynessa, a small smile of familiarity stretched across Elior's face.

"Elior," Torben began, "We'd like you to meet our friend Gwynessa."

"Hi, Elior. It's so nice to meet you," Gwynessa greeted.

::I've been waiting for you.::

Gwynessa looked around the room, unsure where the voice came from.

::It's me, Elior.::

Gwynessa's eyes widened and jaw slackened.

Elior continued, *::I can talk, they just can't hear me.::*

::You've been waiting for me?::

::They told me you would come for me.::

::Who?::

::Our sisters.::

Gwynessa paused in thought. *::The drakkina?::*

Elior nodded. *::You have to bring me to them.::*

::How? I don't have access to Cruxeus.::

Elior pointed to the spot where Gwynessa's cracked and blackened heart sat within her chest. *::Yes, you do.::* He then pointed to his own chest. *::We are connected to Her. You are quadradivinus—quarter divine, and I am dimidivinus—half divine. Spawned by mortal, touched by the divine.::*

Gwynessa lifted her hands and examined them with confusion.

"Quadradivinus," she said aloud.

"Huh?" Torben asked. He, Helaine, and Zohar watched the peculiar connection between the Ice Queen and Electric Prince, puzzled by the loud silence of their exchange.

::The gods call us dimis for short,:: Elior explained. *::At least that's how the drakkina always refer to me.::*

::Like a demigod?::

::No, demigods are totumdivinus—fully divine. They are half god and half mortal, and they always have one parent that is a god. They are more invincible than us. We are closer to immortal than regular mortals, though. Mortals can be gifted with full divinity too, but demigods are always a little stronger. No mortal can turn into a god.::

::Closer to immortal?:: Gwynessa asked Elior.

::Dimis always have one or more fatal flaws,:: he explained. *::Quadras have more.::*

::What's yours?::

::The drakkina told me not to tell anyone.::

::Smart. You should keep that information to yourself. As for me, I have shattered multiple times. I can't possibly be a quarter immortal.::

Elior remained fixated on her dark heart sitting behind the glass flesh of her sternum.

::Did your heart shatter, too?::

Gywnessa laughed, *::Figuratively or literally?::*

::Literally.::

::No. It never shattered.::

::I think your fatal flaw is your heart,:: Elior suggested. *::If it had shattered, too, maybe you wouldn't have survived.::*

::No Glaziene survives a complete shatter,:: Gwynessa said,

::Then maybe your heart can't *shatter. Or maybe it never shattered when it should've because it was protected by your divine connection.::*

::Maybe,:: Gwynessa said, unable to confirm or deny this theory. *::But I know I've never been touched by a god.::*

::Touched by the divine,:: Elior corrected her. *::Specifically, gods, progenies, or totums, which are fully divine mortals.::* He then pointed to the tree-shaped mark on her wrist. *::Some of the Woodlins are totumdivinus. Not all, but some.::*

::Who touched you?::

::The drakkina.::

::I see.::

::Will you help me?::

::I will try.:: Gwynessa returned her attention to the adults in the room. "I need to take Elior with me."

"Where?"

"Back to Crystet, then hopefully Cruxeus."

"Cruxeus?" Zohar asked.

"It's a lot to explain and we are running out of time. I need you to trust me."

Helaine looked to Elior. "Do you trust her?"

Elior nodded and grabbed Gwynessa's hand.

Helaine nodded. "This is bigger than me, I know. I have to trust the universe. I have to let you go."

Elior dropped Gwynessa's hand and darted to Helaine. He wrapped his arms around her torso and squeezed her tight.

"I always knew you'd do great things, and it was a privilege to see you through to this day," Helaine offered, answering the unspoken gratitude gushing out of Elior.

She kissed the top of his head, and he let her go.

"I will keep him safe," Gwynessa promised.

Helaine smiled. "Time to save the world, kid."

Chapter 31

Cerébrum

"It worked!" Noelani repeated.

Small fires ignited across Cerébrum in response.

The scattered flames moved closer, converging around Noelani.

"I will try three minds next time," she announced.

A furious shiver shook the figment of her mind.

Already? she thought.

"We have to hurry," she urged. "I sense that He's already on His way back."

A chorus of pleas ensued.

"Take me next!"

"I want to go home!"

"Choose me!"

"Be warned," Noelani declared, "there is no guarantee that it is safe."

The chorus of pleas continued. They didn't care. They wanted to go home, no matter the risk.

Grette and her quintet of warrior Bouldes circled Noelani, keeping her safe from bombardment.

Noelani spoke over the crowd. "Where are the commondores?"

Cesareo, a lifelong commondore who had chosen his life of servitude, pushed through the crowd. Though he had been set free before this imprisonment, the figment of his mind proudly displayed the version of himself he loved most—solid black eyes and pinned wings.

"We are here," he answered, his black eyes gleaming with hope. "All of us."

"Choose two others."

"Wait!" a familiar voice called out from beyond the faint light of the flickering flames.

Orso rushed through the crowd, pulling a small boy behind him. He let go of the child's hand and thrusted him into the light.

Calix.

"Dear boy," Exton declared upon seeing his nephew. "Are you okay?"

"You're here!" Noelani said, her relief profound.

"I'm okay," Calix reassured his uncle.

"If I had known you were here I would've searched for you," Exton said.

"No need to apologize. I am here now."

"The timing is divine," Orso affirmed.

Exton eyed Orso with suspicion, but said no more.

"Divine indeed," Noelani agreed. "You will come with me on this trip, too."

"Are you sure you want to try four minds this time?" Grette asked her.

"Yes, I am sure. I just saw Gwynessa and she has gone above and beyond to help us. I need to bring him home to her."

"Thank you," Calix gushed, unable to contain his emotion.

"Where have you been?" Exton asked.

"I was lost in the dark," Calix explained. "I saw the light, but it always disappeared before I could reach it."

"I found him deep in the outskirts of Cerébrum," Orso explained.

"Is that where you've been?" Grette asked, referring to Orso's random disappearances.

"I heard crying, so I investigated."

"All that crying we heard came from Calix?"

"No," Calix stammered, trying to salvage his pride. "I only cried once. That's when Orso found me. I heard the baby's cries, too, not recently, though."

"Us either,"Grette confirmed.

Noelani shivered. "We don't have much time. Meld into me if you're coming."

The trio of commondores merged into Noelani's mind.

"It's no surprise that your sister is a hero." Exton extended a hand to his nephew. "Tell her I said hello when you see her again."

Calix bypassed his uncle's hand and hugged him instead.

"I will," Calix promised before letting go.

Calix turned to Orso, who pulled him aside so they could talk briefly in private.

"I'm so glad you found me," Calix expressed.

"Me, too, kid. I'm sorry I couldn't bring you into the light sooner. I had to make sure the timing was right."

"You knew where I was this whole time?"

"Of course. You're the only reason I'm here."

Calix shook his head, confused. "Why let me fester alone in the dark?"

"There were too many moving pieces—you were safer in isolation until I had a better understanding of how this unexpected anarchy would unfold." Calix still looked confused, so Orso further explained, "The prayer called for your safe delivery home, heartfull and whole, and the success of Noelani's trips were unknown until now. You're the King of Crystet! They might've tried taking you too soon."

"I don't understand."

"Your sister will."

Calix sighed.

"While there's no guarantee, the current moment feels safest for you to leave," Orso assured Calix.

"Will you leave now, too?"

Orso smirked and shook his head. "This trip has sparked a beautiful uprising. I want to see how it ends."

Calix nodded. "Thank you for helping me."

"Anything for my fellow rebels," he replied with a wink.

Calix meshed his mind into Noelani's.

Just in time—a wicked tremor gripped Noelani by the spine and yanked her out of Cerébrum.

Orso stared into the darkness, eyes gleaming.

As all the Namatéans dispersed to wait for Noelani's return, Exton hung near Orso.

"Who are you?" he asked the strange fire-burnt creature from an unknown land.

"I am a friend," Orso replied.

"Was he truly lost? Or were you keeping him lost?"

"Sometimes divine time requires divine intervention."

"You aren't divine."

Orso smirked. "Don't be mad. The boy is saved."

Exton grumbled, unable to argue this logic.

"I am a friend," Orso repeated, more sternly this time, before walking back into the darkness.

The three commondores and Calix let go of Noelani's mind as Kólasi tore toward her mindless body.

She was alone with the nefarious god once more, and though she was relieved to have saved four more minds, every moment spent with Kólasi terrified her. Would He sense her betrayal? Would He find a new torturous way to punish her? Or worse—would the repercussions of her actions further harm the captured minds or the survivors?

She held on tight, hoping for the best, as Kólasi entered her mindless body.

Kólasi was obsessed with the mortals of Namaté. Their defiance chipped away at His ethereal confidence; their refusal to surrender scrambled His divine plan.

They had seven days to surrender to Him, yet they continued to resist.

Did they not believe His warning? Did they not fear His wrath?

<<*Where are the other relics?*>> He asked Noelani as He twisted her body into aella form.

I'm still thinking. I was only in Cerébrum for a minute before you removed me again.

<<*You had a full day.*>>

I guess time passes quicker there.

<<*Perhaps I am utilizing the wrong mind,*>> He said, more so to himself.

No! Noelani objected. *I will recall the answers you seek. I promise.*

<<*If you do not reveal something of use before the end of our trip, I will find the information elsewhere.*>>

I understand.

While Kólasi tore around Namaté, hidden in aella form, Noelani frantically debated which small piece of information would be safe to share.

She had to pick something that would satisfy Kólasi without jeopardizing the lives of the survivors.

<<These mortals are insolent,>> Kólasi griped after a long tour of the planet. *<<With the muscas gone, they exist without fear.>>*

Will you bring the muscas back?

<<No. This will be over soon. Either they surrender, or I will send a bloodstorm to Namaté. They have six days left.>>

They still fear You, Noelani offered.

<<If they feared me, they would have surrendered already.>>

Did you learn anything helpful while spying on them? Noelani asked.

<<They spoke of nothing important. It's like they can sense they are being listened to.>>

Impossible.

<<I know. They will not thwart my destruction of this planet.>>

Why not send the storm now? Noelani asked.

<<You want them to fail?>>

No, I'm just curious what's stopping You.

<<For starters, I am a god of His word. I said seven days—it will be seven days.>> He paused. *<<Also, it takes time to brew a bloodstorm. My sons are currently collecting blood from Namatéans in the abyss. Another reason I can't send the filii back here.>>*

I see.

<<You're oddly curious today.>>

I've been thinking more, like You asked of me.

<<And?>>

I remembered something.

<<How convenient. Go on.>>

There are nine relics total.

<<I know of three, what are the other six?>>

I'll need to keep thinking, the memories are so distant, she blabbered. *I never dealt with relics while I was in my body.*

<<Useless,>> Kólasi barked.

Commondores can't shift into aella form, Noelani blurted out. *Only warriors can, and there are no other Gasione warriors in Cerébrum. I am the only mind in Cerébrum that can help you spy without being seen.*

Kólasi was amused. *<<You* have *been thinking. Keep it up. I need your memories.>>*

He left her body.

No one was around.

Wicker was vacant of life.

If He meant it when He said He'd be visiting daily, Noelani had many more opportunities to smuggle minds back.

Five days until the bloodstorm.

Noelani let five minds latch onto her. Their delivery to Namaté was successful, and the fact that she was the only Gasione He could spy through seemed to keep Kólasi placated.

Four days until the bloodstorm.

Noelani let six minds latch onto her.

Three days until the bloodstorm.

Noelani let seven minds latch onto her—Kólasi was so consumed by the forthcoming blood storm, He had made no indication that He sensed her travel companions.

Noelani hoped it wasn't wishful thinking, but decided it didn't matter either way—each successful transport meant more saved minds.

Two days until the bloodstorm.

Feeling ambitious, and running out of time, Noelani let ten minds latch onto her.

They made it all the way to Namaté, and the moment Noelani thought they were in the clear, but before she could instruct the minds to let go of her, Kólasi erupted in laughter.

<<This has been fun.>>

What has?

<<Did you think I wouldn't notice?>>

Notice what?

<<The refugees you've been smuggling home.>>

Detatch! Let go! She urged the minds inside of hers, but Kólasi tightened His grip, trapping them inside Noelani's mind.

Please, Noelani begged. *It's not their fault, it's mine.*

Kólasi laughed. *<<It will all be over soon.>>*

If you knew, why did you let me do it?

<<Because you have doomed every soul you brought back to a far worse fate than Cerébrum. Their minds, bodies, and souls will drown in the blood of their ancestors, with no opportunity for salvation. No nirvana, no rebirth. Only fatelessness.>>

Noelani sobbed.

<<Also, your perceived success strengthened your mind, and now, it is fully formed and ready to deliver what's mine.>>

Please, no!

Kólasi clawed through her mind, tearing her memories in half as He searched for the single piece of information He needed. He rummaged violently, unconcerned by the massive damage He was causing.

Noelani's consciousness flickered in and out as her mind faltered.

Kólasi dug until He found it—a vision of Noelani and another Gasione perched atop a tree on a perfectly sunny day talking casually about the lost relics.

He listened until He heard what He was looking for.

Dagmar's clay lungs.

He released a manic laugh before rocketing Noelani's body, with her mind plus the ten others inside, across the sky. He soared through the clouds, turning them black while churning a violent storm.

Thunder rumbled.

Kólasi's voice echoed into the mind of every mortal below.

<<Noelani, along with the ten minds she harbors, have dishonored the gods. For this, they will leave the comfort of their oasis within my abyss and be cursed with fatelessness. A fate you too shall know if you do not accept my generous offer.>>

His split exited Noelani's body.

She plummeted through the sky, desperately stretching her dormant wings.

A crack of lightning illuminated the night and seared Noelani's wings off her body.

"No!"

Her scream rang louder than Kólasi's next burst of thunder. It carried across all of Namaté, amplified by the ten mortal minds who screamed along with her.

Before hitting the ocean, Kólasi stopped her freefall and lifted her burning body back into the sky.

Kólasi's storm winds toured her blazing carcass over each land of Namaté, ensuring that every surviving mortal witnessed His wrath. She burned alive for hours, her scream never ending.

There was nothing they could do to help.

They could only watch her suffering with horrified empathy.

Noelani's body rained ash over those she had hoped to save.

When she was burnt to bone, Kólasi finally let her perish. The screaming stopped as her bones fell into the sea.

<<*You have one day left.*>> Kólasi warned.

Chapter 32

Crystet

Flaming cinders from Noelani's demise still fluttered from the sky and scattered across the castle's rooftop.

Though Gwynessa had never been close to Noelani, her fate was cruel and undeserved. Her plight for redemption had been cut short by Kólasi's vicious games.

Gwynessa's heart ached.

If Calix hadn't returned yet, he never would.

She felt hopeless, but needed to know her brother's fate. They had already searched for his mindless body in Crystet, but he wasn't there.

"Form a small search team for Calix," she ordered Tyrus. "With the muscas gone, it's safe to travel by sea again."

Tyrus bowed his head in understanding.

Gwynessa continued, "Regardless of Calix's mental state, bring him home. I want his body kept safe within Crystet."

Tyrus gathered a small group of Glaziene survivors and left Crystet.

::We are running out of time,:: Elior warned Gwynessa.

Gwynessa held his hand and led him to the royal grounds. She needed open space to work.

Ruts and ripped terrain from the aftermath of her previous elemental whirlwind still scarred the glassy lawn. She had spent the last few days attempting to reach the drakkina again, to no avail. Fire and ice weren't enough.

She found a patch of untouched ground, and while holding Elior's hand, Gwynessa created another elemental whirlwind. This time, she included extremes from all four elements—ice from the moon, fire from the sun, wind from Neptune, and soil from Earth.

Earth, she had heard of prior to this quest, but Neptune was new. Glimpses of each place came to her as she used the rib cage relic to channel their extremities and siphon their precious resources into her whirlwind.

Orange and yellow flares of flaming hydrogen from a sun named Sol. Pale blue streams of methane wind from Neptune. Dark, fertile soil from beneath the verdant flora of Earth. Daggers of crystallized ice from the dark side of a moon referred to as Luna.

All four elements came from the same solar system, which led Gwynessa to assume that this system was one of Gaia's earlier, more potent models.

Her elemental whirlwind raged across the lawn.

Gwynessa focused, trying to hear the drakkina like she had in the past, but all she heard was the ferocious roar of her tornado.

::We need to be inside,:: Elior suggested.

Gwynessa had no other ideas, so she took his proposal and redirected the violent twister to where they stood, hand in hand, at the top of a small hill. As it tore toward them, a small doorway opened at the base. It crossed over them, and they were swallowed by the whirring of wind, fire, ice, and soil. The door closed, leaving them fully immersed within Gaia's elements.

The voices of the drakkina came through. Elior heard them, too.

::Come to us.::

::How?:: Gwynessa asked.

::Desire it, and it will be.::

Both Gwynessa and Elior focused their desire on reaching the drakkina.

Within moments, the elemental whirlwind morphed into a vacuum portal that sucked them out of Namaté and spat them into Cruxeus.

They had a soft landing in the pink fleshy chamber of Gaia's heart. The seven drakkina lounged around the room in half form—they were gorgeous human females with a mixture of horns, fangs, claws, and scales.

::Welcome,:: Amari greeted them.

::How did I do that?:: Gwynessa asked.

::With Elior's help.::

::But I thought only Gaia could come and go from Cruxeus.::

::A quadra and a dimi working together can summon much greater power.::

Gwynessa shook her head. *::When? When did I become a quadradivinus?::*

::The Woodlins touched you long ago, but it wasn't until you returned your heart to your chest for the last time that Gaia blessed the touch.::

::So it's new.::

::Very new, but you've been chosen by Gaia for a long time. She had hoped you'd be ready when you took the throne, when the Woodlins shared their divine touch, but you needed more time. So she waited to see if you'd live up to the role. Originally, she planned to make you a dimi, but ultimately decided on quadra.::

::She didn't trust me.:: Gwynessa's posture slouched.

Amari shook her head. *::I fear not.::*

::What's the difference between a quadra and a dimi?:: Gwynessa asked.

::Quadras have multiple fatal flaws, but are still more durable than regular mortals. They also possess smaller gifts, like talking to animals, manipulating nature's elements, and communicating with the gods. Dimis are near-immortal with less fatal flaws, sometimes only one, and they possess all the smaller gifts plus some godly powers at reduced strength. Not all dimis are created equally though, nor are they blessed with access to the same godly powers. It's unique case by case. For example, the Woodlins cannot come and go, but they were given access to see all within Namaté. Similarly, totumdivinus non-god progenies, like us, have limitations. We are on Gaia's tight leash, which is why we cannot leave Cruxeus to assist you.::

::And what are Elior's limitations?::

::The correct question is: what is his potential?::

::I don't understand.::

::He has been touched by two gods.::

Elior's eyes widened.

::Which ones?:: he asked.

::Gaia and Kólasi,:: Amari answered.

::Kólasi? When?::

::Inadvertantly by Rúnar,:: she explained. *::During Rúnar's long stay in primordial purgatory, while his heart was removed from his body, he rescinded Gaia's favor and aligned with Kólasi instead. He could've stayed bonded to Gaia, or chose any other primordial god, but he chose the devil. Kólasi didn't make Rúnar divine, but He gave him a totumdivinus touch that only transferred to those Rúnar killed.::*

::So he did *kill me then.::*

::Briefly. You died and were revived. Kólasi's touch stayed with you, and when I further healed you, you gained a second divine touch from us. Both divine touches were sealed by Gaia's blessing.::

::Despite your surplus of blessings,:: Deidra added, stepping into the conversation. *::We still somehow managed to almost lose you.::*

::How?:: Gwynessa asked.

::He and I share the same fatal flaw—internal moisture,:: Amari explained.

::That's why it took him so long to heal after Elixyvette left him to drown in that bassinet,:: Deidra clarified.

Gwynessa looked down at Elior, whose bright azure eyes brimmed with tears.

She thought of her own mother, and though the circumstances weren't the same, she knew too well the everlasting pain caused by a mother's betrayal.

::I'm so sorry,:: she said to the young boy.

He nodded.

::Was it you that I heard?:: Elior asked Deidra.

She nodded, her emerald eyes glimmering with kindness. *::I was there with you, guiding your breaths and helping you float near the top of the bassinet.::*

::How, though, if you were here?:: Gwynessa asked, eager to understand.

::I am the bringer of life—my gift is rebirth. I am highly connected and sensitive to mortal realms. Though I can only do so much from this prison, I am able to gently sway and influence fate from afar.:: Deidra smiled. *::I helped you many times as a child also.::*

::You did?::

::Not through words, but energy. Did you never question the origin of your love for animals? Despite great efforts from your family to choose cruelty, you always chose kindness.::

::Those choices weren't my own?::

::Of course, they were, I was merely a guide. I let you feel the beauty and magic of nature, and you chose to hold on to that instead of succumbing to societal pressure.::

After a brief coughing fit, Rozene added, *::Gaia had us observing you from the start. As always, her choice in mortal was divine.::*

::Your will is stronger than most others,:: Novalee agreed from the corner of the room she hid within. Somehow, despite the lack of sky, she still glowed with silver moonlight.

::She didn't choose me,:: Elior said, feeling glum. *::Technically, neither god chose me.::*

::No,:: Amari answered, her citrine eyes sparking with bolts of electricity. *::The universe chose you.::*

::The universe?::

:: Sometimes, serendipitous events and timing prevail over orchestrated fates.:: Amari smiled. *::In your case, the universe aligned so that you could save the mortals of Namaté.::*

::How do I save them?:: Elior asked.

::You are dual divine,:: Amari said.

::Half strength, but doubly charged,:: Lysandra explained.

::And we intend to help you reach full strength,:: Deidra promised.

::Only Kólasi, Kólasi's progenies, and totumdivinus touched by Him can interfere on His prison planets,:: Rosalee noted.

Gwynessa gasped. *::He can save the mindless?::*

::Yes, but only if we help him reach his full potential in time—his transformation into totumdivinus comes from Gaia's blessing, but he'll forever retain Kólasi's touch.::

Rozalee warned, *::But if Kólasi's edifice falls before He frees their minds from Cerébrum, their mortal bodies will die and their minds won't have a body to return home to.::*

::We only have one day left before the bloodstorm. Can he go to Cerébrum now?:: Gwynessa asked.

::No, he needs training,:: Deidra answered.

::But first,:: Amari said, stepping closer to Elior and cupping his throat in her hand, *::You need this back.::*

She closed her eyes and shared her electricity with him. Buzzing currents tickled his veins as they rocketed through his body. When she let go of his neck, his glow returned. Bright blue and magnificent. Elior was whole again.

His breaths were heavy as he experienced full health for the first time since his birth.

::I'm alive,:: he reveled.

::You need to be whole for what comes next,:: Amari advised. *::Training won't be easy. You need to ascend in a short amount of time.::*

::I am ready.::

::Is there anything I can do to help?:: Gwynessa asked.

::You've done wonderfully by bringing him here,:: Amari said. *::Now, you must go home.::*

::Don't let the others destroy the edifice until Elior frees the minds from Cerébrum,:: Deidra reminded her.

::I will do my best.::

The drakkina could not bring visitors to Cruxeus, but they could send them away. With a unified roar, the seven drakkina sisters collapsed the soft ground where Gwynessa stood, and she was sucked into an exit portal.

Ejected back into Namaté exactly where she had left—the royal grounds of Crystet—except her elemental whirlwind was gone and only its devastation remained.

"Where did you go?" Ario shouted as he ran out of the castle doors to her.

"Home," she answered, more so to herself. Then she recalled the final task she needed to complete. "I need to retrieve the last relic."

"Wait."

"I can't. I'm running out of time."

"We found Calix," Ario revealed with a smile. "He's back, mind intact."

"He's home?" Gwynessa asked, eyes bright with happy tears.

Ario nodded. "In mind and body. He is going to be okay."

"Thank you."

"It was all you," Ario reminded her.

"I didn't find him."

"The stranger that found Calix in Cerébrum said that he was tasked with Calix's safe delivery home. Heartfull and whole. He said you'd understand."

"My prayer," Gwynessa realized. "To the Vorso. That's how I phrased it."

"They heard you," Ario replied in awe.

"They *answered* me."

Gwynessa shook her head, not quite ready to reverse her long-held disbelief.

"I need to see him."

Ario shook his head. "Calix will be okay. The rest of Namaté needs you more."

"You're right." Gwynessa hastily unfastened the rib cage relic from where it hung off her belt. "Take this."

"Don't you need it?"

She shook her head. "I'll have another soon."

She leaned in, gave Ario a kiss, then turned to leave.

Ario caught her hand. "Where are you going?"

"Jökull beach. I need to speak to the narwhals."

"What for?"

"They're going to help me retrieve Rúnar's heart."

Chapter 33

Soylé

Rhoco docked his stone boat in the shoreline muck of Soylé.

He had made the journey alone, despite Stennis and Feodras offering to join. He left Bozrah's skull in Radix de Orewall with his friends and took Amezite's brain for this mission. With the relic securely latched via netting to his waistband, Rhoco jumped over the side of the boat and landed in the thigh-deep mud.

He grumbled as he used his brute strength to push through toward the shore. He had no idea where he'd find Dagmar's lungs, but it was agreed that Soylé was a good place to start the search.

As he reached the shore, the sludge turned to dusty dirt, and his trek became less of a struggle. Covered in mud, he wiped and shook off as many clumps as possible, but there was no salvaging his trousers. They'd be caked in slop until he got home to change. He carried on with the weight of his mud-slicked pants digging into his hips.

Still netted and attached to his belt, he lifted the brain and focused his energy on his desire: finding Dagmar's clay lungs.

Nothing happened.

He had no other leads, so he tried again, unsure if it would work, but determined to try.

This time, the amethyst brain illuminated with faint light. A light tug in the air pulled him to the east, so he followed the feeling. As he obeyed the direction of the wind, the brain glowed brighter.

Was it working?

It led him through a field of tall boulders and dead trees. The sludge grew deeper with every step he took, and he found himself in shin-deep mud again.

He had never seen more than Soylé's shore, and was now wishing he didn't have to go any farther. But the winds pushed him onward.

The mud depth hit his knees and his pace slowed.

In the distance, a tiny figure skated atop the mud. Their movements and pace appeared to be fueled by fury.

As they got closer, he recognized the Mudling.

"Princess Valterra," he mumbled.

She recognized him, too.

Her feral energy filled the space between them as she skated at full speed.

"Stop!" he shouted at her, but she did not slow down.

He aimed Amezite's stone brain at her and trapped her in a prison of light.

"Argh!" she screamed.

"You'll thank me for sparing your body once your mind returns."

"You stone-brained brute! My mind *is* back. Let me out of here!"

"Oh."

Rhoco fumbled with the brain as he tried to figure out how to undo the prison.

"I came back with Noelani before she got incinerated," Valterra explained. "Why are you here?"

"I'm looking for Dagmar's clay lungs."

"They belong to the Mudlings."

"Do you know where they are?"

"No, but I am looking for them, too, and they are mine."

Rhoco stopped fumbling with undoing her cage.

"You know what, you can stay in there."

"No! Come back, you stupid rock!" she hollered at him angrily as he trekked through the muck to search for the lungs without competition.

He focused his desire to find the relic, and the brain resumed its previous job. It led him deeper into the boulder field until he reached what appeared to be a throne room. Except there was no castle, or walls—just a stone dais with five boulders carved into ornate chairs on top. The chair at the center was the largest and had two smaller chairs positioned slightly behind it on both sides. Enormous spiles made of slate encircled the row of thrones.

Amezite's brain beamed with light.

Rhoco circled the area and discovered that it glowed brightest near the center throne.

He carefully placed the relic onto the neighboring chair, then searched all around the center throne.

No lungs in sight.

The thrones were carved from the same stone as the dais—they were attached. But if the relic indicated that it was here, surely it was.

Using all of his strength, Rhoco kicked and punched the solid base of the throne, slowly demolishing it. With his fist, he hammered at the center of the base until he reached a vacant cavity filled with mud.

He moved the relic brain to the floor, and then reached his arm through and felt around. The hollow space was enormous, but his arm was long enough to touch the circular stone walls on all sides.

The issue was he couldn't feel; he had no sense of touch. He was searching for something he'd never be able to detect.

He touched Amezite's stone brain with his free hand.

Let me feel, he thought, hoping the brain might help, and at his command, he felt every stick and stone swirling through his fingers. Now, he was searching for something larger.

It wasn't at the surface or in the middle of this secret mud pit, he had to reach deeper. He leaned in, mud now covering his shoulder and touching his neck, until he reached the base of this mud-filled cavity.

He scraped his fingers along the stone, feeling for anything larger than pebbles, and finally hit an object worth retrieving.

He lifted it out of the mud.

It was the clay lungs.

He found them.

Delighted with himself, Rhoco tossed the dripping wet lungs and stone brain into his netted waist pouch.

As he followed the trail he had made back to the beach, the the thick mud began to soften and rise.

Slick and consuming, every step suctioned his legs, making it increasingly hard to move.

"What's this?" he grumbled, fighting the swell of mud.

It took forever, but when he finally reached the spot where he had left Valterra, she was crouched and seething within her prison of light. Her fingertips twirled in the mud and her dark eyes were bright with fury.

"What have you done?" she barked.

"I'm not doing this, you are!"

"No, I'm not. I'm trying to stop it," she explained, fingers digging deeper.

Rhoco scanned the area. "If it's not you, then who?"

"Did you take the relic?"

"Yes."

"You must've set off a trap when you removed it."

"Oh no," Rhoco griped. "This happened in the mines also."

"Give the relic to me," she demanded.

Rhoco took a step back. "I can't."

The mud deepened, rising to waist-level.

Valterra clenched the soil with all her might, but wasn't strong enough to reverse this disaster on her own.

"Why can't you stop this?" he asked.

"I don't know." The always-present line between her brows softened as she gave up. "I don't think this is ancient Mudling magic."

"Then what is it?"

Dark clouds swirled overhead, followed by a blast of celestial lightning. The thunder that followed was immediate and carried the low rumbling of divine laughter.

"Kólasi," Rhoco said in a horrified whisper.

"Let me out of this cage," Valterra begged.

"Promise you wont fight me for the relic."

"I won't. I just don't want to go back to Cerébrum!"

Rhoco nodded, then reached his hand into the mud, located his waist pouch, and used the brain relic to free Valterra.

The prison of light dismantled.

"How do we survive this?" Rhoco asked.

Valterra tilted her head, her face scrunched with amused pity.

"I think you mean, how do *you* survive this. I can swim in mud. I *am* mud."

"You have to help me. Kólasi can't get the relics."

"You could give the lungs to me."

Valterra lunged at him, but he quickly disconnected his waist pouch and raised it above his head where Valterra could not reach.

She growled as she swam in predatory circles around him. "I can be patient," she said, calming her anger. "The mud will rise, and I will take what's mine."

Rhoco spat. "I should've left you in that cage."

As he fussed to retrieve either of the relics to cage her again, Valterra's temporary calm vanished, and she began clawing her way up his body. Fighting her off made it difficult to get what he needed out of the bag.

He elbowed her and jerked his own body violently, trying to knock her off, but she was feisty, and her climb was successful. Before he could lock his fingers around either relic, she was up his arm and had snatched the lungs.

Valterra screeched with delight before diving off Rhoco's shoulder and disappearing into the rising mud. It was up to Rhoco's lower ribs now. He reached into the mud and searched frantically, trying to locate and seize Valterra, but she was gone.

Rhoco unleashed a furious growl that rang across the sky.

This failure hung heavy on his heart.

He retrieved the brain from the pouch, prepared to try one last trick to summon the lungs back to him, but before he could channel his desire, the mud began to flow.

It started slow, then turned furious, rushing past him like a raging river. He stood unmoving as the mud gushed around his boulder form.

In the distance he heard a gasping squeak.

About a mile down in the flash flood he saw Valterra's bobbing head.

Another mile down, the tree line ended, and the muddy river flowed violently down the swampy beach and into the sea.

"Use the relic!" Rhoco urged Valterra, but she couldn't hear him over the rushing stream.

He trudged his body forward, letting the current push him into a light jog. He was closer to Valterra now, but not yet in reach.

"You're heading toward the ocean," he shouted.

This time, she heard him.

Her light panic amplified as she flailed against the forceful mud unsuccessfully.

"Use the relic!" he repeated.

She fumbled the lungs in her hands while the mud lashed her face and sporadically submerged her in its harsh tide. Up and down, her body thrashed around like a rag doll, and she was unable to get a moment's rest to figure out how to use the lungs.

"Stop fighting the flow and relax. Let the current take you, and use that moment to channel the magic."

She refused to take his advice.

She tried to mesh with the mud, tried to become one with it, but something else flowed within the soil that prevented her from controlling it.

"This isn't natural mud!" she shouted.

"Ditch the relic," Rhoco said, still marching with the flow toward her. "If it's causing this, maybe it'll stop if we surrender it."

Valterra seethed. "Stop trying to trick me!"

"I'm not trying to trick you, I'm trying to save you."

The stubborn Mudling did not trust him, could not trust him, and she fought the unnatural mud futilely all the way to the ocean.

Rhoco raced to catch up with her, but it was impossible. The mud flowed too fast.

He watched helplessly as the raging mud spat Valterra into the sea, where the salt water dissolved her muddy body immediately upon contact.

It happened so fast, she disappeared without making a sound.

The moment she was gone, the current stopped and the mud levels dropped.

The sky crackled with sparks of gold lightning and a thunderous laugh followed.

Furious, Rhoco raced into the sea to get the lungs. He wasn't sure if they had dissolved too, but he had to try to find them.

Five steps in, he submerged and opened his eyes.

The dark water had terrible visibility as it was, and all the mud made it worse.

He retrieved the brain relic and summoned the lungs to him. To his great relief, the relic darted through the water, only stopping upon collison with his chest. They were a little beat up, but seemingly immune to the effects of water.

With both relics in his possession again, Rhoco marched out of the water.

"Thought we'd lose the relic at sea, huh?" He shouted at the sky. "Not today, buddy."

As the storm overhead churned viciously, Rhoco climbed the ladder rungs carved into the side of his boat.

"Funny how the mud only began to flow after the little Mudling possessed the relic," Rhoco added as the wind whipped his face. "Will Gaia see Valterra's death as a direct or indirect interference?" Rhoco shrugged. "I'm not a god, I wouldn't know."

A blast of wind lashed Rhoco so hard, he felt the sting. Then the storm stopped.

Rhoco used a long stone pole to dislodge his boat from where it anchored itself into the mud. Once safely out to sea, Rhoco lowered his hand to touch the relics hanging from his waistband, then directed his energy toward Soylé.

As far as he knew, Valterra had been the only returned Mudling. If so, the Mudling race would end with Valterra.

Rhoco held very little endearment toward the Mudlings, but never wished them true harm. This was a great loss for Namaté, assuming Namaté survived the forthcoming days.

The swamp-ridden isthmus of Soylé vanished beyond the horizon, leaving Rhoco with views of the black ocean on all sides.

He retrieved the lungs from his netted pouch and channeled a deep, magic-enhanced breath. After choosing his words carefully, he made an announcement in a volume that all of Namaté could hear.

"Mission complete."

Chapter 34

"It's time to unite! Meet in Amesyte Valley, Orewall," Ciela and her warriors announced as they flew over all the lands of Namaté. Though their message was cryptic, everyone knew what it meant—all the relics had been found, and it was time to unite them and use them against Kólasi.

Everyone obeyed, including Elixyvette. Though her army was small, she had enough Voltains to man her giant electric tanker. She brought every surviving Voltain with her. In her worsening mania, each electrified life had become a prized possession to her, and she would not let any of them out of her reach. They were too precious, too important. The endurance of their race hinged on their survival.

They sailed southwest across the vast ocean, water bubbling where it touched the buzzing tanker.

When they arrived, only Feodras stood at the shore to greet them.

"Where is everyone else?" Elixyvette shouted from the tall tanker.

"Elsewhere," Feodras replied, his tone cold. "Where are the eyes?"

"I have them."

Feodras extended his hand.

Elixyvette sent a blast of electricity into the sky and lassoed the lightning bolts of her storm, riding them to where Feodras waited. She landed gracefully in front of him, but did not yet fulfill his request.

"I want to be part of this."

"You cannot go where I am going."

"Why not?"

"You are not welcome."

"Then I will not give you the eyes."

"You must."

Elixyvette smirked. "Silly of you to think that I operate at your command."

"If you do not cooperate, we all will die."

"So be it." Her gaze turned vacant. "I'm dead anyway."

"And your people?"

She shrugged. "There's no world to rule if the rest of you are dead, too."

Feodras grumbled as he squeezed the Occavas stone in his grip. By his will, shadow ribbons wrapped around Elixyvette's head, covering her eyes and rendering her blind.

"What magic is this?" she asked, panicked.

"Follow my voice," Feodras said as he walked away.

"I can't leave my people!"

She tried to illuminate the darkness with her electricity, but the shadows were impenetrable.

"You either follow me and partake as a willing volunteer, or I will paralyze you and search for the eyes myself."

Elixyvette hesitated.

Feodras added, "This choice is a kindness that the others would not have offered. I suggest you take it."

His voice grew softer as he walked farther away.

Elixyvette reached her arms out in front of her and stumbled blindly toward Feodras's voice.

He had no desire to talk to her, so he whistled an old mining tune instead. The haunting melody served as an auditory guide as he led her toward the portal in the wildflower field within Amesyte Valley.

The walk was long and they didn't have time to waste, so Feodras used the stone to subtly hurry their pace. The adjustment was undetectable to Elixyvette, as the ground beneath their feet moved with them, carrying them faster toward their destination.

Amesyte Valley was still destroyed from recent battles. Large chunks of the surrounding mountains were blown off and the once beautiful amethyst castle lay in shimmering ruins.

The wildflower field had since regrown and, due to a lack of maintenance, taken over much of the valley. Vibrant blossoms bloomed and vined wherever there was soil to take or structures to climb. An overgrown jungle of color with many of the flowers growing taller than Feodras. The flora was a mix of natural and Boulde-made—the destructive blossoms created by the botanists had survived and mixed with the naturally growing flowers, creating a dangerous minefield.

"Give me your hand," he requested of Elixyvette. "And keep the other by your side."

She gave him her hand. "Why?"

"We are surrounded by bombs."

She gripped his hand tighter, but said no more.

He followed the well-worn path made by the survivors that led straight to the portal. It was the safest route, as they hadn't had time to differentiate the dangerous flowers from the benign.

The small patch of soil atop the portal was covered in tiny purple and yellow flowers.

"Brace yourself," Feodras warned before stepping into Occavas.

Elixyvette followed, and as the lurching sensation of the portal turned her stomach, she released a terrified scream.

They landed in Radix de Orewall a few moments later—Feodras on his feet and Elixyvette in a shaking heap on her knees.

"Why is she here?" Cybelle barked.

"You were supposed to get the eyes and leave her behind," Ciela said. She and her warriors were back with unexpected stragglers also—Calix and Ario stood beside Adaliah and Lovise.

"Why are *they* here?" Feodras countered.

"They are here on behalf of Gwynessa. They have the lost relic of Gaia and Brixton's rib cage."

"Where is she?"

"She is still waiting on delivery of Rúnar's heart."

"Delivery?"

"A narwhal is retrieving it for her from Seakkan's depths."

Feodras unraveled the shadows wrapped around Elixyvette's eyes.

"You could've left the blindfold on at least," Cybelle quipped.

"Where am I?" Elixyvette asked in awe of the dark yet shimmering world around her.

"Just be grateful that you're here," Feodras replied. "Where are the eyes?"

Elixyvette reached into the mess of coiled curls atop her head and retrieved the glowing eyes of Jasvinder. She dropped them into Feodras's open palm.

"We're just waiting on the heart?" Feodras asked.

Ciela nodded. "And for the Bonz and Woodlins to join."

As the words left her mouth, the ground shook. Everyone looked to the west to see Beaumont crossing the ocean. His giant roots propelled beneath the sea and carried him forward. The

Woodlins had caused enough damage to the edifice's base that it was safe to travel again by sea.

"A ceremonious unification of lands!" he declared upon arrival, his roots digging into Radix de Orewall soil to reestablish him there. "A glimpse at what it's like to be friends!"

Moments later, Chesulloth and Azmon joined from the south. Their massive skeletal forms moved so fast, they skittered atop the water. Upon reaching Radix de Orewall, they removed their drakkina skull helmets. Chesulloth scanned those in attendance with her six pretty eyes, while Azmon visually searched for their relic.

A Marble-Obsidian Fused Boulde held it in his hands.

"Where did you find it?" Azmon asked.

Stennis looked down at the relic he held, then back up at Azmon.

"I didn't find it. She did." He pointed to Adaliah.

Azmon turned his attention to Adaliah.

"It was hidden in a Woodlin trunk," she answered. "I don't know whose."

Azmon shifted his attention to Beaumont now. "Why?"

"A hunch, a guess, a suspicion," Beaumont explained. "The clues we saw suggested danger, and we trusted our intuition."

Azmon crossed his bony arms over his bony chest. "Yes, I guess the relic would have been lost forever if it had remained in Radix de Fibril."

"Unretrievable beneath the edifice," Chesulloth agreed.

"When did you remove the skull from our resource chamber?"

"When the drakkina battled Rúnar," Beaumont answered. "We sensed the darkness growing from afar."

"I suppose we ought to thank you," Azmon offered, his internal battle between pride and humility apparent. "But if we survive this, the skull returns with us."

"Of course."

Everyone stirred anxiously, waiting for the last piece to arrive.

"I think we should assemble what we have," Ciela suggested.

"Good idea," Rhoco agreed. He walked forward and placed Amezite's stone brain on the ground. Cybelle retrieved Barzalai's finger coils from her pocket and placed them beside the brain.

Stennis placed Bozrah's skull over top of the brain.

Feodras stepped forward and inserted Jasvinder's fuchsia eyes into two of the skull's eye sockets.

Ario, who cradled Brixton's wooden rib cage, latched the top of the spine to the base of the skull.

Ciela fastened Elzaphan's glorious black feathered wings to the back of the rib cage.

Rhoco nuzzled Dagmar's clay lung up inside of the rib cage.

Calix still held the lost relic of Gaia.

"We will place it once Gwyn is back with Rúnar's heart," he announced.

No one challenged him.

Nothing would happen until Gwynessa arrived with the final piece to this puzzle.

Chapter 35

Crystet

Gwynessa walked into the lapping waves until the icy sea water touched her knees.

::Come to me,:: she beckoned the narwhals. *::I need your help::*

She waited.

No reply.

She lowered her hands, letting her fingertips touch the surface of the black ocean.

::My loves, please come with Rúnar's heart. It is urgent.::

Her worry heightened the longer she was kept waiting.

::The fate of this planet depends on my retrieval of Rúnar's heart.::

The lightly lapping waves rose with intensity, crashing harder now.

Gwynessa took a few steps back.

The narwhals never arrived with such force.

"Show yourself!" Gwynessa shouted, aware that something else, something nefarious, had come to greet her.

Five waves from the shore rose a jagged diamond crown adorned with rubies. A moment later, Rúnar's foggy red glare crested the water's surface.

Gwynessa gasped and backstepped out of the water and onto the beach. She was unarmed with no access to magic—all the relics were in Occavas.

Rúnar trudged through the water toward her, expression vacant as his menacing form approached. He lifted his arms, palms cupped and holding his charcoal heart. Though Rúnar was mindless and seemingly hollow, the cracks in his heart pulsated with a vibrant glow. It was very much alive, even if he wasn't, and it appeared to be the source of his current motivation.

If she could knock the heart out of his hands, she might stand a chance, but after a quick scan of the beach, there was nothing long enough to assist.

Rúnar was only a few paces away.

She was at his mercy.

Gwynessa closed her eyes and raised her arms to cover her face. She did not want to see the end when it arrived.

Nothing happened.

Rúnar grunted impatiently.

Gywnessa opened her eyes and found Rúnar within arm's reach, shoving his heart at her.

"You're giving it to me?" she asked, amazed but doubtful.

He nodded.

"Why?"

He could not answer verbally, but a single sea salt tear streaking down his cheek and leaving a raw rut in his glass flesh answered her question.

Remorse.

"Your fate is sealed," Gwynessa reminded him.

He nodded and took a step closer, urging Gwynessa to take the heart from him.

She opened her waistpouch, allowing Rúnar to drop the heart inside.

"Thank you," she offered cautiously.

Rúnar turned without acknowledging her gratitude. He walked back into the sea, shoulders slouched under the weight of his eternal damnation. He'd surely endure Kólasi's everlasting wrath for this betrayal.

Gwynessa felt a ping of sympathy for him—their mortal journeys had many parallels. Though she chose Gaia's light now, and forever more, and hoped that would be enough to salvage her fate.

Rúnar disappeared beneath the sea.

Gwynessa used his heart to fly to Wicker, then launched herself through the looking glass portal.

A whistling wind carrying snowflakes swept across the land.

"Wait!" Gwynessa shouted as she landed harshly and stumbled. "Wait," she repeated.

"We *have* been waiting. For *you*," Ciela quipped. "Do you have Rúnar's heart?"

"I do, but we can't combine all the relics yet. We need more time."

"More time for what?" Ciela asked. "In a few hours, the red moon will rise and we will drown in the blood of our ancestors."

"Elior is going to free the minds from Cerébrum."

"Excuse me?" Elixyvette cut in, her face paled. "Who?"

"Your son," Gwynessa spat. "He isn't dead."

"Yes, he is! I buried him myself."

"Do you mean you *killed* him yourself?" Gwynessa seethed. "You shouldn't even be here with us. You aren't worthy. You will rot in Kólasi's abyss for what you have done."

"He is dead," she repeated, though her conviction had softened. Her fear and confusion read plainly across her face.

"Explain," Ciela demanded.

"Only Kólasi, His progenies, and His totumdivinus can free those trapped on His prison planets."

"I don't understand how that allows him access to the lost minds."

"Elior is dualisdivinus—he is touched by two gods; Gaia and Kólasi. Kólasi's touch came when Rúnar briefly killed him as an infant, and Gaia's touch came when the drakkina healed his voice. Gaia blessed the drakkina's touch, and granted Elior the potential to become a totumdivinus. He is with the drakkina now receiving expedited training to become fully divine."

"How long will the training take?"

"I'm not sure."

"We can only wait so long," Ciela urged. "While I want to see the mindless restored, we cannot sacrifice our lives for theirs."

"Understood, but let's wait and see. We haven't run out of time yet."

"Fine."

"Thank you. I'll go above to observe the mindless. As soon as their minds are back, I will return with Rúnar's heart."

"No," Ciela corrected her. "At the first sign of blood rain, you will return with the heart. Dasan and Lovise will go with you."

"Ario and Calix also," Gwynessa replied.

"Leave the lost relic of Gaia here," Ciela requested.

"No," Gwynessa countered. "We may need it. We will return with both relics."

"We'd like to help also," Rhoco said, pointing to himself and Stennis.

"Yes, you can come also," Gwynessa agreed.

The Bouldes led the small group to the portal in Radix de Orewall. They crossed through into the overgrown wildflower field and carefully traversed the well-worn path over the crumbled tunnel and into the desert.

"How will we observe the mindless?" Dasan asked. "They're scattered all over."

"Aerial reconnaissance," she said pointing to Dasan and Lovise, then motioned to herself, Ario, Calix, and the Bouldes. "Relic reconnaissance."

"We shouldn't split up," Dasan said.

"How else are we supposed to see everywhere at once?"

Dasan grumbled. "Fine, where will you be if we need to find you?"

"Crystet, Vapore, Fibril, Soylé—where most of the mindless are gathered."

Dasan nodded, then reiterated Ciela's order. "At the first sign of blood, we return to Occavas."

"Yes."

Dasan and Lovise lifted into the sky and flew in opposite directions.

"Where are we actually going?" Ario asked.

"Wicker," she replied. "There's a looking glass portal there. I'll be able to watch all the mindless at once."

Using both relics, the Glaziene and Bouldes swiftly transported themselves across the ocean to Wicker.

While Gwynessa had her head buried in the looking glass portal, the others stood guard.

After the first hour passed, Rhoco started a nervous game of stick piling with Stennis.

"Anything?" Ario asked after another hour of tense silence.

"Nothing yet."

Ario and Calix joined the Bouldes' game to redirect their anxiety.

The day passed with no positive news.

The sun set and night had arrived.

"We've run out of time," Stennis said as they waited for the first moon to rise.

It never arrived.

In its place rose a ferocious red moon.

Bright and fearsome, its light beamed through the storm clouds and bathed the lands in a crimson haze. The air swelled with moisture. Teardrops turned into deathly raindrops as the blood of their ancestors prepared to deliver their fate.

The crimson clouds shuddered, and a drop landed on Gwynessa's cheek. Upon wiping it off, she smeared blood all over her face and hand.

"It's begun," Calix said in a low voice.

"We can't tell them yet," she urged. "It will take a while for the blood rain to seep into Occavas. Let's give Elior a little more time."

"I don't want to die either, though," Stennis countered.

"You won't. None of us will. We won't wait too long."

The blood rained down harder.

Stennis gave Rhoco a worried look.

"I trust her," Rhoco offered. "Do you trust me?"

Stennis grunted. "Okay, fine."

The small group waited in the pouring blood, praying for a miracle.

Chapter 36

Cerébrum

Elior arrived in Cerébrum, healed and holding the wisdom of a thousand lifetimes. His bright azure glow illuminated all of Cerébrum, revealing multitudes of minds trapped on this prison planet.

Drawn to the flame, the figment minds flocked to him.

He floated above them, scanning their desperate faces. Noelani hadn't come back in days and their fear filled the massive space.

Though young in appearance and age, Elior radiated divine confidence.

"Creatures of Namaté, I have come to avenge you." His azure eyes carried a hint of citrine—fire blazing atop a crystal sea.

"And what of everyone else?" Orso called from the crowd, shadow smoke billowing from his figure.

"Renegade," Elior said, tilting his head in consideration. "What are *you* doing here?"

"I am an advocate for these mortal minds."

"You are a menace. What trouble have you caused here?"

"Just a little bit of anarchy, delivered in the form of guidance. I came here to help."

"You were only tasked to help *one* of them."

"I've grown fond of the others."

"You can go home now."

"Who will you leave trapped in this prison? Who will you set free?" Orso challenged.

Thousands of minds from planets beyond Namaté were mixed into the crowd. They murmured among themselves frantically.

Elior addressed the minds. "I will set you all free. Where you go after is out of my control."

Murmurs of excitement traveled among them.

"But first," Elior declared. "Namatéans, gather beneath me."

The Namatéans in the crowd assembled directly under Elior. His blue glow blanketed them.

"Those of you who were living when your mind was stolen will return to your bodies," he informed them. "If your mindless body perished after you arrived here, you will be sent to either Gaia's nirvana, Kólasi's abyss, or Incarna's holding room—the life you led while living will determine your fate."

Elior extended his arms and, using his newly learned divine magic, tried to send them all at once, but only one went through. Panicked, he scanned the massive crowd.

"We don't have time," he said to himself.

"We have to try," Grette shouted up at him.

Elior nodded. "Everyone, step out of my light and create a single file line. You will depart one by one."

Desperate squabbling ensued—a discord of pleas, shouts, and curses. The crowd surged like a living tide pressing toward the blue light. Everyone wanted to go first.

"Cooperate, or no one goes home," Elior demanded.

Half of the group surrendered, while the other half continued to push and shove each other.

Elior relocated, removing his blue light from the quarrelling Namatéans to those who waited patiently in line.

Exton of Crystet was first in line. He stepped into Elior's light.

"The stranger among us, is it who I think it is?" he asked Elior.

Elior sensed Exton's suspicions. "It is."

"Thought so," Exton grumbled. "I never knew she could do good. I guess there's still time to change an old man's views."

"There's always time for change," Elior agreed, then instructed, "When you return to your body, find Gwynessa and tell her that I have to send the minds back one by one."

Exton grunted in acknowledgement.

Elior scanned the long line. Grette stood at the back.

"What's your name?" he asked her.

"Grette."

Elior spoke to Exton again. "They will know I am done once Grette returns."

"Understood."

Exton disappeared into the blue light.

"Next!" Elior shouted.

King Adamek of Soylé entered the light next.

The blue light surged, and the royal Mudling vanished.

"Next!"

One by one, the line moved. Though it was swiftly growing shorter, they had a lot of minds left to go.

At the back, Grette patiently waited her turn.

Orso joined her.

"I guess this is goodbye," she offered.

"We never had a proper hello," Orso said before twisting his smoky form into knots and bursting into a flurry of charred embers.

A woman stood in his ashy remnants.

"Who are you?" Grette asked.

"Rebelene," the beautiful progeny answered. "The Bouldes never believed in us, but the Glaziene were always devout."

"Bouldes believe in Gaia, ghosts, and superstitions."

"I am one of Gaia's Vorso children. I am one of Her progenies."

"I believe now," Grette said. "Thank you for everything. You sparked the fire of rebellion in us all."

"You've always had the fire inside of you, I just fanned the flame," Rebelene offered.

"If you can come and go, why didn't you just take Calix with you?"

"I am Gaia's progeny, not Kólasi's. I can come and go, I can influence, but I cannot make changes. Only Kólasi, His children, and His divine can create tangible interferences here."

"Does that mean Elior is connected to Kólasi?" Grette asked.

"Yes. He is also, and more profoundly, connected to Gaia. He will do right by all of you."

Grette nodded, her sudden fears allayed.

"Good luck," Rebelene said. "I hope you beat Him."

The rebel goddess disappeared in a contained explosion of orange, blue, and silver sparks.

Grette focused on the mission ahead. Approximately fifty minds were still ahead of her in line.

She'd be home soon.

Freedom from this prison was finally in reach.

Chapter 37

Wicker

The blood flood brought forth grave darkness. Visibility through the crimson haze was dismal, which heightened their other senses.

The stench of metallic death singed their nostrils. The echoing roar of rushing blood and screams from other lands, paired with the thunderous laugh of Kólasi observing from beyond, filled their heads. Worst of all was the searing muscle aches making it increasingly difficult to withstand the strengthening current.

The blood flood rose to waist level.

Calix, still child sized, was neck deep in blood. As the blood flowed past, it splashed into his eyes and mouth, causing him to gag.

"Climb onto my shoulders," Ario offered, who held on to Rhoco's arm for support with one hand and Calix's hand with the other.

"How much longer will we wait?" Stennis asked.

"As long as it takes," Calix answered as he climbed Ario's back.

Stennis and Rhoco stood sturdy despite the destructive rise and flow of blood, but they weren't immune to the nightmarish sensory overload—each droplet that dripped into their eyes stung just as fiercely as it did for their Glaziene companions.

Gwynessa was beneath the rising blood, shoulder deep in the tree stump portal. Though she could breathe there, she couldn't hear the others.

Ario used his foot to feel for her body beneath the blood. Once he found her, he gave her a light tap.

She emerged, covered in blood.

"What?" she asked, her eyes burning.

"We have to go back!" Stennis urged. "We have to tell the others!"

"I can see them," Gwynessa reassured Stennis while wiping the blood away from her eyes. "There's no blood in Occavas. They are safe."

"Are *we* safe?" Stennis countered.

"I saw movement in Crystet. I have to go back."

Before she could dive back under, Lovise and Dasan arrived in a furious whirlwind.

"We've been looking all over for you!" Dasan squawked.

"Where are the relics?" Lovise demanded.

"Hold them back," Gwynessa commanded before diving back into the blood.

The Gasiones dove to follow, but Rhoco and Stennis caught them by their ankles.

They flapped their wings, trying to reemerge.

"Pin her wings!" Rhoco instructed Stennis.

Stennis fully constrained Lovise while Rhoco did the same to Dasan.

The large Bouldes had full control over the Gasiones. As they lifted their faces out of the blood, the winged warriors gasped for air.

"What are you doing?" Dasan demanded.

"We were supposed to go back at the first sign of blood," Lovise added.

"She thinks she sees abnormal movement among the mindless," Rhoco informed them.

"Surely you see how fast this blood is rising," Lovise challenged. "We don't have time."

"Give her a minute," Rhoco urged.

"Trust her," Ario doubled down. "She doesn't want to die. And she certainly wouldn't let her brother die."

"Seems we have no choice," Dasan griped, still trapped in Rhoco's grip.

Beneath the blood, Gwynessa located the tree stump and shoved her face into the looking glass portal.

Safely inside, she gasped for air.

After cleaning the blood out of her eyes, she zeroed in on Crystet. As she had noticed before leaving, the mindless were no longer standing idly in the waist-deep blood—they were flailing, swimming, and panicking. Debris from the cities and villages rushed past, creating dangerous obstacles for the already struggling Glaziene to dodge. One full force hit from a rocketing sofa could break them in half. Some floated aimlessly, getting tossed and dragged under by the violent flood, while others clung to makeshift rafts. The thunderous collapse of buildings and the deafening surge of the raging current overpowered the screams of the fraught Glaziene. She could see their distraught expressions, but could barely hear their cries.

Among them she found her uncle—he clung to a wooden tabletop while wading toward higher ground.

Gwynessa grabbed the air over her homeland and pulled, tugging herself through the portal until she was closer.

"Exton!" she called out.

He reached the top of the hill and looked up.

Gwynessa hovered above the royal grounds—she hadn't fully left the looking glass portal; she needed it to return to Wicker.

"What is happening?" Exton asked her.

"Kólasi is flooding us with the blood of our ancestors."

"Indirect, but effective," he noted. "How is Calix?"

"He's home. He is well. Are all of the minds back?"

"I was the first in a long line. There is a Boulde woman who will be the last." He paused to recall her name. "Grette."

"Thank you," Gwynessa offered. She did a quick search for Grette within Crystet before zooming out and reentering the looking glass portal.

With a bird's eye view of Namaté, she searched for Grette.

Terrifying screams of confusion echoed across every land as minds were returned to their bodies amid this bloody hellscape.

Gwynessa searched Orewall next, hoping Grette hadn't strayed far from home, but she wasn't there.

Her weathered heart pounded ferociously against her glass ribs as she turned her search to Soylé and then Coppel—no sign of Grette.

The blood rose fast, now at chest level for most.

Gwynessa swiped a shaky hand across the looking glass toward Elecort. Outside their shield, most of the mindless had returned to normal and were swimming through the blood to seek safety in the tall castle. Grette was not among the few mindless still wandering outside the shield.

Breath quickening, she frantically swiped the air of the looking glass until she was facing the lighthouse of death in Fibril.

All the former mindless clinging to the edifice had let go and were now wading in the dark ocean. None of whom were Grette.

Wicker had no mindless there before the bloodstorm, so her last place to look was Vapore.

She yanked herself toward the gaseous dome and pulled herself through without losing grip of the portal.

There, swaying beneath the black-moss willow tree, was Grette.

The mindless around her had resumed consciousness and were desperately climbing the surrounding trees to escape the flood.

"How many were left in line?" Gwynessa shouted down to them.

The mix of Bouldes, Mudlings, and commondore Gasiones looked up at her from where they climbed, unable to answer—they were too distracted by this new nightmare they had to survive.

"How many?" she demanded.

"About ten," a small Mudling finally replied, she grimaced as the blood poured down on her. "Grette wasn't far behind me."

Gwynessa nodded, relieved, but taking note of the Mudling's struggle.

"What's wrong?"

"The blood, it burns. It won't kill me as fast as water, but I can't stay here much longer."

"As soon as Grette returns, I will depart and save everyone."

The Mudling nodded.

Gwynessa turned to where Grette's mindless body stood in the chest-deep blood.

Eyes vacant, expression slack, muscles disengaged—Grette swayed ominously with the flowing blood.

She was the last mindless left in Vapore, and Gwynessa waited anxiously for life to return to her eyes.

A strong current pushed Grette's limp body forward, and she fell face first into the blood.

"Someone help her!" Gwynessa shouted, unable to leave the portal fully.

Those climbing toward their own safety could not assist.

Gwynessa touched Rúnar's heart hanging in a pouch from her waistband and reached its magic through the thin wall separating the looking glass portal from reality. She sent an invisible arm beneath the blood where Grette had fallen and lifted her back to the surface.

As Grette's face hit the air, she coughed up blood and then screamed. Her limp body became rigid with fear.

"Are you back?" Gwynessa asked, still holding Grette above the blood via magic.

"What is happening?" Grette asked while wiping the blood off her face.

Gwynessa released a long-held breath. "You're back."

"What did I come home to?"

"Death," Gwynessa answered. "I have to go. Do your best to ride this out."

"I can't swim!"

Neither could the other Bouldes clinging to the treetops. She then glanced at the Mudlings, who were latched desperately to their branches and suffering a slow death beneath the bloodstorm—every drop chipped away at their bodies.

"I can't bring you all with me."

"Please," Grette begged.

Unable to waste any more time, Gwynessa made the impulsive decision to save the twelve former mindless left stranded in Vapore.

One by one, she lassoed them using Rúnar's heart and pulled them through the veil and into the looking glass portal. She then tossed their bodies outward toward the dark waiting room before retrieving another. Once she had them all, she pushed herself backward until Namaté was so far zoomed out it became a floating orb once more. The blood-covered Namatéans waited for her there.

"Stay here," she instructed. "I'll be right back."

Gwynessa took a deep breath before popping her head out of the tree trunk and reemerging under blood.

She kicked her legs and swam through the ever-deepening blood until she reached the surface.

Gasping for air as she breached the surface, she panicked upon realizing the blood depth was now taller than her.

"I can't reach the bottom," she said, bobbing up and down, blood splashing into her mouth as she spoke. "Help!"

She caught the attention of her allies, who were preparing to abandon this station if she hadn't returned.

Ario and the Bouldes were taller than her, so the blood was neck-deep for them. Rhoco passed the ankle of his captured Gasione to Stennis, who now constrained two, then reached under Gwynessa's arms and held her above blood level.

She relaxed in his sturdy grip, catching her breath and spitting the blood out of her mouth.

"They're all back," she announced. "All the minds."

"Let's go," Ario urged.

"Link up and follow me," Gwynessa said, taking Stennis's hand. She dove under the blood and guided the others to the portal. She entered first, tugging Rhoco along behind her. Barreling in behind him was Ario, Calix, Stennis, Dasan, and Lovise.

The small waiting room was now overcrowded with blood-covered Namatéans.

There was no time to explain why the former mindless were waiting there.

"Everyone," she instructed. "Flip upside down."

As she and Rhoco maneuvered their hovering bodies to somersault, the others mimicked them.

The orb switched from rich shades of pastels to shimmering shades of neons.

Gwynessa grabbed the orb and rocketed herself and everyone with her into the orb.

They broke through the thin veil and landed in huddled heaps a few yards from where Ciela and Feodras waited with the other survivors.

"Took you long enough," Ciela squawked.

"Are the mindless saved?" Feodras asked.

"What was the hold up?" Cybelle barked.

But as the new arrivals lifted to their feet and began shuffling toward them, those who hadn't left Occavas had a moment to take in their blood-drenched appearance.

All of their questioning ceased.

Before anyone could question what had transpired in their absence, a bead of crimson fell from the sky and landed on Ciela's forehead.

She wiped it off, saw the smear of red on her fingertips, and her orange eyes widened with horror.

The first droplet of blood had fallen in Occavas.

Chapter 38

Radix de Orewall

"The bloodstorm has started."

"Technically, it started a few hours ago," Gwynessa confessed.

"We gathered based on your appearance," Ciela quipped.

"But it was worth the wait. All the minds are back. We saved them."

"You brought them back just in time for them to drown," Cybelle remarked.

"They've found higher ground. We still have time if we hurry."

The combined relics sat perched like a little lifeless creature.

Gwynessa shoved Rúnar's heart into the rib cage near the lungs.

The blood rained heavier now, speckling everyone with red.

Calix stepped forward with the lost relic of Gaia. He removed its chain from around his neck and draped it over the Bonz skull, letting it rest on the top bones of the wooden rib cage.

As soon as all nine relics touched, each piece of the assembled creature stirred with life.

Jasvinder's fuchsia eyes beamed like beacons, while Rúnar's heart thudded like a war drum. Amezite's stone brain created a purple glow within and around Bozrah's skull. The creature spread and shook Elzaphan's wings, adjusting its body to its new form. Barzilai's finger coils unraveled, not only becoming fingers, but also arms and legs. Brixton's ribs expanded and contracted as the creature took its first breath through Dagmar's lungs.

Beautiful and awe-inspiring, Conexus came to life, repositioning itself to stand on two coiled legs.

"Who is my master?" Conexus asked.

The possessors of each relic scanned each other nervously, wondering who would claim this power, but Feodras answered before any singular individual stepped forward.

"We all are," he stated. "We have one task for you before you're dismantled."

"What is my task?"

"Destroy Kólasi's edifice."

Conexus nodded, then noted, "I sense power equal to my own."

"The scepter of alchemy," Beaumont explained. "Its magic courses underground, chipping away at the edifice's inner binds. We can defeat chaos with our forces combined."

Conexus understood. "The scepter will crumble the inside while I demolish the outside."

The blood pouring from above now pooled on the ground, creating puddles.

"Please, hurry," Feodras gently urged Conexus.

Without further delay, Conexus pounded Elzaphan's glorious black wings and took off toward Radix de Fibril.

Ciela and her Gasione warriors followed, flying through the torrential blood to monitor the relic's progress.

Beaumont departed to oversee the scepter and ensure that it continued to operate at its fullest capacity.

The rain fell faster, harder—worsening everyone's visibility.

"What now?" Elixyvette questioned, her jet-black ringlets drenched and elongated by the weight of the blood. She tucked the strands in front of her face behind her ear.

"We wait," Feodras answered. "We hope for the best."

"We try not to die," Cybelle added, lifting her stone foot out of an ankle-deep blood puddle.

"I want to see what's happening," Gwynessa commented, to which many mumbled in agreement while wiping the blood from their eyes.

The terrain shook violently—a prolonged tremor that forced everyone to pause and brace themselves. When it finished, the group shared cautionary glances.

"We may not be able to see what's happening, but I think we're feeling it," Cybelle offered.

Circling the base of the edifice in Radix de Fibril, Ciela and her warriors observed the slow destruction. Large in numbers, their rotation moved like black ink on a red canvas—a fast break in the storm.

The ground still tremored above, occasionally adding large chunks of terrain to the rainfall. Though they were relatively easy to dodge, the enormous splashes of blood caused by their landing were not.

While the scepter of alchemy ate away at the edifice's roots, Conexus rammed its magic into the walls, creating new fissures and reopening the gold-fused cracks.

"Is there anything we can do to help?" Ciela called out to Conexus through the pouring blood.

"As I crack the sealed fissures, use your talons to carve out the gold putty," it replied.

"We can't touch the lighthouse," Ciela reminded the relic. "Doing so would capture our minds."

Conexus paused its attack on the edifice to send a surge of enveloping magic to the Gasiones. A silver-blue shield of light blanketed their bodies.

"It cannot take you now," Conexus assured them before resuming its attack on the lighthouse.

The Gasiones wasted no more time. Like a surging breath, they stopped their rotational flight, leaned back, then dove inward. They latched to the edifice, tearing apart every bit of loosened gold sealant.

Conexus continued pulsating its magic at the edifice, hitting it with powerful blows that rattled its core.

They worked in synchronized unison—Conexus sent a wave of forceful magic, the Gasiones flew in, wreaked havoc, and flew out just in time for another blast.

The top of the edifice could not be seen within Occavas—it had jetted through Fibril's portal and stood erect in Namaté—but its thick base had demolished all of Radix de Fibril. Bits of stone crumbled off its façade—a slow demolition from the bottom up.

Conexus continued its strikes while the Gasiones chipped away at the gold.

The blood pouring from the sky was torrential now and caused the sea level to rise.

Ciela worried about her allies stationed at ground level, but kept her focus on the task at hand—worrying and wondering was futile, only the destruction of the edifice could save them.

Screeching squawks accompanied the Gasione's frenzied destruction. Talons to gold—scratching, scraping, clearing. Their work sped up the process, and each emptied crevice destabilized the edifice further.

Small pops sounded where the hollowed-out cracks collapsed.

Like a symphony of tiny fireworks, the edifice trembled as its interior snapped and cracked.

Then, the rumbling of an enormous collapse sounded from above. Partially muted by the deep blood, but still loud enough to recognize it as the demolition of the edifice's top half.

"We're halfway there," Ciela encouraged her warriors. "Keep at it!"

Conxeus amped up its power, sending steady, rhythmic blasts. In between each blast, the Gasiones tore at every open lesion in the stone, ripping at the rock and widening the cracks.

It was a beautiful manic dance of destruction.

As they waltzed in harmonious timing, a new disruption boomed across the echoland. Louder than their work, louder than the falling blood, the sound of terror thundered for all to hear.

Conexus was unfazed, but the Gasiones paused their dance to locate the source.

Far in the distance, blurred by the red rain, fire joined the storm with a mighty roar.

"Is it Kólasi?" Adaliah asked.

"I don't think so," Ciela answered, eyes squinted, attempting to see through the veil of blood.

Another blast of fire and whiplashing wind.

Out of the red emerged the fury of the heavens.

Massive, scaled, and fanged—a drakkina took form.

Her silhouette dwarfed the Gasiones, and as she rocketed past them, the wind she created tumbled them through the sky.

The Gasiones erupted into hysteria.

"How many?"

"They're on our side, right?"

"Did Gaia send them?"

The drakkina circled the edifice and ripped past the Gasiones again, knocking loose their stronghold of the air and forcing them to scramble to reposition themselves again.

Ciela watched in awe, unsure what this arrival meant.

The drakkina circled again, this time slowing its ferocious flight and hovering in front of Ciela.

From the nape of the drakkina's neck emerged a young boy. His azure glow illuminated fiercely despite the thick rain.

Unconcerned by the blood dripping down his forehead and into his eyes, he spoke with grave authority.

"Where is my mother?"

Chapter 39

The young boy stood at the nape of Rozene's neck. He clutched two of the many spiked horns that protruded down and around her spine.

In full form, the drakkina of sickness and storms roared with infectious fire. Her thunderous presence amplified the storm raging around them, causing the blood to fall faster.

The onslaught was debilitating.

The storm amplified, and the blood pounded so hard, Gasiones dropped from the sky.

"Make it stop!" Ciela begged.

"Rozene!" Elior commanded, to which Rozene reversed her energetic output and slowed the bloodstorm.

Ciela took a few deep breaths, calming her panic, before speaking again.

"Can she make it stop?"

"No," Elior answered. "I brought her to calm the storm. She can only manipulate Kólasi's ploys, not eradicate them."

Ciela was enamored by this child's poise, confidence, and knowledge.

"Who are you?" she asked.

"Elior Lucien Ignatius Boaneres."

Ciela's eyes widened. "How? You were born mere months ago."

"I was touched by the divine."

"I thought only Gaia could release the drakkina."

"She blessed my transition into full divinity and allowed the release of one drakkina to accompany me on my mission."

"Gaia knows what's happening here?"

"She does now. I am here to end this."

"Please, hurry!"

"First, my mother. Where is she?"

The terrain above trembled, causing all of Occavas to shake.

"You can see her later," Ciela urged. "We need to destroy the edifice now!"

"She cannot survive its fall," he explained. "The sovereignty of Namaté depends on her elimination."

"You wish death upon her?"

"As she wished upon me." His voice was clear and unwavering.

"Well, I don't plan to stop you, just hurry, please. The Namatéans above will drown if this storm doesn't cease soon."

"Where is she?"

"Radix de Orewall."

"Onward!" Elior commanded Rozene, who obeyed with feverish delight. Her sapphire eyes speckled with sickly yellow spots as she carried Elior to his final destination.

Wherever Rozene flew, the storm's intensity lessened.

When they reached Radix de Orewall, they found the survivors there scaling the mountainside of Amesyte Valley to escape the rising blood levels.

Rozene roared to announce their arrival.

"The drakkina," Gwynessa said, elated.

Everyone else paused their climb to cower wherever they landed.

Rozene flew in circles over the mountain.

::My sister,:: Gwynessa said in greeting. *::Why are you here? Did Gaia send you to aid?::*

::I am here, too,:: Elior replied.

Gwynessa could not see him from this angle.

::You did a wonderful job freeing the minds. It wasn't easy getting the others to wait, but we succeeded. All the minds are home::

::Thank you for all of your help.:: Elior offered. *::Gaia thanks you also.::*

"Did Gaia send it?" Cybelle asked.

"How many of them are here?" Stennis followed up.

::Is it just you?:: Gwynessa asked Rozene.

::Just me,:: she replied. *::To help slow the storm and transport Elior. He didn't need the fleet for what he came here to do.::*

"Just one," Gwynessa answered the Bouldes. *::And what did you come here to do?::*

::Eliminate the last threat to peace after this storm clears.:: Elior responded.

::Say more.::

::My mother.::

::Are you sure this isn't vengeance?::

::And what if it is?::

::I wouldn't blame you.::

Elior silently appreciated her reply, then added, *::I can see her aura—it's black. She will bring turmoil to the new world.::*

::Do what you have to do.::

Elior pushed Rozene's neck spikes upward, which redirected her flight path. She lowered, flying slower now as they hunted for Elixyvette.

The Voltain queen stood on a rocky mountain ledge alone; none of the others were nearby.

"Mother!" Elior shouted. His voice caught Elixyvette's attention, but she looked around confused. She could not see Elior where he crouched between Rozene's wings.

"Mother!" he repeated.

His voice was directed at her—she felt it, but didn't understand.

"Me?" she asked.

Elior rose between Rozene's wings, his azure glow unmistakable.

"Yes, *you.*"

Elixyvette hesitated a moment, deciding how best to respond. There was no denying who stood before her on the back of a furious drakkina—he looked exactly like Lucien.

"Your glow, it's back!"

Elior seethed silently.

"You're so big!" she continued. "How? You shouldn't even be a year old yet."

"You're right, I shouldn't be. I should be dead, throat slit and body swallowed by the sea—isn't that right?"

"My boy—"

"I am not your boy."

"Elior, I'm sorry."

"Do not lie to me."

"I thought I was doing you a favor."

"By killing me?"

"Yes. This world is cruel, and I did not want you to suffer."

"Your love would have been enough."

The world quaked, causing giant boulders to tumble down the mountainside.

"Please forgive me," Elixyvette begged.

"That's not up to me." Elior touched the side of Rozene's neck. *::End her.::*

Plague-ridden steam blasted from Rozene's mouth, encasing Elixyvette in a deadly cloud. Millions of microscopic toxins crawled across Elixyvette's flesh, entering every orifice of her body. They chewed at her veined cords, corroded her bloodstream, and nestled into her tissue. Little by little, the disease ate away at her from the inside.

Within moments, the inner corrosion reached her outer flesh. Tiny bugs chewing holes through her flesh crawled through her peeling skin.

She screamed.

The infection spread fast.

"My boy!" she pled, begging for mercy.

Elior ignored her.

Elixyvette fell to her knees, flesh rapidly disintegrating and revealing her wire-wrapped skeleton.

"Forgive me!"

He shook his head.

Elixyvette took her last breath as the plague seized her life.

Elior held no remorse in his grave stare.

"May the gods have mercy on your soul."

Chapter 40

A swirling black cloud joined the fray. It stretched across the entirety of Occavas, worsening the storm as it spread.

::Rozene! Do something!:: Elior implored

Rozene used all of her power to stop the downpour, but to no avail.

::It's Him. There's nothing more I can do.::

Elior and Gwynessa scanned the sky, awaiting Kólasi's wrath.

"What is happening?" Feodras asked.

"He's here," Gwynessa answered.

"Where?"

Gwynessa exhaled slowly. "Everywhere."

The survivors, still precariously perched on the side of the mountain, experienced unified tension as they awaited their fate.

<<You had your chance to choose deliverance,>> Kólasi bellowed. *<<Instead, you chose condemnation.>>*

"The edifice needs to fall!" Gwynessa shouted to Elior, who heeded her urgency and steered Rozene back to Radix de Fibril.

<<I am here to finalize your judgment.>>

Red lightning bolts struck the mountainside. The illuminated blood inside burst on impact, creating massive rockslides and a gushing red deluge.

The survivors scrambled, scaling the rock as quickly as they could to avoid the falling rocks and rushing blood.

Kólasi's laugh carried across the echoland as He sent another round of lightning at Amesyte Valley.

Simultaneously, He watched Conexus blast devastating blows to His edifice. Kólasi tossed a rage-fueled lightning bolt at the combined relic, only to watch His spear of fire whittle into a skinny spark before making contact.

He could not intervene, could not stop the magic-fueled creature—it belonged to Gaia and its pieces were impervious to Kólasi's indirect attempts at elimination.

Kólasi growled, creating a rolling thunder that shook Occavas.

His weakened edifice trembled violently.

<<No!>>

Conexus gave one final slam, accompanied by a lethal blast of fire-fueled wind from Rozene, and the lighthouse crumbled to dust.

The edifice vanished, along with Kólasi.

Afraid to celebrate too soon, Elior waited until the blood levels began to lower.

Inch by inch, the flood drained, dissipating back into the ether. He summoned Conexus, which separated its pieces back into singular relics upon his command. He shrank and placed all the pieces into his waistpouch—each relic would return to its respective homeland after the blood fully drained.

Joy filled his heart as he directed Rozene back to Radix de Orewall.

"We've won!" he announced. "Kólasi and His edifice are gone, and the blood is receding!"

As he arrived at the mountainside, the scene was chaotic.

Stennis and Grette clung to Rhoco's limp body, which hung over the side of a cliff.

"What happened?" Elior asked.

"He fell!" Grette replied.

"At the same time we heard the edifice collapse," Stennis added.

"Help him, please!" Cybelle begged.

Elior ruminated, then asked, "When did he die?"

"What do you mean?"

"Was it while he was mindless?"

"He died before the edifice arrived," Feodras answered. "But he came back. He was alive again!"

Elior shook his head. "He wasn't only mindless, but also lifeless."

"I don't understand."

"The edifice reanimated many deceased bodies, Rhoco's included," Elior explained.

"And the golden muscas gave the bodies motivation and purpose," Gwynessa said, understanding the intricate formula. Ario held her hand. Their love for each other radiated despite the death and chaos surrounding them.

"Without the edifice or the flies," Elior further explained, "the lifeless will resume their eternal slumber."

"But his mind came back!" Cybelle challenged. "He didn't need the flies for purpose or motivation. He was himself again after we got rid of the flies."

"You need a mind, a soul, *and* a body," Elior explained. "Without the edifice here, his body remains deceased. The edifice was the only thing giving his body life."

Grette sighed. "We failed."

"You saved so many," Gwynessa countered, side-eyeing Calix with a smile.

"You saved everyone that you could," Ario added.

"It's time to let him go," Elior encouraged the Bouldes.

"We need to give him a proper burial," Grette objected, grimacing as she and Stennis struggled to hold Rhoco's weight.

"We will find him again after the flood recedes," Cybelle promised. "I won't let his soul flounder without a proper farewell ceremony."

Feodras shook his head. "He had a ceremony when he died the first time. His soul is already beyond."

"A ceremony for his mind and body then," Cybelle quipped.

Grette and Stennis couldn't hold him any longer.

"We will find you," Grette promised before she and Stennis let go.

Rhoco's enormous body free fell into the ocean of blood below, sinking immediately upon contact.

Deep into the depths.

Deep into the unknown.

Chapter 41

The ocean beckoned.

Body lying on the coarse sand, he let the waves lap over him—swallowing him whole and then spitting him out. Over and over.

The sun rose and set.

The moon did the same.

Was it tomorrow yet?

He tallied the never-ending waves, losing count often then starting over again.

Rhoco watched the sun rise, defiant in his choice to stay put.

The waves surged and retreated, as they always did.

He sighed, wondering how much time had passed. He lifted his head to scan the world around him—there was no one around, no one in sight.

Alone, as he had been for however many days.

He couldn't remember how he got here, and he suspected nothing new would come his way.

Every day was exactly the same.

Was this heaven? Had he found peace?

Or was this hell? Was he forever stuck holding on to his greatest regrets?

Back in this mundane purgatory, teetering between the desire to live and die, he contemplated if he even had a choice. He had faced death many times, close calls and finality, yet fate had resurrected him and dropped him here. Back in this solitary, introspective place he used to cherish.

Since experiencing the stimulation of adventure, connection, and knowledge, Rhoco craved excitement.

Being back at his dune felt lonely now.

The monotony had lost its charm.

For the first time since he could remember, he forced himself to sit upright.

The urge to swim washed over him.

Bouldes can't swim, he thought. *Bouldes sink.*

Still, he could not quell the urge to try.

He stood and wobbled—his balance askew.

One step into the water, then another.

Knee-deep, he paused.

Bouldes can't swim.

The thought was concerning, but he felt no fear. He took another four steps until the water level reached his waist.

Arms extended, hands hovering atop the water, he hesitated. Though he could not feel the water's chill, he felt its luring pull.

The ocean beckoned, enticing him to tread deeper.

Feet lighter with every step, the water carried him forward. When it reached his chin, he paused again.

Bouldes sink.

He shook his head. *I will swim.*

Deep breath held, he took another step forward and was underwater.

Stone feet weighted firmly into the sand, Rhoco scanned the darkness surrounding him, then shifted his focus upward at the sunlight beaming through the water.

He waved his arms, trying to gain lift, but he remained fixed to the ocean floor.

He was too heavy to swim.

This feeling of defeat was familiar—an ancient disappointment he had forgotten until now.

Determined to succeed, he tried again. This time, he bent his knees and launched his body toward the surface. Pure strength propelled him closer to the light.

Arms stroking, legs kicking, his body pushed against the resistance of the water, rising despite his heaviness.

Lungs filled with air, his buoyancy activated.

Flotation—an unfamiliar feeling.

He had never gotten this far before.

Determined now more than ever, Rhoco paddled upward, water rippling around his massive form.

No struggle, no fight—he ascended gracefully, gliding through the water like he'd been doing this his whole life.

He was doing it—a long-held ambition finally realized.

Rhoco swam toward the light.

The Gods

as seen across Nicoline's books thus far—more to come!

Inaugural Gods

Cretus – God of ALL creation and destruction (gods included)

Cretia – Goddess of ALL creation and destruction (gods included)

Primordial Gods

Matrigaia – Goddess of all mortal life

Kólasi – God of mortal death and chaos

Kólasi's Prison Planets:

Corpeus – prison for mortal bodies

Spirtus – prison for mortal spirits/souls

Cerébrum – prison for mortal minds

He can not create mortal life—He can only take it away. Each captured mind, body, and spirit nourishes Kólasi's dark ecosystem, fortifies His chaotic dominance, and feeds His tyrannical ego.

Incarna – Goddess of souls and reincarnation

All souls see Her before being assigned to the abyss, nirvana, or reincarnation.

Tempus – God of time

Obscuro – God of darkness

Lumine – Goddess of light

Natralis – God of natural resources

Emovere – Goddess of emotions

Veritus – God of truth and logic

Idem – God of identity

Fantasia – Goddess of imagination

Elder Gods

Solédon - God of all suns
Progeny of Matrigaia and Lumine

Lunéss - Goddess of all moons
Progeny of Matrigaia and Obscuro

Mortacia - Goddess of death and mischief
Progeny of Kólasi and Rebelene

Sensi - Goddess of mortal minds and thoughts
She keeps deceased ancient minds in Her vault. This is why mortals can't remember their past lives.
Progeny of Incarna and Fantasia

Viscus - God of mortal casing
He creates the integumentary system (skin, flesh, membranes, etc) for mortal bodies. He does not collect bodies after they perish—He could, but He lets the cosmos deliver the pieces as they organically decompose.
Progeny of Incarna and Natralis

Vigor - God of mortal spirits
Progeny of Incarna and Emovere

Marlodon - God of the seas
Progeny of Matrigaia and Natralis

Contemporaneous Gods

Filli Diaboli – the devil's sons

Progenies of Kólasi

They serve the many different hells assigned to different mortal worlds. The deepest levels of their hells connect to Kólasi's Abyss.

Kólasi often sends the Filli on missions, disguised in various forms, to cause mayhem and do his dirty work. In golden fly form, the Filli are referred to as MUSCAS.

For reference: Lucifer, one of Earth's primary and most recognizable devils, is a Filli.

Vorso – 17 Gods tasked to guide Namatéan personalities

Progenies of Matrigaia

**In the timeframe of these books, only the Glaziene continue to worship the Vorso.

Altrudene – benign goddess of kindness and altruism
Clevren – benign god of logic and reason
Devotene – benign goddess of loyalty and guardianship
Romanel – benign god of romance

Aberand – dualist god of the weird, strange, and abnormal
Avarese – dualist god of greed
Droma – dualist goddess of drama and belligerence
Imperiup – dualist god of control and rigidness
Karmandel – dualist god of karma and fate
Melanel – dualist goddess of melancholy
Narcesse – dualist god of narcissism and selfishness
Rebelene – dualist goddess of mischief and rebellion
Reculese – dualist god of isolation and social aversion
Timoro – dualist god of timidness and fear
Trepedene – dualist goddess of suspicion and doubt

Deraingla - malignant goddess of violence and psychosis
Vindicene - malignant goddess of vindictiveness and malice

Non-god Progenies

all progenies are totumdivinus (fully divine)

Drakkina – Half human woman, half dragon

Progenies of Matrigaia

- They live in Cruxeus—Matrigaia's heart. Though it is a cozy home, it is also a prison. They can only leave with Matrigaia's permission.
- They feed on all forms of adoration, both positive and negative. (ie; fear and jealousy.)
- Genuine hatred weakens them.
- They can morph in and out of drakkina form.

Diedra – The bringer of life. She is driven by rebirth and creation. Her colors are emerald and brown.

Amari – The possesser of electricity and justice. Her colors are amber and citrine.

Caliza – The lawless child of the sun. Her colors are gold and amethyst.

Lysandra –The fearless shadow of chaos.
Her colors are crimson and ruby.

Rozene – The storm of misfortune and illness. Her colors are sapphire and yellow.

Novalee – The lonely child of the moon. Her colors are silver, pearl, and aquamarine.

Gwyneria – The snow ghost of death. Her colors are white and diamond.

God Levels

all gods are totumdivinus and immortal

1. **Inaugural Gods** – There are two, and no other gods are older or more powerful than them.
   When they create a god together, it is automatically a primordial—though they rarely have need to make new primordials. If they create a new god with a lesser god, the resulting progeny's ranking is determined by lesser god's ranking—it will be the same or lower.
2. **Primordial Gods** – Gods born from inaugural gods
3. **Elder Gods** – Gods born from primordials, or any combination of primordial + progeny
4. **Contemporaneous Gods** – Modern day gods, created by necessity within specific worlds. Born by any combination of primordials, elders, and progenies.

Progenies – a term to refer to the child of a god

- Can apply to any level of god besides Inaugural, or to non-god creatures birthed directly by a god. Must be born from the god's divine form.
  Examples: Primordials are progenies of Inaugurals. The drakkina (non-god progeny) and Vorso (contemporaneous) are Gaia's progenies. The Filli/muscas (contemporaneous) are Kólasi's progenies.
- Never applies to creatures birthed by mortals.
- Non-god progenies only serve their parent god, and are often under tight control by their parent god.
- All progenies have special access to their godly parent's planets and powers.
- Any levels of gods can create progenies.
- Some progenies may be older than Elders or Contemporaneous gods.

Divinity Levels

1. **<u>Totumdivinus</u>** - Totums - fully divine
    - All gods and progenies are totumdivinus, plus a very few select mortals.
    - For mortals, the divine touch from any progeny or totumdivinus mortal must be blessed by a god to take effect. The god decides their level of divinity.
    - All gods are immortal.
    - Totumdivinus mortals and non-god progenies are immortal, but can expire at the discretion of the gods.
    - Totumdivinus mortals and non-god progenies possess godly powers, but never more than the gods. They also have a special connection to the god who blessed or birthed them, as well as access to their planets.
    - Totumdivinus mortals and non-god progenies possess differing yet rivaling levels of power.

2. **<u>Dimidivinus</u>** - Dimis - half divine
    - All mortal dimis have one or more fatal flaws, but are immortal otherwise, or until a god/totumdivinus chooses to expire them.
    - They possess some godly powers at reduced strength.
    - They possess smaller godly gifts, such as, but not limited to: talking to animals, manipulating nature's elements, and communicating with the gods.

3. **<u>Quadradivinus</u>** - Quadras - quarter divine
    - All quadras have a few fatal flaws, but are far more durable than mortals without divinity.
    - They possess smaller godly gifts, such as, but not limited to: talking to animals, manipulating nature's elements, and communicating with the gods.

<u>Dualisdivinus</u> - Dualis - dual divine

- A mortal who receives a divine touch from two different gods, via the god directly or through their progenies/totumdivinus mortals.
- They can be given any level of divinity—totum, dimi, or quadra.

- Dualis possess connection to and powers from both gods they are touched by.

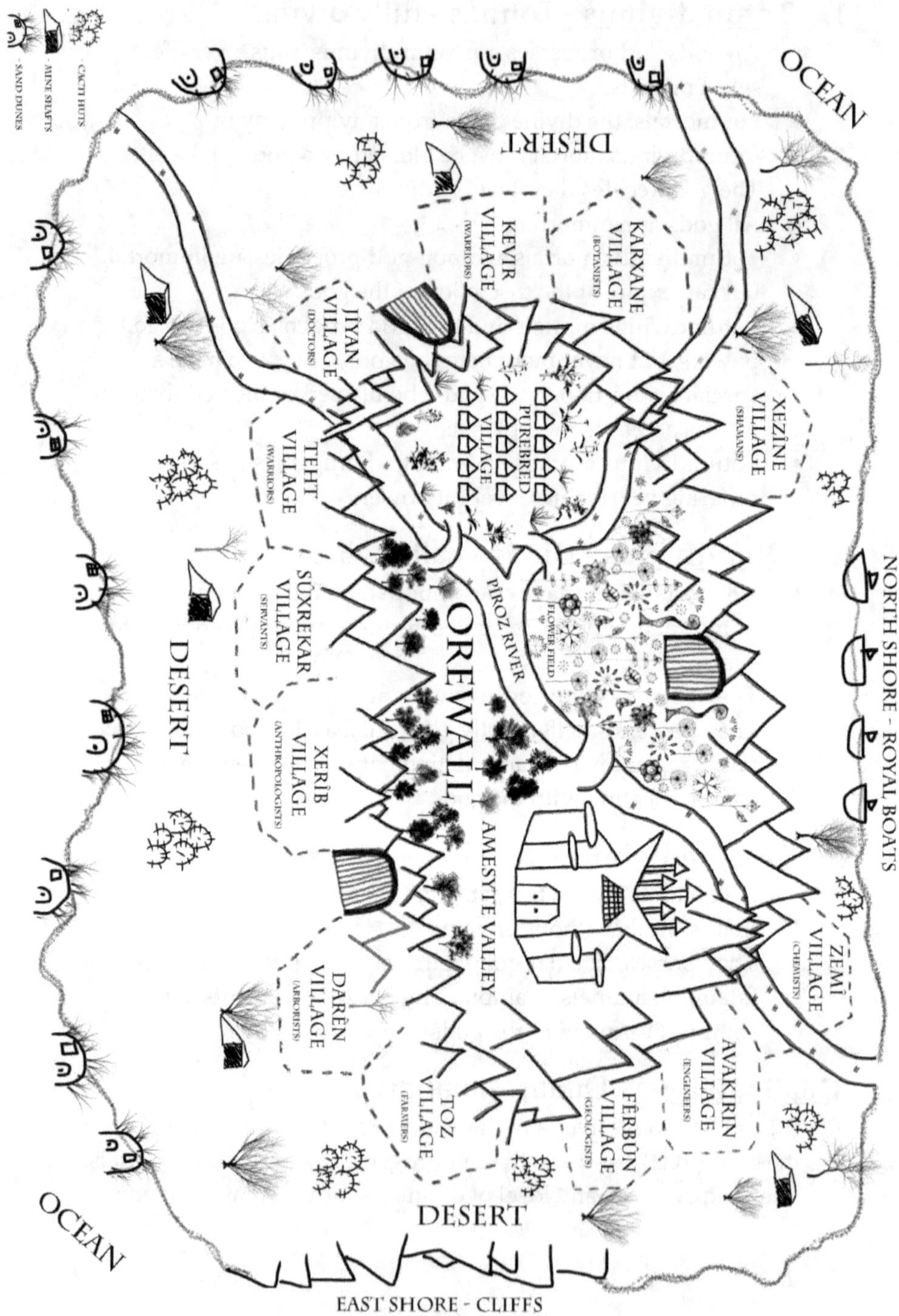

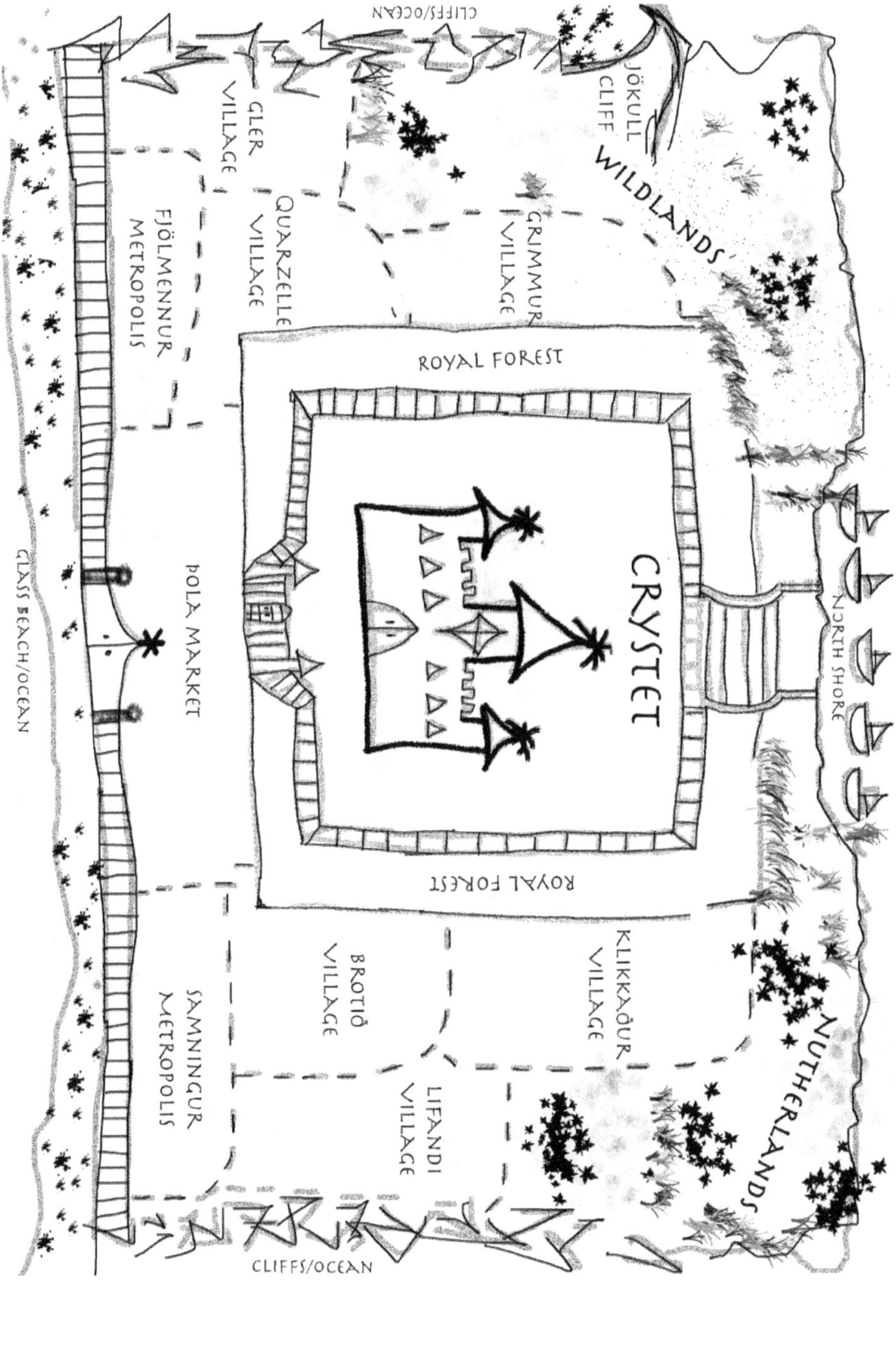
CLIFFS/OCEAN
JÖKULL CLIFF
WILDLANDS
GLER VILLAGE
QUARZELLE VILLAGE
GRIMMUR VILLAGE
FJÖLMENNUR METROPOLIS
ROYAL FOREST
CRYSTET
POLA MARKET
NORTH SHORE
GLASS BEACH/OCEAN
ROYAL FOREST
KLIKKAÐUR VILLAGE
BROTIÐ VILLAGE
LIFANDI VILLAGE
SAMNINGUR METROPOLIS
NUTHERLANDS
CLIFFS/OCEAN

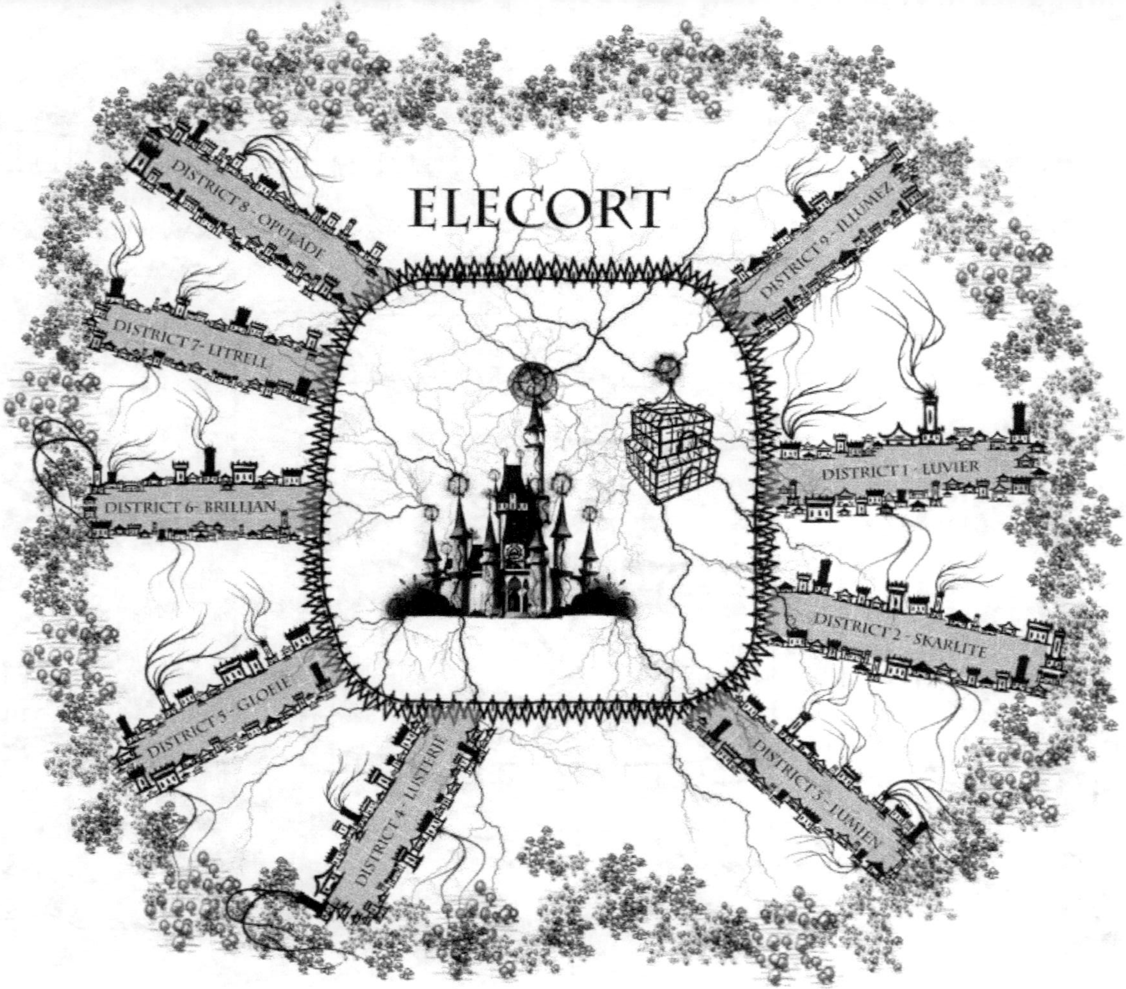

ELECORT
DISTRICT 1 - LUVIER
DISTRICT 2 - SKARLITE
DISTRICT 3 - LUMIEN
DISTRICT 4 - LUSTERIE
DISTRICT 5 - GLOEIL
DISTRICT 6 - BRILLIAN
DISTRICT 7 - LITRELL
DISTRICT 8 - OPULADE
DISTRICT 9 - ILLUMEZ

Thank you for reading *Cerébrum* – I hope you enjoyed it! If you have a moment**, please consider rating and reviewing** it on Amazon, and sharing your thoughts with me via social media. All feedback is greatly appreciated!

Amazon Author Account:

www.amazon.com/author/nicolineevans

Facebook:

www.facebook.com/nicolinenovels

Instagram:

www.instagram.com/nicolinenovels

To learn more about my other novels, please visit my official author website:

www.nicolineevans.com

www.ingramcontent.com/pod-product-compliance
Lightning Source LLC
Chambersburg PA
CBHW051333020726
47501CB00007B/2068
* 9 7 8 1 9 5 6 5 4 5 1 1 1 *